I turned my full attention to Vivian. "Do you mind if I ask you a few questions about David Smith?"

Her mouth puckered. "I really don't wish to speak of the dead, ill or otherwise."

"What about Dan? What can you tell me about him?"

Vivian frowned and refused to meet my eye. "He couldn't have hurt David if that is what you are implying. Dan Jacobson is a fine young man." A blush ran up her neck. I wasn't sure how to interpret that.

"Do you have any idea who might have killed Mr. Smith?"

Vivian looked up, eyes hovering near my chin. "Don't you think you should ask Rita and her little flock that? They were jealous of David, I tell you. He could sweet talk just about anyone, and they knew they were in trouble the moment they heard him speak. He could have recited the pledge and won the teapot for us." Her voice hardened. "If you are looking for a murderer, you best look in your own back yard."

Books by Alex Erickson

DEATH BY COFFEE

DEATH BY TEA

Published by Kensington Publishing Corporation

Death by Tea

Alex Erickson

KENSINGTON PUBLISHING CORP.
http://www.kensingtonbooks.com

KENSINGTON BOOKS are published by

Kensington Publishing Corp.
119 West 40th Street
New York, NY 10018

All Kensington Titles, Imprints, and Distributed Lines are available at special quantity discounts for bulk purchases for sales promotions, premiums, fund-raising, and educational or institutional use. Special book excerpts or customized printings can also be created to fit specific needs. For details, write or phone the office of the Kensington special sales manager: Kensington Publishing Corp., 119 West 40th Street, New York, NY 10018, attn: Special Sales Department, Phone: 1-800-221-2647.

Kensington and the K logo Reg. U.S. Pat & TM Off.

ISBN-13: 978-1-61773-753-4
ISBN-10: 1-61773-753-4
First Kensington Mass Market Edition: December 2015

eISBN-13: 978-1-61773-754-1
eISBN-10: 1-61773-754-2
First Kensington Electronic Edition: December 2015

10 9 8 7 6 5 4 3 2 1

Printed in the United States of America

1

A steady beeping tried to drown out the gunfire and pounding of my own heart. Officer Paul Dalton lay atop me—fully dressed unfortunately—as he shielded me from an unknown assailant who seemed to have an endless supply of ammo. I knew I should have been scared, but with him that close, I couldn't think about anything but his firm muscles flexing as he held me, and those wonderful dimples of his that were creasing his cheeks. Even in the heart of danger, he could still find time to smile.

The beeping continued, louder, more insistent than before.

"Do you think it's a bomb?" I asked as I dreamily stroked Paul's bicep.

"No, Krissy, my love." His smile was enough to make my head swim. "I think it's an alarm."

"An alarm?"

Panic flared through me as I surged from the dream and into the waking world, arms and legs flailing. My cat, Misfit, who had been sleeping next to me, was unceremoniously dumped onto the floor as I sat up, eyes darting to the clock, which read an alarming 8:31.

"Crapcicle!"

I nearly fell out of the bed as I scrambled to my feet. There was no time for a shower, so I went straight for my closet, where I grabbed the first thing my hand fell upon. I was supposed to be at work at half past eight. Somehow, I'd managed to oversleep my alarm by a good hour.

"Stupid dream," I grumbled as I ripped off my pj's, tossed them onto the floor, and scrambled into my clothes. I hopped on one foot into the kitchen as I tried to walk and slip on my shoes at the same time. Misfit was sitting next to his food bowl, watching me with a kitty grin.

"Enjoying this, are you?" I asked him. "Next time, I'll let you starve." I filled his dish and he promptly buried his face in his bowl. The cat normally woke me up well before my alarm, yet this time he'd intentionally let me sleep, more than likely because of something I'd done that he didn't approve of. He's devious like that.

I looked longingly at my coffeepot before darting back down the hall and into the bathroom. My hair was sticking up every which way in massive tangles that would take hours to fix. Either I'd spent the night twisting and turning my head on the pillow, or Misfit had been at my hair with his tongue and claws again, kneading away. I swear that cat has it in for me.

I grabbed my brush from the drawer and yanked it through my hair a few times. When that didn't work, I snatched up a hair tie and did my best to tame the mess on my head into a ponytail. It was uneven and lumpy, but it would have to do.

Next came a quick once-over with my toothbrush— there was no way on God's green earth that I was going to go out without at least making an attempt at brushing my teeth—and then it was back to the kitchen, where I grabbed my purse and keys and headed out the door. The curtains next door swished open as my neighbor, Eleanor

Winthrow, leaned forward at her window seat to watch me. It was becoming a routine. The woman probably knew my schedule better than I did. She really needed a hobby other than spying on me.

I paid her little mind as I got into my black Focus, started the car, and backed wildly out of my driveway in a spray of dusty pavement. And then it was a mad rush to work, as I prayed I wouldn't come across one of the local cops along the way.

At least I wasn't supposed to open Death by Coffee today. My best friend, Vicki Patterson, and one of our new hires, Lena Allison, were scheduled for that, so the doors should already be open, but that didn't make me feel any better. I didn't like to be late, especially on a day like today, when we were to finally have Wi-Fi connectivity for our customers. It was a big day for us.

I found a parking space just down the road from our shop. I made one last futile attempt to tame my hair and then headed down the sidewalk. I could see Lena hanging something on the front of the store, and when she glanced up, I gave her an apologetic wave.

"Sorry," I said, hurrying over. "My alarm didn't go off." A little white lie never hurt anyone.

"It's cool." Lena gave me a crooked smile. A fresh scrape on her chin told me she'd crashed her skateboard again. The poor girl was practically a living scab. She'd recently cut her hair short and dyed it from dark brown to something a little more wild. I had to admit, the purple really did bring out her eyes. "Everything's taken care of." She motioned to the FREE WI-FI sign now hanging in the window.

Lena had wanted to go to college after high school but didn't have the grades or money for it. So, instead, she'd chosen to work at Death by Coffee in order to make some money so she *could* go. She was smarter than she let on and deserved an opportunity.

"Good." I sucked in a deep breath and then hurried past Lena into Death by Coffee.

The combination bookstore and coffee shop was doing much better after a slow start. I'd managed to solve a murder on my first week in town. Apparently, the people of Pine Hills enjoyed a little excitement every now and again, and I was viewed as something of a minor celebrity. It was the reason we were finally able to hire a couple of new employees, rather than close up like I thought we would have to. The money coming in wasn't as good as I thought it should be, but at least it was enough so the workday wasn't left totally up to Vicki and me.

I barely paid any mind to the nearly packed store as I hurried behind the counter and into the office. My apron was hanging from a hook just inside the door. I grabbed it, threw it on around my neck, and then headed out to face the world.

Vicki was busy ringing up a book order upstairs. She gave me a quick wave before turning back to the customer, dazzling him with her million-dollar smile. She really should have been an actress—something her parents had pressed on her since she was little—but she'd chosen the life of a store owner instead. She was wearing shorts today, showing off those legs of hers. I sighed and turned away, feeling even worse about myself than I had before, and found myself looking right into my dad's smiling face.

Something akin to "Gah!" garbled its way out of my mouth. My hand went reflexively to my hair to smooth it down as I staggered back a couple of steps. I was about to start babbling explanations to my appearance and late arrival when I noticed Dad's body was shiny and decidedly flat.

"Oh, I knew you'd approve!" Rita Jablonski, the resident gossip, said. She stepped around what was apparently a life-sized cardboard cutout of my dad.

"Approve of what?" My heart slowed down from its rapid pounding as I leaned on the counter. I loved my dad, I really did, but I didn't want him showing up at Pine Hills unannounced, especially with Rita lurking about. He is a retired writer, and Rita considered herself his number one fan. I didn't want her to go all *Misery* on him.

Rita patted the fake James Hancock on the shoulder. "Of having him as your store mascot!" She just about swooned. "I hate not having him in my bedroom looking out for me at night, but I think he belongs here, don't you?"

"He was in your bedroom?"

"Of course, dear." She giggled in a way that made my stomach do a flip. It sounded bubbly, lustful, and just a little crazy. I so didn't want to think about what she did with the cardboard cutout. "I was lying there this morning, looking at him, when I realized how fitting it would be to bring him in here. I mean, the store *is* named after one of his books, right? This is where he belongs, at least for a little while—I'll want him back eventually." She whispered it almost conspiratorially before going back to her normal shout. "With us having the book club meetings here, and reading one of his books, it just made sense."

"Wait, what?" My mind was unsuccessfully trying to catch up. I was still stuck on the fact that she kept him in her bedroom. I mean, ew. "What book club?" And where had she gotten a cardboard cutout of my dad? I didn't even know such a thing existed.

Rita waved a hand at me. "Oh, it's no matter." She glanced over her shoulder. Andi Caldwell and Georgina McCully—Rita's elderly gossip buddies—were standing near the two stairs that led up to the bookstore portion of the store with a man and woman I didn't know. "I best get over there," she said. "It's the first day, you know!"

She carried my dad over to the plate glass window and set him up so he could look out into the street before she walked over to where the others waited. Together, they went upstairs, forgetting me and my confusion.

I stared dumbly at the cardboard cutout. "What just happened?"

"Rita happened." Lena rolled her eyes as she stepped behind the counter. She walked over to the register to take an order.

Vicki came sauntering down the stairs then and walked over to me. "Are you feeling okay?" she asked. "You're looking a little pale."

"I'm not sure." I tore my eyes away from the cardboard Dad. "What's going on?" I nodded toward where Rita and the others were talking with another group of five strangers.

Vicki glanced back before turning to me with a grin. "Rita asked if they could have their book club meeting here, and I told her it would be okay. I figured it couldn't hurt business. In fact, it will probably help. She brought a few chairs to set up in the bookstore so they won't disrupt anything down here." She paused and frowned at my expression. "That's okay, isn't it?"

"I . . . Yeah." I was still reeling from Rita's assault and didn't know what else to say. I mean, it wasn't like having more people in the building was a bad thing. If they ordered coffee for their meetings, that could only help, right?

"Okay, good." Vicki breathed a sigh of relief as she tucked a strand of blond hair behind her ear. "She asked me on your day off, and I didn't want to call you and bother you with it. It seemed harmless enough, especially since you are a part of her writers' group and all."

"It's okay." And really, outside the cardboard Dad in the window, I didn't mind it all that much. Rita practically lived here, anyway. She spent a large portion of her day sitting in the corner of the store, typing away at her little pink notebook, torturing innocent prose.

Rita's arms suddenly flew up into the air and she stamped her foot. She said something harsh to the man in front of her, who responded in kind. Georgina and Andi stood beside the two strangers behind Rita, while another four people I didn't know stood behind the man Rita was yelling at. They were leaning forward as they argued, fists clenched, eyebrows bunched. It looked like a scene out of one of those movies where a pair of street gangs would argue right before breaking out into song and dance.

"I think I best go up there and see what's going on," I said, slipping around the corner. I doubted Rita and her crew would be dancing any time soon; this fight looked as if it might actually come to blows.

"I'll come with," Vicki said. She didn't sound worried about the fight that appeared to be escalating by the moment.

We marched across the store, leaving Lena to handle the register. She didn't seem to mind. Ever since we hired her, she'd focused hard on her job. She might look like trouble with all of the scrapes and bruises, and now with the purple hair, but she was truly a good kid. I couldn't have asked for better.

"I don't see what the problem is," Rita said as we neared. "We agreed to the book months ago!" She waved a paperback copy of *Murder in Lovetown* in front of the man's face. It was one of my dad's earlier works, one that he was embarrassed by, even today.

"We didn't know you'd be holding the thing in a store named after the author!" The man practically shouted it. He stood less than five and a half feet tall, weighed no more than a hundred and twenty pounds, and that might be generous. He looked as if he could stand to gain a few pounds. His hair was parted right down the middle in a vain attempt to conceal his rapidly retreating hairline. "We believe another book should be chosen."

"Isn't it a bit late for that?" Rita asked with a smug smile. "We've already started reading and have had the first of our local discussions."

The man's jaw clenched as he leaned forward and grabbed a silver teapot from the table in front of him. His fingers went white where he gripped it, and I had a sudden vision of him whacking Rita upside the head with it. I rushed forward and, before anything unseemly could happen, snatched it out of his hand.

"Everyone calm down," I said, holding the teapot behind my back, out of everyone's reach. I looked from face to face. "Anyone want to tell me what's going on?"

Rita straightened and thrust her impressive bust outward, practically poking the man in the eye with it. "Albert here doesn't approve of where we are holding our meetings. He thinks we should read something else."

"It gives you an unfair advantage!" Albert said at a near whine.

"Why *don't* you read something else?" I asked. "Like Agatha Christie? She's pretty popular." And wasn't my dad.

"Pah!" Rita waved a hand dismissively at me. "It's too late to make a change now." Her gaze moved past Albert to a man standing behind him. He was holding close a woman wearing a pearl necklace and diamonds on her fingers, as if protecting her. "Besides, *they* are the ones who should be ashamed. There are rules to membership, and *he* hasn't lived in Cherry Valley long enough!" She nodded toward the man.

"Rules? Cherry Valley?" Once again, I was operating at a loss.

Rita sighed and gave me a pitying look. "It's simple, really. Each town's team can have five members, but the members have to be a citizen of the town for at least one year before they can be an official part of the book club competition."

"Competition?"

"We talk about the book, and whoever understands it and can articulate it best wins the prize," Albert put in.

"Prize?" I wanted to break out of my rut of asking one word questions so I added, "What prize?"

"The silver teapot, silly!" Rita said with a gesture to the teapot in my hand.

I looked at Vicki, who simply shrugged. Who'd ever heard of a book club competition? Without having to ask, I knew Rita had been the one to come up with it. No one else would have thought of something so . . . odd.

I knew I was going to regret it, but I asked anyway. "How do you determine who the winner is?"

Rita gave me a look like I'd just asked her if the world was round. It was Albert who answered.

"We hold a public discussion. We alternate towns, and this year Pine Hills has the honor of hosting the event. We discuss the book amongst ourselves during the evening for a week, and then we have the big public discussion. Quite a lot of people turn out for it. The crowd votes for the winner."

I had a hard time believing what I was hearing. I mean, a book club competition? Really? I plowed on anyway. "Doesn't that skew the results?" They both gave me a blank look. "Won't the people from Pine Hills vote for the Pine Hills team and vice versa?"

"Oh no," Rita said. "This is much too important for that."

If she said so, I wasn't going to argue. None of this was making much sense to me.

"So, you are going to have the meetings here?" I asked, still trying to feel my way through.

"We are," Rita said. "We usually hold them at the library, but Jimmy here has kindly agreed to move it here this year." She leaned toward me as if she was about to share some deep, dark secret. "He's the local librarian, you know."

Jimmy gave me something of an annoyed smile, telling me he wasn't all that happy with the move. He wore a sweater vest and brown slacks with loafers that just about screamed librarian. His hair was buzzed short and his jaw square, juxtaposing the nerd with military. He was a good six feet tall, and I caught a hint of muscle beneath his plaid undershirt.

"It's nice to meet you," he said in a surprisingly nasal voice. "It's Jimmy Carlton." He put his arm around the short, round woman next to him. "And this is my wife, Cindy."

Since introductions were already started, I turned an expectant look on the Cherry Valley group.

"Vivian Flowers," the oldest member said with a shrug when my eyes landed on her. She looked to be at least eighty and probably weighed not much more. Her dress was covered in white lilies. I wondered whether she chose it because of her name, or if she simply liked the pattern.

The next man in line squinted at me through thick, black-rimmed glasses. "Orville Rush." He was clutching the paperback copy of his book close to his chest, and even then his hands shook. His hair was but a wisp on his head.

The tall man whom Rita had indicated earlier smiled at me. He wore a fedora, pulled down low over his eyes, and an unbuttoned suit coat over a white shirt. "David Smith." He tipped his hat toward me, and I nearly swooned. The man's voice did something strange to my insides. He was clearly from across the pond, if his accent was any indication.

"Sara Huffington," the woman with the pearl necklace said in a bored tone of voice. She snuggled in closer to the Brit and promptly ignored the rest of us.

"And as you know, this is Krissy Hancock, daughter of our beloved author." Rita put an arm around me. "She has kindly agreed to host the event this year, so I do hope you can show her some respect." The last was aimed at Albert, who looked away, frustrated.

I tore my eyes from David and handed Rita the teapot. "I guess I should get back to work, then." The argument seemed to be over, and I wanted to get as far away from these people as I could before another one broke out. "It was nice to meet you all."

"Likewise," David said in his silky smooth voice. It was followed by a wink.

I made a little squeak before spinning and hurrying away, Vicki hot on my heels.

"Cute, isn't he?" she asked as soon as we were back downstairs.

"Uh-huh." It was all I could manage. I fanned myself off.

"Do you think it will be okay to allow them to have

their meetings here? If they argue like that all of the time . . ." Vicki looked worriedly back up the stairs.

"I think they'll be fine."

And if it meant I got to sit back and watch David Smith while I worked, I don't think I'd mind a little arguing, either. I mean, what could possibly be the harm?

2

I spent the rest of the day with half of my mind on work, the other half on the book club. Rita and the others left the store an hour after I talked to them, claiming they'd be back for the real meeting that night, yet every few minutes I'd find myself looking upstairs where they'd sat, wondering how it was going to play out.

The bell above the door jangled, and Mike Green walked in. He was a tall and lanky man with shoulder-length brown hair swept back from his face and liberally coated with hairspray or some sort of gel. He was one of those people with such a baby face, he was still carded at the movies, despite the fact he was in his mid-twenties. I even went as far as to make sure his ID was legitimate when he'd applied for the job. Pimples speckled his chin and forehead, and he was sporting his best attempt at side-burns, though it looked more like peach fuzz to me.

"Hey, yo," he said with a nod to me. "I'll take the register."

"Thanks," I said. "Been a busy day."

His eyes gleamed at that. "Can't wait."

I went to the back to return my apron to its peg, feeling only mildly guilty for the shorter day. Lena had left an hour ago, and I was off in five minutes. Vicki, who'd been there all day, planned on staying until close with Mike. When I'd tried to tell her I'd stay later, she shook me off with a "You have a long day coming up."

In a way, I was thankful. At least now I wouldn't have to stare at Cardboard Dad any longer. Every time my eyes passed over him, I shuddered. Something about it bothered me, though I couldn't quite pinpoint what it was. Maybe it was just the idea that it had been in Rita's bedroom and was now standing in my shop, staring out the window, scaring off customers.

Or maybe it was just because it was my dad, and darn it, no one wanted a life-sized cutout of a parent hanging around while they worked. It's downright creepy.

By the time I was on my way home that evening, my feet were killing me and I was mentally exhausted. I still couldn't wrap my mind around the idea of a book club competition, and no amount of thinking about it helped. It was just another one of those strange quirks of Pine Hills, I supposed. The town was like nowhere else.

I pulled into my driveway and parked. I had a fleeting thought about adding a garage but dismissed it pretty quick. You had to have money for that, and while I wasn't eating out of trash bins, I wasn't rolling in the dough, either. A garage would have to wait.

I made a pointed effort not to look toward Eleanor's house as I got out of the car. I could feel her staring at me with those binoculars pressed to her eyes. I focused instead on the sedate looking Phan household on the other side of my property. His pink car was nowhere in sight, but a white SUV was parked out front. I'd seen it a few times since I'd moved in and could only assume it was owned by his significant other, Lance. I would need to head over and officially meet the man sometime. So far,

I'd only seen a picture. From what I gathered, he kept himself busy, often out of town doing whatever it was he did for a living.

But the introductions could wait until another night. I dragged myself to the front door, rubbing my eyes. You'd think that with the extra sleep, I would have had more energy, but no siree. I felt dead to the world, and after about fifteen minutes inside, puttering around, I figured I *would* be.

Yawning, I fumbled for my keys. I stepped up to the door and just about face-planted when I kicked something lying on my front stoop. My hand made a solid *smack* as it slammed against the door as I caught my balance.

A wrapped package lay at my feet. Pink paper was tied together with a long length of twine. I picked up the package and shook it, just to make sure it wasn't a bomb or maybe a bag of dog poop. It wasn't very smart, I'll grant you, but I was tired, so I could be forgiven. There was a faint, decidedly foodlike rattle from inside. A little card was taped to the top. It read, "To Krissy. From your loving neighbors, Jules and Lance."

"How sweet." I glanced toward the Phan house, but the lights were all off. Either they'd gone to bed early or were out running around somewhere. I'd have to save my thanks for later.

Unlocking the door, I tucked the package under my arm and headed into the house. Misfit darted for the door, but after years of practice I knew how to deal with the fuzzy demon. I pushed open the door far enough to insert my foot, gently pushing him away as I eased inside. The screen slammed closed, and I stepped aside to close the inner door. Normally I'd get a good swipe on the ankle for my effort, but tonight all I earned was an annoyed kitty huff.

"You feeling okay?" I asked the cat. He was sitting on the floor, staring at me, tail swishing from side to side. Okay, maybe he wasn't looking at *me*, but rather the box in my arm. "I don't think so," I told him, holding the package even higher. "It's a gift for me and I get to open it first."

Misfit followed me into the dining room where I set my purse and package onto the island counter. He jumped up and immediately made for the colorful packaging. I snatched it up before he could get his greedy claws into it.

"Can't you be good for a whole minute?"

He gave me a look that quite clearly said, "Of course not, moron. Who do you think you're dealing with here?" before pawing at me.

Holding the package away from him, I turned it over in my hand. The pink paper was covering what felt like a flimsy cardboard box, about the size of a shoebox. The twine itself was one continuous piece that wrapped around the entire thing in a way I could never manage on purpose.

I opened my junk drawer and removed a pair of scissors, knowing I'd never figure out how to get it open otherwise. I snipped the twine close to the knot and unwound it. The paper came next, and I set the wrapping and twine on the counter, next to the sink—which was about as far from the cat as I could get it without leaving the room. He gave me an annoyed look but remained firmly planted on the island, eyeing the box.

"I don't think you'll be eating these," I said, peeking under the lid. It was filled nearly to the brim with freshly baked chocolate chip cookies. I removed one and sampled it.

Misfit's eyes narrowed as I chewed. His tail picked up speed as he watched me, growing more and more annoyed by the second.

"Sorry," I said, wiping drool from my lips. The cookies weren't just good; they were *amazing*. I might have to hire on whoever made them, because there was no way I was ever going to make something this delicious. "You can't have chocolate."

Misfit hopped from the counter and sauntered off toward the bedroom. I considered following him, knowing he was going to get back at me some way, but I decided against it. Better now than when I was trying to sleep.

I looked at the cookies in the box and knew I should put them away, but they were just too darn good. I grabbed a chipped mug from the cabinet, turned on the coffeepot, and went about creating bliss.

After the first sip, I realized I could die right then and there and be content. Little bubbles escaped from where the cookie sank to the bottom of the mug to absorb the chocolaty, sugary goodness. The smell of coffee and chocolate filled the kitchen as I sat down at the dining room table to drink.

A horrible hacking sound came from down the hall, followed by the sound of rampaging elephants as Misfit hurried away from the mess he left me, like I wouldn't realize it had come from him. I swear that cat revenge pukes. He ran straight down the hall and into the laundry room, where he would more than likely play the game of *Miss the Litter Box*. It looked like I'd be dealing with two messes tonight.

The thought nearly pulled me away from the bliss of the cookie. I tried hard to focus on drinking and chewing the little chunks that broke free from the whole, but other thoughts invaded. I kept seeing Rita's smug smile as she held up the cardboard cutout of my dad. I could deal with the book club and listening to them bicker for a week or so, but that? No sir. I don't think I could handle going to work every day with *that* looking at me.

I finished my coffee and grabbed a spoon. I could try to talk to Rita and see if she would take Cardboard Dad back home, but somehow I knew it would be pointless. Just asking would probably offend her enough that she'd make a scene. I supposed I could ride it out, but what would that do to my sanity? I had the tendency to let the smallest of things bother me, and having a flat version of my dad waiting for me at work day in and day out would drive me insane.

That did it. I scooped up the cookie and ate it. I am sure it tasted like pure heaven, but I hardly noticed. I took the mug to the sink, rinsed it out, and then just stood there, staring at the remains.

If I didn't do something, I'd have to look my dad in the face every single day for the rest of my life, or at least until Rita decided to take him back. It would feel the same either way.

I glanced up, toward the window that looked out over the Phan property. Night was coming on fast and it would soon be dark.

A plan started to form.

Now, I'll admit, I'm no evil mastermind, able to concoct elaborate plans to foil my enemies. I didn't even register on the devious scale. I might have said a few choice things in my time, might have used my wiles to trick a police officer into taking me into a crime scene, but that hardly counted.

But I couldn't just let this go. If I didn't get rid of Cardboard Dad, it would eat at me until I either did something about it or exploded. I dwelled on stuff like this, much to the annoyance of anyone who knew me. It would be far better to take care of this now.

I calmly grabbed the paper towels from the counter and the can of Spot Shot from beneath the sink and headed to my bedroom. Not surprisingly, Misfit had left his mess right where I'd normally step if I was getting in or out of bed. I knelt down, cleaned it up, and then took the wet, lumpy paper towel to the trash. The spot would be wet until morning, but I could deal with that.

Misfit watched me from the hall and I made sure to smile at him, as if his actions didn't bother me. If I showed him my frustration, he'd only do it again.

"That's a good kitty," I said, patting him on the head as I headed for the laundry room. His ears flattened and he bolted for the living room as if I'd just threatened him with a trip to the vet. It took me a moment to realize that those were indeed the words I usually used when I *was* taking him to see the kitty doctor. Oh well.

I would have apologized, but having him out of the way made things easier. I didn't like him watching me, especially since I was planning to do something shameful once I was done cleaning up after him. It was like having him sit there and watch me while I am on the toilet; there are just some things that are never comfortable, no matter what.

I quickly cleaned up the mess he left outside the litter box, sprayed the room with air freshener, and then headed into my bedroom to wait.

Time ticked by so slowly, I very nearly fell asleep. The smart thing to do would have been to work on a few puzzles, maybe watch TV or browse the Internet for a few hours, but I wasn't being very smart right then. It should have been a sign, warning me that leaving the house tonight would end in disaster.

But I couldn't go to work tomorrow with Cardboard Dad there. I'd quit first.

After about twenty minutes, I couldn't take just sitting around anymore, so I began to organize my closet. When I'd unpacked the moving boxes a few months back, I'd haphazardly shoved my clothes onto hangers and put them into the closet with no apparent organization, which wasn't like me. I removed everything and sorted my shirts and dresses into separate piles. All of my dressy clothes—what few there were—went on the right. T-shirts in the middle. Everything I never planned on wearing ever again went on the left.

Once that was done, I hung everything up, except for a plain black shirt, and moved to my dresser to repeat the process with my drawers. I left out a black pair of yoga pants I'd bought in a fit of insanity and had never worn. I removed the tag, tossed the pants next to the shirt, and found a pair of white tennis shoes, which would clash with the darks but would have to do.

"Am I really going to do this?" I asked the clothing. I knew what I was doing was stupid. I could suck it up and just tell Rita the cutout had to go. If she took offense, well, I'd apologize and stand firm.

But there was a sense of excitement now that I was started, something that I hadn't felt since I'd chased down a murderer and nearly gotten killed. I wouldn't call myself an adrenaline junkie, but I definitely was feeling it as I considered my plan.

After a moment of silent contemplation, I slipped out of my work clothes and got dressed into the mostly dark ensemble. From there, I went into the bathroom to look at myself in the mirror.

A groan escaped my lips as I viewed the result. The yoga pants made it evident I hadn't worked out in a long time, and the shirt, though black, clashed with it. The yoga pants went down to mid-calf, so I was thankful I couldn't see most of my legs. I could only imagine how white they looked—probably as white as my shoes.

I considered changing but decided there really was no reason to. I wasn't doing anything *that* illegal. And when I got home, I could slip off my shoes and lounge around in the rest. The yoga pants weren't as uncomfortable as I'd thought, and with the way they looked on me, they might motivate me to do a few lunges and sit-ups before bed.

Misfit was curled up on the couch. He opened one eye, started to close it, and then raised his head to look at me.

"Shut up," I said, turning to the kitchen. It was still too early for me to leave, so I filled my mug with coffee, dropped in a cookie, and then took my time to enjoy it.

At a little past ten, I got up. Nearly everything would be closed by now, and I hoped most of the people would be tucked safely away in their beds. I turned off all the lights in my house and then started for the front door, where I hesitated. I could almost feel Eleanor's eyes through the wall. It very nearly made me reconsider.

Of course, when did I ever listen to reason, even when it was coming from my own head? Slowly, I turned the knob and eased out the front door. I closed it quietly behind me and then guided the screen door closed. From there, I walked on tiptoes to my car, slipped inside, and started the engine with a wince. At least I'd made it this far without making much sound. I just hoped it would be enough.

I backed out of my driveway, turned on my lights, and then headed for Death by Coffee.

Now, if there is one good thing about breaking into a place you own, it's that you don't actually have to break in. All the lights were off inside, and only a couple of cars rolled down the street. I waited until they passed before hurrying out of my Focus and running to the door. I unlocked it, eyes focused on the silhouette of my dad just inside the window. I pushed my way in, started to reach for the light, and then thought better of it. I was here for only one thing and it was here, right by the door.

"Sorry, Dad," I said with a giggle. My heart was pounding and I was breathing hard as I grabbed the cardboard cutout around the waist. I had every right in the world to be in my store in the middle of the night, but it felt as if I was breaking into a bank.

A twinge of guilt made me hesitate. I promised myself that after a week or so, I'd return the cutout to Rita, claiming I found it somewhere. Maybe then she'd realize how dangerous it was to leave the thing at the store and she'd keep it at home.

The thought made me feel a little better about what I was doing. I wasn't *stealing* it; I was just borrowing it without permission. There was a difference.

I carried Cardboard Dad outside, locked the door, and then took him to my car. The cutout wouldn't fit into the trunk without bending it, so I put it into the backseat at an angle. I closed the car door, hurried around to the driver's side, and got in. I was gasping for breath by the time I was on the road again, heading for home, but I was pretty sure no one had seen me.

Once I was safely back in my driveway, I checked to make sure Eleanor Winthrow's curtain wasn't moving, noted that Jules's pink car was now parked in his driveway and a light was on somewhere in the back of his house, and then removed the cutout carefully from the backseat. I carried it to the front door, slipped inside, and then leaned against the wall, still breathing as if I'd just run a marathon.

I looked over at Dad and smiled. "It looks like you'll be staying with me for a little while. Hope you don't mind."

Thinking of where he had been spending his nights lately, I was pretty sure he wouldn't.

3

A crash brought me sitting straight up in bed, and face-to-face with my attacker. I screamed and flailed my arms, which didn't have the desired effect of allowing me to escape. Instead, I found myself trapped even farther within the confines of my covers. I rolled sideways and promptly fell off the side of the bed, where I hit with a solid *thunk*. I crawled across the floor, toward the bathroom, in the hopes I could escape before the man who'd broken into my house could kill me.

I made it halfway there before my arm bumped into cardboard.

It all came together then.

Cardboard Dad was leaning against the wall where I'd knocked him. My bedroom door was closed, just like I'd left it when I'd gone to sleep. I'd brought the cutout into the bedroom because I was afraid Misfit would claw the dickens out of the thing if given the chance.

No one had broken in. I'd simply scared myself.

I breathed a sigh of relief as I picked myself up off the floor with as much dignity as I could manage. I glanced at the clock and found that my alarm wasn't due to go off for another hour, but with the way my heart was racing, it was unlikely I'd ever get back to sleep. Early morning sunlight drifted in through the parted curtains. Birds sang. It was going to be a good day.

I started for the bathroom to relieve a bladder that had come within a fraction of releasing when I'd woken up to my dad looming over me. I made it to the doorway when there was a loud thump somewhere within the house.

My entire body went icy cold. I opened my mouth to call out, but snapped it closed again. I didn't want to alert whoever was out there that I knew they were there. I wasn't sure how they'd interpret my screams and my falling out of bed, but I didn't have time to worry about it, either. I looked toward where I usually kept my cell phone overnight to charge. The nightstand was empty. I'd left the darn thing in my purse.

Which was on the dining room table . . .

In the room where my attacker might be lurking . . .

Okay, Krissy, you can do this. I looked around my bedroom but found nothing I could use as a weapon. I really needed to invest in a baseball bat or a high-powered rifle or something. Being defenseless sucked.

With nothing but a lamp evident in the bedroom, I went into the bathroom and opened a drawer, quietly so as not to be heard. I grabbed my flat iron and considered plugging it in and warming it up before using it, but another crash, followed by a pained yowl, stopped me.

Misfit!

I rushed for the bedroom door, flat iron in hand, cord whipping my legs behind me. If the intruder so much as laid a finger on my cat, I'd, well, watch as the cat ripped him or her to shreds. Those claws of his should be registered deadly weapons. He could take care of himself.

Unless the intruder has a gun, of course.

I stopped at the bedroom door and pressed my ear

against it. There were a few more thumps, but I couldn't tell for sure where they were coming from. I licked my dry lips and then turned the doorknob. I opened the door slowly, knowing it was going to squeal as I did, and sure enough it let out one of those ominous *creeeeaaaakkks* you hear in scary movies. I winced, and then rushed out, figuring I might as well leap in headfirst, rather than give the intruder time to prepare.

No one was in the hall. A crash from the living room sent me running that way, flat iron held above my head, ready to smite down whoever dared wake me . . .

. . . and rushed right into a disaster.

Misfit was standing between the dining room and living room, back arched, fur standing on end. Chairs were knocked over. My purse lay on the floor, contents strewn across the linoleum. One of the lamps in the living room lay busted on the carpet. The front door was closed, and even from where I stood, I could see that it was still locked.

My head jerked from side to side, looking for someone, yet it appeared Misfit and I were alone.

And that is when I saw it.

Hanging from his fluffy orange tail was a piece of twine. My gaze traveled from Misfit to the counter where I'd left the wrapping after I'd opened Jules and Lance's gift. The pink paper was lying on the floor, torn into tiny little bits.

The rest of the twine was nowhere to be seen.

Misfit's head jerked back toward his tail. He licked twice, let out an annoyed yowl, and took off toward the couch, where he ran along it sideways, claws tearing, and then around the side, where he vanished behind it.

I leaned against the wall, heart hammering. "Why did you have to scare me like that?" I asked him. I couldn't catch my breath. The morning was already warm, and my terror only made it worse. I made my way across the mess of the floor, stepping around large balls of orange and white fur, and opened the front door. I made sure the screen was fully closed before taking a deep breath of fresh air. There was a breeze and it felt good on my skin. I turned to find Misfit sitting in the middle of the room, rapidly licking his backside.

"Come over here, silly," I told him. "It's just stuck to you."

Misfit gave me a frantic look and then tried to climb the wall.

"Stop that!" I rushed over and grabbed him, which was a huge mistake. As soon as my hands landed on him, he turned into a whirling, writhing dervish that was made of nothing but claws and teeth and fur. I yelped and dropped him, arms screaming from at least a dozen scratches. Misfit bolted for the kitchen, running as if his tail were on fire.

I sucked at an especially deep scratch on my left hand and approached him warily. Misfit was standing in the middle of the room, back arched, tail swishing wildly around him. He was panting, and I could tell the twine was just about driving him crazy.

"If you'll just let me help," I said in as calm a voice as I could manage, "I can make it all better."

He glared at me, swished his tail a few times, and then charged at me like a bull.

I had only an instant to think. He was coming right for me, intent on getting past me—*through* me if he had to. I dropped to my knees, rapping them hard against the floor, but it was my only shot. Misfit tried to change course, but he was on tile. The fuzz between his toes meant he had little in the way of traction. His feet flailed wildly on the floor and he turned sideways, where he slid directly into me. I latched onto him, tucking him firmly against my chest where he couldn't move.

"I've got you!" I practically screamed it in triumph. Misfit struggled for a moment before he sagged in my grip, panting.

Carefully, so as not to give him a chance to free himself, I adjusted my grip so I could see his tail. There, on the underside, was the twine. I grabbed the end and pulled, thinking it would simply fall off and he'd be fine.

Boy, was I wrong.

Misfit let out a tortured yowl that reverberated throughout the house and probably woke the neighbors if all of the screaming and crashing hadn't done so already. A dog started barking somewhere down the road. The twine pulled taut, only moving a tiny fraction before becoming caught on something.

"Now, what in the world?" I lifted Misfit's tail and instantly saw the problem.

The twine wasn't just wrapped in his fur like I thought; it was coming out of his, well, you know, backside.

"Oh no," I moaned. I'd completely forgotten about the twine while planning my not-so-daring heist. He must have eaten it after I'd gone to bed. I knew better than to leave something like that lying around. I might as well have sprinkled it with catnip and set it in his food dish.

Misfit looked back at me with a "This is your fault" look on his face. I tugged gently on the twine, pulling it an inch. Misfit squirmed in my arms, clearly not liking the sensation of a long piece of twine being pulled out of his rear. Really, I don't know many people who would.

"It will be over in just a few moments," I told him as gently as I could. "Maybe this will teach you not to eat things you aren't supposed to." I grinned, despite the situation. "Everyone could use a little cleaning out every now and again."

"Why are you flossing your cat?"

The sudden voice startled me so badly, I slackened my grip on Misfit while jerking back with the hand holding the end of the twine. Misfit shot toward the couch so fast, he was nothing but an orange blur. The twine whipped out of him at high speed.

I looked up with a grimace to find Officer Paul Dalton standing just outside my screen door, in full uniform, sandy brown hair tucked under his police hat, with a perplexed look in his startling deep blue eyes.

"I wasn't flossing him," I said, standing. I could feel my face flaming, but what could I do? He'd seen me pull something out of my cat's butt; I'm not sure how a relationship—no matter how limited it might be—could recover from that.

"Are you sure?" he asked. "It looked like you were flossing him to me."

I dropped the twine into the trash. "I'm sure. I was definitely *not* flossing the kitty. He'd eaten some twine and . . ." I trailed off, knowing how silly it sounded.

Paul stood there a moment, looking bewildered, before glancing toward the door. "May I?" he asked.

"Sure." What else could I say? I wasn't about to tell him to go away, no matter how unflattering I must look. I was still in my black outfit and my hair had to be a mess.

As he entered, I patted my head, winced at the tangles of my hair, and then tried to adopt a relaxed posture.

"Don't mind the mess," I said. "Misfit went on something of a rampage." I plastered on a fake smile. "So, what's up?" The smile slipped when I saw the look on Paul's face.

Normally, he was all dimples and bulging muscles, but

today he was anything but. Even after witnessing what would probably be forever known as the Flossing Incident, he didn't even show a hint of being amused. That was definitely not a good sign.

"What's going on?" I asked, straightening. I felt a sudden urge for coffee and headed into the kitchen to turn on the pot.

"I wouldn't do that," Paul said, voice grave. "You won't have time for it."

"What? Why?" I turned to face him, a feeling of dread creeping into my gut. "Has something happened?"

Paul stood there a long moment. He'd taken off his hat and was fiddling with it. The brown of his hair was slowly turning a dirty blond during these warmer months. What I wouldn't give to run my fingers through that hair. Maybe once he delivered the bad news, he could make me feel better by taking me to my morning shower.

Instead, he just stood there, staring at his hat. He opened his mouth a few times as if he was going to speak, but nothing came out. Definitely not a good sign.

"Paul?" I said. My hands were starting to shake. "Is everything all right?"

He shook his head.

My mind wanted to go to the worst possible places, but then I remembered Cardboard Dad sitting in my bedroom. A smile found its way onto my face as my shoulders eased.

"Look, I can explain . . ."

Paul held up a hand. "Don't," he said. "Not yet. Not here."

I frowned. I mean, how much trouble could one person get into for stealing a cardboard cutout from her own store? I knew Rita loved the thing a little more than what was healthy, but to call the police over it? It didn't make sense.

"Krissy," he said with a heavy sigh that seemed to take

all of the strength right out of him. "I'm going to have to ask you to come down to the station."

"What?" I gawped at him. "It's not that big of a deal!"

He looked up at me. "Don't say anything until we get there, okay?"

I nodded, feeling light-headed. He held a hand out to me and I walked over. He gently took my arm and started to lead me to the front door, despite the fact I wasn't wearing shoes.

This can't be good.

"Can you at least tell me what's going on?" I asked as we stepped outside.

Paul led me over to the cruiser and opened the back door for me—the *back!* I slid inside without protest.

"There's been a murder," he said. "And it happened at Death by Coffee."

4

There's something unnerving about sitting alone in a police interrogation room—even if it does look more like a lounge than a place where hardened criminals are questioned. My foot jiggled up and down, and I kept looking at the wall behind me as if there was something more than a dartboard there. I swear I could feel eyes on me. Did they make see-through walls like those one-way mirrors? It sure felt like it.

Paul didn't zip strip me up like I thought he would. He didn't answer my questions on the ride over, either. After I gave up trying to talk, we rode all the way to the police station in silence. He spoke to me again only once we were inside the interrogation room, where he told me to sit tight before walking out.

I eyed the coffee machine across the room. The pot was halfway empty, and I knew it had probably sat there for the last two hours, but I was thirsty and headachy. I hadn't had time for my morning coffee, which was usually a recipe for disaster.

Eventually, the door opened and Chief Patricia Dalton entered. She was flanked by her son, Paul, and the one cop in the entire world I didn't want to see right then, Officer

John Buchannan. He was grinning as if he'd been the one to apprehend me, which seemed to be his normal expression anytime I got myself into trouble. He'd caught not just me, but Paul, at the scene of a crime, poking around where we shouldn't have been. He'd arrested us with much gusto, but we'd gotten off pretty easily—probably because Paul is the chief's son—which had to rankle Buchannan to no end. Ever since then, he'd had it in for me.

I stood as they entered, and opened my mouth to speak but had no idea what to say. Proclaiming my innocence right off the bat was probably the wrong thing to do, especially since I had no idea whether they viewed me as a suspect or not. As far as I knew, I was there only for my protection, though looking at Buchannan, I was guessing it was a bit more than that.

"Is Vicki okay?" I asked, suddenly worried about my best friend. If the police had me here for my protection, they'd have to have a reason for it, wouldn't they? And since Vicki was often working before I ever showed up . . .

"She's fine," Chief Dalton said. She pointed to a plastic chair pushed against the table in the middle of the room. "Sit."

I stepped away from the couch, more worried than ever. I'd never been told to sit anywhere but on the semicomfortable couch when in the interrogation room, which was happening more than I would like. Something was different this time, something that had my stomach in knots and my forehead breaking out into a cold sweat. I eased down slowly, looking from face to face as I did. Buchannan was still grinning. Paul and Patricia looked grim.

"Please . . ." I trailed off as the chief's eyes rose to meet mine.

"Where were you last night?" she asked in a businesslike tone.

"After work, I went home."

"And afterward?"

"I went to sleep."

Buchannan lunged forward and slammed his open palm down onto the table. I just about toppled over backward as he leaned in, putting his face as close to mine as he could with the table between us.

"Liar!" he screamed. "We know what you've done. You won't get away with it."

The room fell silent as Buchannan's shout finished echoing off the walls. Both Daltons stared at him like he was an idiot, which I wholeheartedly agreed with. I think the chief was more disappointed in him than anything. With a sigh, she took him by the arm and pulled him away from the table. His chest was heaving and his grin had turned into a sort of sinister glower.

"John, I think you need to take a walk. Go. Cool off." Chief Dalton gave him a little shove toward the door with one hand while keeping a firm hold on him with the other. "Now."

Buchannan turned incredulous eyes on her, clenched his jaw, and then jerked his arm from her grip. I had a sudden flashback to all those police dramas on TV where one cop would act the friendly part while the other was the rampaging psycho. It was obvious which part Buchannan was playing.

He raised a finger and pointed it at me—well, jabbed it, really. "I knew about you from the start." He was practically snarling. "I only wish I'd been there to see you do it. Then I wouldn't have to hold back."

"John!" Patricia barked his name. "Out."

He turned and stormed through the doorway. He slammed the door behind him hard enough to cause the dartboard to rattle.

"Jeez," I said. "He seems a little uptight today."

Nobody cracked a smile. I swallowed as best as I could due to my parched state and chose to study my hands rather than meet their unhappy gazes.

"Now," Chief Dalton said, leaning on the table in front of me. Paul remained near the door, like he was afraid to come in any farther. "Buchannan wasn't entirely wrong. We have a witness who claims she saw you leave your house last night, dressed in black, acting like you were up to something." She looked me up and down.

My stomach clenched as I crossed my arms over my shirt, as if to hide it. I had to take a few deep breaths before I could answer, lest I be sick all over the table. "Eleanor?" I asked, knowing the answer already.

Chief Dalton didn't so much as twitch. Behind her, Paul gave the faintest of nods. I guess at least someone was still on my side.

"I suppose I did leave last night," I admitted, face flaming for being caught in the lie. "I had something to do at Death by Coffee."

"In the middle of the night?" Patricia asked. "Dressed like . . ." She gestured at my outfit and frowned. "Like that? Why not wait until morning? What was it you had to do?"

"It was nothing. I forgot something and had to pick it up. I was wearing this for bed." I tried not to wince at all the little white lies I was telling. I was afraid of what they'd do to me if they knew the truth. When I thought about it, the whole thing sounded silly, so much so I was worried they wouldn't believe me.

Patricia sighed and rubbed at her temples. "Please tell me you didn't kill him."

"I didn't kill him." I paused. "So, who didn't I kill?"

"When you went to the shop, did you see anyone?" Patricia asked, ignoring my question.

"No." I shifted in my seat. The plastic was hard and uncomfortable. "It was dark. I only ran in for a minute and was out again. I didn't even turn on a light or go much farther than the entrance. I promise I didn't kill anyone, and I swear I never saw a body!" I started to hyperventilate.

Paul moved from where he stood to the coffee machine. He poured some of the thick goop into a Styrofoam cup and carried it over to me. I took it with a muttered "Thanks" and took a sip. The bitterness was enough to cause me to grimace. What I wouldn't give now for one of Jules Phan's cookies.

"Now, think hard," Chief Dalton said as Paul stepped back. "When you went into Death by Coffee, did you see anything at all that seemed out of place? Hear anything?"

I shook my head. The only thing out of place was the cardboard cutout of my dad, but I'd removed that. "No one was there." My blood ran cold. But what if someone *had* been there, waiting inside the darkened shop. "Oh, my God." My hands were trembling so badly now, I had to set the cup down lest I spill lukewarm coffee on myself. "Do you think the killer could have been waiting in there for me?"

"We don't know," Patricia said.

"Oh, God." I very well might have been within inches of my death. If I'd turned on the light, I could have seen a masked man, knife poised and ready, or perhaps a gun would have gone off. I shuddered.

"What can you tell me about David Smith?" Patricia asked.

I jolted out of my thoughts. "The British guy?"

The chief nodded.

"Not much. He was in the store yesterday because he's part of a book club competition Rita is running."

"I know of it," Patricia said, her expression stony.

"That's all I know about him. He came in and . . . wait! Is he dead?"

Paul and his mom shared a look before the chief nodded. "He was found this morning by your partner, Vicki Patterson."

Holy crap! What was it with me and meeting guys who ended up dead shortly after? The sad thing was, I sort of liked David. Well, it was his looks and voice I'd liked, but I didn't actually know anything else about him. It would have been easier if he'd been a jerk.

I sniffed and a tear found its way onto my cheek. "Who would do such a thing?" I asked, genuinely shocked.

"We were hoping you could tell us."

I looked from the chief to Paul and back again. "I have no clue. There was a little spat earlier that day, but it was between Rita and Albert—he's one of the guys from out of town." Patricia nodded as if she already knew. "I had to step in when Albert was about to clunk Rita over the head with some stupid teapot. . . ." I trailed off at the look the two police officers were giving me. "What?"

"David Smith was bashed in the head with a silver teapot," Paul said, speaking for the first time since he'd left me alone in the room. "It was next to the body. We found quite a few fingerprints on it and hope one of them belongs to the murderer."

I groaned. "Some of the prints will be mine. I had to grab the teapot from Albert."

"Did anyone else touch it that you saw?" Patricia asked.

I thought back, but my head was a jumble. I mean, I couldn't believe someone else had died so soon after talking to me. It was starting to become a trend, and I'd been in Pine Hills for less than a year.

"I don't know," I said with a shrug. "I think Rita might have taken it from me, but I can't be sure. There were so many people there. Any one of them could have touched the thing. And if they left it out on the table and then went home, I'm sure Vicki or Lena or maybe even Mike could have moved it so someone didn't steal it."

Chief Dalton produced a pad of paper from her shirt pocket. She tossed it and a pen in front of me. "Write down all of their names, if you would."

I went about scribbling the names I could remember in my frazzled state. It wasn't easy. I kept seeing David's face, the way he smiled, the way he winked. I didn't have any real desire for the man, nothing I'd act on, anyway. But I sure hadn't minded looking at him or listening to him. To think that he'd never speak again brought yet another tear to my eye.

Could someone have killed him because they were jealous of him? With those looks and that voice, any man would be intimidated. Or could it have been someone from Rita's group, angry because the rules had been broken by his inclusion? It seemed ridiculous, but stranger things have happened.

And they seemed to be happening to me more and more.

"Krissy." Paul spoke right next to my ear, causing me to jump and jerk the pen across the page. I'd managed all of three names before getting lost in my thoughts.

"Sorry," I said. I hurriedly wrote the other names I could remember before sliding the pad across the table to Chief Dalton. "I think that is everyone. Some of them are from out of town, so I might have misheard their name or confused them with someone else."

"Thank you." She tucked the pad back into her pocket after only a cursory glance. "Now, I for one don't believe you had anything to do with the murder. We don't have an official time of death yet, so I can't completely rule you out. Our witness was able to give a general time of your return, so once we have a better timeline, I'm sure we'll be able to dismiss you as a suspect."

I nodded, though I had no idea what I was nodding for. I couldn't believe this was happening. Again. It was like I was a magnet for trouble.

"Still," the chief went on, tone serious. "I don't want you leaving town. You can go about your life like normal, but if I catch you leaving Pine Hills for any reason, I'm going to lock you up until we figure this thing out. Do I make myself clear?"

"Very."

"Good." Chief Dalton rose from her place at the table. "Paul will drive you home." She walked out.

I looked at Paul, hoping to find some sort of comfort in his gaze, but instead I found him looking down at his hands, frowning. When he glanced up, he didn't meet my eyes.

"Let's go," he said, turning away.

Officer Buchannan was waiting for us outside the room. He was glaring, and his teeth were clenched so tightly, I was positive his face was about to explode. He narrowed his eyes at me and gave me the "I'm watching you" hand gesture. I hurried past before he popped.

This time, Paul let me sit in the front seat as we got into his cruiser. It was an upgrade from the back, sure, but still made me feel like a criminal. As soon as he got into the car, I felt the need to defend myself.

"I would never kill anyone," I said. "I swear. I didn't even know the guy. Please, you have to believe me."

"I do," he said, though he didn't sound too confident. "It isn't my fault!"

He glanced at me, tried on a smile that failed miserably, and then started the car.

We rode in silence yet again, which wasn't all that bad of a thing. It gave me time to think. I wasn't sure how I could prove my innocence sitting at home, doing nothing. My fingerprints were on the murder weapon and I'd been caught sneaking out of my house like an idiot, thanks to my nosy neighbor. Even if I told the police why I went to Death by Coffee, I had a feeling they wouldn't believe me. My reasoning sounded lame, even to me.

I had an intense desire to solve the case, to prove my own innocence. I knew the police would do their best to make sure the right person was apprehended—or at least, most of them would. Buchannan had it in for me, meaning he would do everything in his power to make sure I ended up arrested for the murder. It would mean he'd be looking in all of the wrong places while a murderer was running loose.

I glanced at Paul, saw his contemplative frown, and realized that telling him my plan to poke around in the case would only end up with me behind bars or handcuffed to my bed.

I cleared my throat, suddenly embarrassed at where *that* thought had led me, and looked out the window as we pulled into my driveway. Paul stopped the cruiser beside my car but made no move to shut off the engine. He didn't even look my way, outside a quick glance. He bit his lip and then pointedly looked away. I could only imagine how we looked to Eleanor, who was inevitably watching, even now.

"Do you want to come in?" I asked. Maybe if I could talk to him alone, I could convince him I had nothing to do with this. I could show him Cardboard Dad and make him understand.

Then again, with the way my luck was going, he was just as likely to arrest me for stealing the darn thing. It might have been in my store, but it belonged to Rita.

"No," Paul said after a moment. "I best not."

"What about later? If there's a killer out there, I could use the company, just in case he has it in for me." I winced at how pathetic that sounded.

Paul shook his head. "I need to focus on the job. There's still a lot to do. You'll be fine."

My heart sank. "Okay." There was no talking my way out of this one, not as long as everyone assumed I knew more than I was letting on. "Then I'll see you sometime soon?"

"Sure."

I opened the car door and started to slide out. Paul's hand landed on my wrist and I just about threw myself into his arms. The worried look on his face was the only thing that stopped me.

"Be careful," he said before letting me go. "I really hope you had nothing to do with this."

That last bit stung. Where was the loyalty? Where was the innocent until proven guilty? It felt as if he'd punched me in the gut.

I got the rest of the way out of his car and then slammed the door a little harder than necessary. I caught Paul's wince before he turned and backed out of my driveway. I felt betrayed, horribly so. I mean, we'd gone on a date! Sure, it had been one measly date that hadn't yet developed into anything more than a few sweaty dreams, but that didn't mean he had the right to turn on me so easily. I really thought we could have had something.

As Paul's car vanished down the street, I turned away,

determined to get to the bottom of this murder and prove my innocence, not only to Paul but to everyone who even considered for an instant that I might have killed David Smith. I would leave no stone unturned, wouldn't sleep until I found the true killer!

And I would start, just as soon as I showered.

5

Smelling of flowery soap and shampoo, and with legs that didn't feel like sandpaper as they rubbed against each other, I headed for Death by Coffee. I felt rejuvenated, alive, but the feeling was quickly dashed when I saw my poor store. Ugly yellow and black police tape was strung across the door. A few gawkers stood on the sidewalk, trying to see past the few policemen still working the scene. It had been hours, yet they were still looking around. I vaguely wondered if the body was inside but quickly buried the thought. I didn't want to know.

I hurried past, forcing myself to look straight ahead after my first curious glance. I wasn't going in to work today; no one who worked there was. I had a sinking feeling we'd be closed for a week or two, or at least until the murder was solved. I only hoped we could weather the storm without going under.

Stop it, Krissy. You're not that bad off, and you know it.

Business might have been picking up lately, but it still felt like we weren't making enough money. I didn't know if we were pricing our coffee too low, or if it was something else that was causing the numbers to look so pathetic.

Vicki handled the money, so if there was something wrong, I was sure she would have told me by now.

I found a parking spot and pulled in. I shut off the car and then hurried across the street into a place called Scream for Ice Cream. It wasn't as bad of a name as a lot of the other stores in town, but it wasn't great, either. One of these days, a store called Bob's or something will open up. I don't care what kind of place it is; if a store opens with a simple name, I'll be the first in line.

An electronic ping sounded as I opened the door and stepped inside the ice-cream shop. Vicki was sitting at a table in the middle of the room. As soon as she saw me, she waved me over, smiling as if nothing was wrong. Half the guys in the place were watching her, and half of those didn't even have anything to eat. It was like she was a sun and every man on the planet had to fight with one another to orbit her. It was disgusting, really.

"How are you doing?" Vicki asked as I sat down across from her.

"I'm alive," I said, wincing as I realized how it must have sounded. "Can you believe the police actually questioned me?"

"I believe it." She nodded her head and shot a glance past my shoulder. I turned to find Officer Buchannan settling into a chair near the wall. He grinned and waved when he saw me looking.

"Great," I said, turning back. I wondered how long he'd been following me.

"I already ordered for us, if that's okay," Vicki said. "I know you love Rocky Road when things go wrong, and well, I think this whole mess qualifies as a Rocky Road event."

As if on cue, a kid who was no more than sixteen came around the counter with two bowls in hand. He set them down in front of us before scurrying back, as if we might bite.

"I don't know if I can take this," I said with a sigh. "Everyone keeps looking at me like I killed the guy."

"Did you?"

I gasped in shock. "How could you ask that? Of course I didn't!"

"Then you have nothing to worry about." Vicki shoved a spoonful of strawberry ice cream into her mouth and smiled.

I would have felt better if I believed it. I was sure there were more than enough women locked in a prison somewhere who were innocent of the crime they were convicted of. If I couldn't clear my name, Buchannan would make sure I joined them.

I leaned forward and lowered my voice. No sense letting Buchannan overhear our conversation if it could be avoided. "Did anything happen last night after I left?"

Vicki shrugged one delicate shoulder. "The meeting got a little loud and heated, but nothing anyone would kill over. I can hardly believe anyone would kill that poor man. He seemed so nice."

"What about after? Were they still arguing after you locked up?"

Vicki actually looked embarrassed. "Well, I didn't actually lock up last night."

That surprised me. One of us always closed, just as one of us always opened. I trusted both of our employees fully, but that didn't mean I wanted them in the store alone without either Vicki or me there to supervise them.

"Why not?" I asked. "Did something come up?"

"Not really," she said between bites of ice cream. "Trouble didn't like all the yelling. We left as everyone was packing up. Mike closed up for me."

"Oh." Then that wasn't so bad. Besides, if one of those people was a murderer, I'd much rather have Mike there to deal with them than Vicki. I had nothing against him, but if I had to choose between them, I'd take Vicki's survival every time.

Does that make me a bad person?

I shoveled some Rocky Road into my mouth and chewed, feeling as low as I could go. I glanced back at where Buchannan sat and hurriedly looked away. He was staring at me still, in almost the exact same position I'd last seen him. It was downright creepy.

"Don't worry about him," Vicki said. "He's just fishing right now. The police will realize you are innocent soon enough. It's not like they have anything on you, right?"

Sure, if you didn't count my fingerprints on the murder weapon, being placed at the scene on the same night as the murder, and, well, me being me. My life really did suck sometimes.

I took another large bite of Rocky Road and spoke around it. "Did the police talk to you already?"

Vicki's nearly ever-present smile slipped. "A little. They questioned me when they came to see the body. I called it in." She shuddered. "It was horrible."

I suddenly felt like the world's worst friend. In all of this, I really hadn't considered how finding the body would affect Vicki, or what condition he was in. All I knew for sure was that David had been hit in the head with the teapot hard enough to kill him. A shudder worked its way through me.

"Are you doing okay?" I asked, pushing my bowl away. I was only halfway through, but I was getting the chills thinking about the case and the cold ice cream wasn't helping.

"I suppose." Vicki sighed dramatically. "I was worried

they'd blame me, but they only asked me a few questions before kicking me out. And then when they told me the store would have to remain closed while they investigate, I put my foot down. There wasn't a mess and they are going to get all of the clues from there today, so there is no reason to remain closed longer than necessary. The police chief agreed with me, and we'll be opening tomorrow."

"Really?" I wasn't all that surprised Vicki had managed to talk them into letting us open so soon. She could sweet-talk just about anyone. There was a reason her parents had pushed her so hard to follow in their footsteps and become an actress. She had the charisma for it, not just the looks.

Still, the thought of reopening Death by Coffee after such a horrible tragedy had me worried.

"Do you think that's such a good idea?"

"Why not?" Vicki asked. "It isn't our fault the man was killed." She frowned. "I don't mean to disrespect him, and it is terrible what happened, but we shouldn't be punished for what someone else did. If we remained closed, our customers might go elsewhere."

She didn't need to mention that those customers had only recently started coming to Death by Coffee for their morning jolt in the first place. If they stopped coming now, it was unlikely we'd ever get them back.

"Besides," she went on, "if I have to sit at home and think about what happened, it'll drive me crazy. I'd much rather work." She paused, her frown deepening. "I do think I might skip out on the audition I was considering, though."

I looked up, surprised. "What audition?"

Vicki's face broke into a shy smile. "There's a local theatre that puts on a play every now and again. It's small-time stuff, really, but that's perfect for me. One of the leads had to bow out and her understudy is sick, so they're scrambling to find someone to replace her." She shrugged. "I thought I might give it a try. I might not want to stand in front of a camera, but I don't hate acting. This kind of thing would be perfect."

"Then you should do it."

"I don't know. . . ." She trailed off and looked toward the window. "With everything that's happened, it might be in bad taste. I should focus on making sure Death by Coffee survives this. I'd feel as if I'm abandoning you."

"Don't." I took her hand and squeezed. "If you want it, you need to do it. Don't let this stop you."

She eyed me a moment before breaking into a wide grin. "I was hoping you'd say that."

I laughed. "What kind of play is it?"

"Well . . ."

She never got to finish.

"Oh, my Lordy Lou!"

I groaned inwardly and turned to face Rita as she hurried across the ice-cream store to where I was sitting.

"Can you believe what happened, right in your own front yard? I mean, good Lordy! It's like something straight out of a James Hancock novel!"

I grimaced. Of course she would think so. In a way, every murder was like something out of one of my dad's books. If they kept happening, I was going to have to move elsewhere, somewhere where no one had heard of James Hancock and wouldn't constantly remind me I was his daughter.

Rita looked around the shop, mouth pursed, and waved at Buchannan, who only grimaced. She then turned back to me.

"It's just terrible David was killed, but I can't say I am sorry to see him go. He wasn't fit for the book club. I don't think he cared one lick about the book we were reading.

He hardly said a word the entire time we were there! He spent the whole meeting making eyes at all of the women." She took a breath. "And now that he's gone, and the teapot is all dented and in police custody, I just don't know what we are going to do." Another breath. "And that's not even the worst part! The killer stole my James!"

I just about choked. "You don't say?" My face felt warm, and I knew I was blushing as red as a carnation. I grabbed my ice-cream bowl and shoved a spoonful of melted Rocky Road into my mouth in the hopes it would cool me down.

"It's just plain awful!" she wailed. "I couldn't believe my eyes when I went to see what all of the ruckus was about and James was gone. I made the young man in the cute police outfit look for him, but he was nowhere to be found! What could James have possibly done to deserve being taken like that? He might have seen what happened, but it's not like he can talk."

"Do you have any idea who could have killed him?"

Rita shook her head sadly. "I just don't know. David upset a lot of people but not so much I could see someone killing him." She clapped her hands together. "Maybe if the police can't figure this one out, we can call your dad in! He'll know what to do."

I tried really hard not to show any emotion as I said, "I doubt he'll be interested."

"Oh, pah," she said with a wave of her hand. "I'm sure he could make something of this. That's what he does!" She looked at her watch and then heaved a sigh. "Well, I best be going. I haven't had my morning coffee yet, and I just don't know what I'm going to do now that your place is closed." She turned to Buchannan and raised her voice. "And I hope you are out looking for my James. Like I told you before, whoever took him is your killer, mark my words." Back to me. "I'll see you." She waved and strutted out the door.

"Talkative one, isn't she?" Vicki asked, grinning.

"Too much so." I glanced at Buchannan, who was watching Rita leave with an annoyed expression on his face. I wondered if he was the officer she'd had searching for Cardboard Dad; I kind of hoped so. I turned away and lowered my voice. "She's going to get me into trouble."

"How so?"

I leaned in so I was practically prone on the table. "You know that cardboard cutout she's all worked up about?"

Vicki nodded.

"Well, I took it."

"You what?" Vicki just about shouted it.

Wincing, I leaned in even closer. "I couldn't stand the thought of the thing hovering over me while I worked, so I went to Death by Coffee last night and took it."

Vicki's eyes widened. "Did you see David?"

I shook my head. "No one was there as far as I know. I only went inside the front door, grabbed the cutout, and took off." I paused. "Where did you find him, by the way?" It seemed strange I wouldn't notice it, even in the dark. David Smith wasn't a small man, so I should have seen something—an outline, or looming shadow perhaps.

"Up behind one of the bookshelves," Vicki said. "You had to just about trip over him to see him, which I did." She pushed her mostly empty bowl away.

"Ah." I guess that explained why I didn't see anything. And if he was all the way back there, there was a chance the killer could have been crouched behind the stacks without my knowledge, watching me.

The back of my neck started prickling. I glanced over my shoulder, but Buchannan was gone. I breathed a sigh of relief.

"Well, I think I'm going to spend the day shopping," Vicki said, pushing away from the table. "And you're coming with me."

"I am?"

"You are." She took my arm and led me toward the door.

"I . . . I have a lot to do." Like clean up after my cat and look into David's murder.

"You can do whatever it is you think you need to do later," she said. "You really do need to get out more." She stopped just outside the ice-cream store and turned to face me. "Have you done anything for fun since you've gotten here?"

"I went on a date." It came out at a near whisper.

"One date." She gave me a flat look. "And?"

"Well . . ."

She took my arm again and steered me down the walk. "That settles it. We're going shopping, and then afterward we're going to have a little fun."

6

"Bowling?" I said, staring at the building. "You can't be serious."

Vicki grinned at me as she started for the front doors. "It'll be fun."

I wasn't so sure about that, but I followed her in, anyway.

Vicki had driven to the bowling alley after we'd finished shopping. She'd refused to tell me where we were going, rightfully assuming I'd complain about it. I mean, bowling? Really? The last time I'd gone bowling was in high school, and that had turned into a disaster. I'd stepped on the slippery lane after tossing my ball, causing my feet to go out from under me as if I'd tried to walk across an icy lake. Vicki had been there, with a large portion of my high school class. She knew how mortified I'd been, how I'd sworn off the game since.

And yet, here we were.

I hoped the few bags of clothes I'd bought when we'd gone shopping earlier would be okay in my car. I'd left the Focus sitting outside Scream for Ice Cream, locked, sure, but with how my luck had been going lately, I wouldn't be shocked to come back to find the thing stripped down to the frame.

McNally's Alleys—another fine specimen of Pine Hills's naming—looked like any other bowling alley. There were eight lanes, three of them taken, and a small arcade off to the side, where a pair of college-aged kids stood, heads nearly touching as they giggled over a pinball machine. Ah, young love.

Vicki led the way to the counter, where a husky middle-aged woman sat. Her hair was flat and tired, as were her eyes. She looked as if she'd spent the last few years sitting in that exact same spot, watching the endless routine of balls rolling down the lane, crashing into pins that would reset after only a few seconds. When she turned her head our way, she showed no reaction.

"Just the two of us," Vicki said, approaching the counter. She gave the woman our shoe sizes, which surprised me. I couldn't believe she remembered mine after all this time.

The woman grunted and spun to pick out a pair of blue and red shoes for Vicki and a pair of green and pink ones for me. The color combination left a lot to be desired, but at least the shoes looked somewhat new. She sprayed them each once, killing any remaining bacteria and germs, before setting them onto the counter.

"That'll be fifty even," the woman said, sounding as bored as she looked.

"Fifty!" My eyes just about bugged out of my head. When did bowling get so expensive?

Vicki paid for both of us without complaint, and then scooped up her shoes.

"Lane three," the woman said, gesturing toward the lane with the big number three over it. "Once the first game starts, you have an hour. It'll be ten dollars per person for each hour after."

I picked up my shoes and followed Vicki toward the indicated lane. I could get through an hour, and would refuse to stay any longer. Fifty bucks was too much for throwing a ball at pins, and while another hour would cost only twenty dollars more, I still felt guilty that she'd paid for me when I was perfectly capable of doing it myself.

"Relax," Vicki said as she sat to change her shoes. "We're supposed to have some fun here."

I snorted as I pulled off my own shoes. "Fun. Kinda hard after, well . . . you know."

Vicki shook her head. "We're not going to think about that. We'll let the police take care of their business and then we'll get back to work. Life will go on like normal. I won't stress over it." She leveled a finger at me. "Neither will you."

"Yeah, okay." I found it highly unlikely I'd be able to ignore David's murder. First off, it had happened in Death by Coffee. It's kind of hard to forget something like that. Second, Buchannan thought I was involved somehow. Even if I wanted to forget about it ever happening, he'd be sure to remind me every chance he got.

Vicki finished putting on her shoes first and then wandered off to find a ball she liked. They were lined up against the far wall, presumably placed by weight if the numbers on the wall were any indication. I knew how quickly organization got ruined, so I doubted they were placed correctly. Most people didn't pay attention to where they picked something up, depositing it instead wherever was convenient when they were done. Even as I watched, Vicki went to pick up a ball that was on the lighter end and just about dropped it on her foot when it was heavier than she'd expected.

"This is going to suck," I grumbled, getting to my feet. My shoes were a little tight, but serviceable. I guess my feet had grown more than I thought. It was either that or these shoes were sized incorrectly. *One hour*, I reminded myself. I could do an hour.

The sound of balls crashing into pins wasn't quite deafening, but it was loud. The acoustics of McNally's could have been better. Instead of dampening the sound, the walls seemed to amplify it.

Vicki found a ball just as I approached. She grinned as she hefted it and then carried it back to our lane. "I'll get our names put into the machine," she called over her shoulder.

I eyed the bowling balls distrustfully a moment before picking up what I hoped would be one of the lightest, but with large-enough finger holes to fit me. I didn't have sausage fingers or anything, but I didn't have the super-thin appendages Vicki sported. I shoved my fingers inside, found it to be snug but not so much that they'd get stuck, and then carried the ball over to where Vicki was waiting.

"You're up," she said, with a grand gesture toward the lane.

I approached it with a hint of trepidation. I so didn't want a repeat of my high school fall. It hadn't hurt much more than my pride, but I remembered the sound of laughter, of my butt hitting the floor, feet flying up over my head. Just thinking about it caused a blush to rise up my neck.

"I will not fall. I will not fall." I repeated it like a mantra as I scuffed my feet across the floor. I stopped about a foot from the line and heaved the ball down the lane. It hit the floor with a thud that caused me to wince, bounced twice, drifted to the left, and then promptly went into the gutter. I kept my head down as I went to the ball return and waited. I could almost feel eyes on me from nearby lanes.

At least there was a lane between us and the nearest group of people.

My second try was better. I took out three pins, and then went to sit down while Vicki took her shot. As she weighed the ball in her hand and judged her toss, I looked around at the other groups in the room.

While I'd been embarrassing myself with my first throw, one of the groups had left, leaving only two still bowling, other than Vicki and me. The couple was still in the arcade, lost in their own little world.

My eyes traveled to the group near the far wall, in lane eight. It was a group of four, two elderly men and what was presumably their wives. They had on matching bowling shirts, telling me they were more than likely in a league together. I watched a woman who looked to be ninety if she was a day snatch up her ball, stride to the line, and toss it without considering it for more than a heartbeat. The ball hit the floor and made a satisfying hum as it sped down the lane. It crashed into the pins, sending all ten of them flying as if a bomb had gone off beneath them.

I groaned and looked away. Great, I was going to get shown up by someone's grandmother. It was a good thing Paul wasn't there to see me embarrass myself.

I turned the other way, to lane one, where three guys were playing. They were my age, and all of them looked as if they could have been on the cover of *GQ* or some other high-end magazine where all the men looked yummy in suits—unbuttoned or not. Two of the men were up by the lane. One was ready to throw while his buddy teased him mercilessly. I glanced toward the other man, who was seated, and found him looking at me.

I jerked my head away to watch Vicki as she took her second shot. She only had a pair of pins remaining, one right next to the other. She lined up her shot and strode forward with confidence. Her ball didn't move quite as fast as the old woman's had, but it was right on target. Both pins went down, and she did a little hop and a skip as she spun with a clap of her hands.

"Spare!"

"Nice shot," I said, rising. I snuck a glance back at the men. The guy wasn't watching me any longer but was instead getting his own shot ready. His dark, near-black hair was clipped short and styled. He was wearing a light-weight button-up shirt with the sleeves rolled so as not to get in the way. There wasn't a tan line or anything, but something about the way he held himself told me he normally wore a watch. Even with the lane between us, I could tell he wasn't wearing a ring.

I felt my face get hot as I turned toward my lane. *What are you thinking, Krissy,* I reprimanded myself as I approached the line. The guy was hot, but I was already sorta, not quite taken by Paul Dalton.

There's nothing wrong with looking.

I snuck one more quick glance to find him finishing up his shot—a strike, of course. He turned my way and grinned as if he'd known I'd been watching, causing me to just about drop my own ball as I spun to look away.

Suddenly, I didn't want to look like a fool and mess this up. I eyed the pins at the far end of the lane as I adjusted my grip on the ball. They stood there, mocking me with their innocent appearance. The lane, I noted, sloped toward the gutters with only a thin strip of flatness in the middle. I aimed for that as I started forward, and let fly.

The ball didn't bounce this time. It hit the floor and crept slowly down the lane. About halfway down, it started drifting to the left again.

"No, no, no. Come on," I muttered as it neared the pins. "Don't make me look like an idiot."

The ball didn't cooperate. It nudged the far back pin, which wobbled but didn't go down.

"Almost!" Vicki called cheerfully. "You'll get it next time."

Mortified, I trudged back to the ball return, picked up my ball, and then carried it back to the line. I knew I was still being watched, but at this point I just wanted to be done. I lined up my shot, tossed the ball toward the center, and watched as it guttered out a good foot from the pins.

Vicki, oblivious to my embarrassment, leapt up. "Isn't this fun?" she asked, going to her ball.

"Yeah," I said, not feeling it at all. I glanced toward lane one to find the other two men there, changing their shoes. It appeared they were done and leaving. *Thank God for small favors.* At least now I could stop embarrassing myself in front of a cute guy.

"You should aim to the right." The voice came from behind me.

I yelped and spun to find the man with dark hair standing behind my seat. He was leaning, arms straight, hands pressed against the back of my chair, as he smiled down at me.

"Excuse me?" I asked, heart hammering. Why did everyone always have to sneak up on me?

"When you throw," he said. "You cause a natural spin on the ball that sends it to the left. If you aimed to the right of center more, you'd have a better shot at hitting the pins."

Oh, God, kill me now. My face felt hot as I forced a smile. "Thanks," I said. "This is my first time in a really long time."

He chuckled. "I can tell. But that's okay. You should see

me when we go golfing. I might as well dress for fishing with as often as my ball hits the water." He straightened and held out a hand. "Will Foster."

"Krissy Hancock," I said, shaking his hand. I noted he was now wearing that watch I'd assumed he had. "It's a pleasure to meet you."

"The pleasure is mine." His eyes flickered toward Vicki and then back to me. "If you ever want some more practice, I'd be happy to show you," he said. "I'm not as good as Darrin and Carl over there, but I can hold my own."

I assumed Darrin and Carl were his two buddies but didn't ask. I was too busy trying to determine if he was doing what I thought he was doing. *Could a cute guy actually be flirting with me?* It seemed ludicrous.

"I, uh . . ." My vocabulary suddenly took a break and left me sitting there like a dope, mouth opening and closing while I thought of something to say.

Will laughed and glanced toward his friends. They were busy with their own conversation, pretending not to watch what he was doing. "It's okay if you don't want to," he said. "I know this is kind of sudden." Was that a ring of red creeping up his neck?

Oh, my God! He is *flirting with me!*

"I don't know if I like bowling," I said after I managed to swallow back my pounding heart. "I feel stupid every time I get up there."

"Me too," Will said with another laugh. His eyes were sparkling. They were a deep brown that made me think of warm, freshly baked chocolate chip cookies. "But you'll get over it eventually." He cleared his throat as his friends started our way. "But if you aren't interested . . ."

I was struck with a sudden fear that he would turn and walk away and I'd never see him again. It was stupid considering my heart belonged to Paul Dalton, but I couldn't help it. It wasn't every day a guy hit on me with Vicki in the room.

"I am!" I just about shouted it. "Well, maybe." I looked down at my hands. Why couldn't I say what I meant? "Maybe learning wouldn't be so bad."

"We've got to get back," one of Will's friends said as he approached. He winked at me before patting Will on the shoulder. "You can hit on the girls later."

Will checked his watch and frowned. "I'll be out in a minute."

His friends, grinning, walked past him, talking and laughing. I knew, without having to hear them, that they were making fun of me.

"You don't have to stick around," I said, feeling about as small as I could get. "It's okay."

Will's eyes darted to his retreating friends. "Don't mind them," he said. "They're both married already and think I need to get on board with the program. Of course, if you'd met their wives, you'd wonder why anyone would ever trap themselves like that. We're talking stuck-up snobs here." He smiled. "Just don't tell them I said so, all right?"

"Sure." I found myself smiling right along with him.

With a sigh, Will spread his hands in defeat. "But I really do have to go. We shouldn't have stayed out this long."

"Oh, okay," I said. The brief moment of flirting was nice, but it was good that it was over. He couldn't honestly be interested in me.

"Let me give you my number." He patted his pockets and frowned. "Do you have a pen and paper by chance?"

I winced. *Foiled by lack of stationery?* That was just my luck. "Sorry," I said.

"How about a cell phone? I left mine in the car."

This time I groaned. "Mine's in my purse, which I also left in the car." Go figure.

"Ah well." He smiled. "We'll figure something out." Another glance at his watch. "I best get going."

"Death by Coffee!" I shouted it at him like I'd completely lost my mind.

He raised his eyebrows at me in confusion.

"I work there," I said. "Well, own the place, really. You could stop by. We can work things out then."

He smiled. "Okay, then, Death by Coffee." He nodded slowly, and I could tell he had no idea where that was. "I'll see you sometime soon." Another quick peek at his watch and then he started away. "Have a good time, Krissy."

"I will, Will."

He chuckled and walked away.

"Look at you," Vicki said, grinning. "Making friends."

It was then I realized she'd been done with her turn long ago and had stood back to watch our little interaction.

"It's nothing," I said. "He's going to show me how to bowl."

"Uh-huh." She was smiling so wide, she looked like she might split her face in half. "You're going to let a man show you how to handle balls, all right."

"Vicki!" I looked around to make sure no one had heard her.

She laughed and gestured toward the ball return. "It's your turn, by the way." She sat down, still laughing.

I picked up the bowling ball and moved to the line, head still spinning from what had just happened. I didn't think it was possible for me to forget about David's murder, but right then it was the furthest thing from my mind.

Instead, I was thinking about Will, about his willingness to help a hopeless girl out with her ball-handling skills.

And I thought about Paul Dalton. Would he be jealous I'd talked to another man? Would he even care?

As I strode forward and threw my ball, I realized that at that moment I didn't really care either way.

7

Red and blue lights spun, illuminating the front of my house. I sat in my car at the end of the driveway, backseat full of things Vicki and I had bought on our free day together, and stared at the two police cars, not quite believing what I was seeing. Eleanor Winthrow stood outside her house, nodding as if she'd known this day was coming all along, which seemed to be the norm with most of my detractors. Chief Dalton stood, arms crossed, facing the front of the house. She turned as I started forward again. She motioned for me to park behind her cruiser.

"What's going on?" I asked, getting out of the car. "Did someone break in?" It would be just my luck to come from having something good happen to me, in the form of Will, to having someone break into my house and steal all of my things. Couldn't I ever catch a break?

Patricia frowned at me before handing me a piece of official-looking paper. I looked at it and gasped.

"A warrant? Why did you get a warrant?"

"We have reason to believe a stolen object that might pertain to the murder investigation could be inside the premises."

"Wait. What?" My heart started pounding. What could

they possibly think was inside? "Why would you think that?" I looked down at the warrant in my hand. "And how did you get this so fast?"

"Local judge," Patricia said, leaning against my car as if we were simply shooting the breeze. "Helps expedite things." She chewed on her lower lip a moment before narrowing her eyes at me. "Did you actually admit to stealing something from Rita Jablonski?"

My stomach fell. Of course. No wonder Buchannan had left the ice-cream shop so quickly. Apparently, he'd overheard my confession to Vicki, and after the scene Rita had made over her stupid cardboard cutout, he'd surely assumed I was up to something nefarious, especially since I hadn't told the police I'd taken it.

"I can explain . . ."

"Got it!" Buchannan strode out of my house, Cardboard Dad tucked under his arm. "She had it in her bedroom." His eyes fell on me and a grin split his face. "And there she is."

I went immediately defensive. "I didn't kill anyone!"

He sauntered my way, clearly enjoying every second of this. "Oh? Then why do you have this?" He held out the cutout as if it proved my guilt.

I reddened. "Because it was an eyesore." I glanced at the chief. "I was going to give it back."

He snorted a laugh. "Or is it because there are blood-stains on it that would implicate you in the murder?"

"What? Where?" I started forward, intent on scouring every last inch of the cutout in search of blood, but Chief Dalton stopped me with an arm across my chest.

"That's far enough, Krissy."

"But there isn't any blood! I took it from the front of

the store last night. That's all I did! I didn't kill anyone. Honest!"

"We'll see about that." Buchannan opened the back door of his cruiser and shoved the cardboard cutout into the backseat. Apparently, there were no evidence bags big enough for the cutout, or I was sure he would have made a show of sliding it inside. Once satisfied, he crossed his arms and stood expectantly in front of his cruiser.

"I guess we're all done here," Patricia said. She heaved a sigh. "Please stick around, okay? I'm sure you have a perfectly good reason for taking this thing, but until we check it over, this puts you at the very top of our suspect list, whether I like it or not."

"But . . . but . . ." But what? It was all happening too fast.

"Aren't you going to arrest her?" Buchannan asked as Chief Dalton started for her cruiser.

"Why?" she asked, clearly annoyed. "She isn't going anywhere."

"But she is our best suspect! She might make a run for it now that we have evidence."

Patricia glanced back at me. "Are you going to leave town?"

"No." It came out as a mumbled whisper. I sounded like I did back when I was a little girl caught with my hand in the cookie jar before dinner.

"Good." She got into her cruiser and started it up.

Buchannan stood, mouth agape, as he watched Chief Dalton turn the car around—driving over my yard, no less. As soon as she was at the end of the driveway, his gaze turned toward me and hardened.

"We're going to get you," he said, pointing a finger.

"Even if I have to follow your every step for the next month, I'll make sure you don't get away with this."

"Buchannan!" Chief Dalton was leaning out her window. "Let's go."

He glared at me a moment longer before he stormed around to the driver's side of the car, got in, slammed the door hard behind him, and then jerked the car into reverse. His tires spun and he nearly lost control before he managed to find his way back onto the road. He gave me one last furious glare before shoving the car into drive and speeding off in a flurry of dust.

I stared after the retreating cruisers in disbelief. Did they actually search my house while I wasn't there? Was that even legal? Somehow, I didn't think it was, but I doubted I'd make much headway if I tried to argue it, especially in a town like this. I was quickly learning that Pine Hills wasn't like other places. Things were done differently here and I'd best learn to fit in or else I was going to find myself in a whole lot of trouble.

Something warm and fuzzy barreled into my legs just then, startling a scream from me. I staggered forward, arms pinwheeling, and just barely managed to keep from falling. A sharp yip came next, and before I could turn around a white Maltese was standing on his back paws, front paws pressed against me, begging to be pet.

"Maestro, no!" Jules said, rushing to my side. "I'm so sorry." He picked up the little dog and held him close to his chest. "He just gets so excited sometimes."

Jules Phan was my neighbor—the one I actually liked. He appeared to be of Asian descent, though I'd never asked him if he was born here or immigrated. It seemed rude somehow. He had caramel skin you could lap up and stylized hair that made him look as if he could fit right in with a boy band. When at work, he often dressed in outlandishly colorful outfits, but today he was wearing white Keds with tan shorts and a tight-fitting T.

"It's okay." I swallowed back my heart as I brushed hair from my face. I ruffled the dog's ears.

"I saw what was happening," Jules said. "It's absolutely terrible how they're treating you, isn't it? I heard through the grapevine that Mrs. Winthrow is responsible for a lot of your troubles." His gaze traveled to the Winthrow house, but Eleanor had already retreated inside.

"I suppose," I said with a sigh. "I brought a lot of it upon myself." At Jules's widening eyes, I hurriedly added, "I didn't kill anyone. But I did take a cardboard cutout of my dad that belongs to Rita Jablonski. She left it in my shop, and well . . ."

Jules nodded as if he completely understood. "She's a special one, isn't she?" He clucked his tongue. "I just hope this doesn't interfere with the book club competition. It would be a real shame if they had to cancel it."

"You actually go to that thing?" I asked completely shocked. I mean, a book club competition? Really?

"Of course," Jules said with a smile. "Everyone does." He glanced over his shoulder to where a tall, well-built blond man was walking our way. "Ah, here he is." He waved. "Lance was dying to meet you." He paused. "Well, figuratively speaking."

I'd seen Lance only in pictures before now, so it was quite a shock to see how well defined he was. He reminded me of a professional swimmer. His skin was tan, without a hint of sunburn anywhere. He wore a teal polo shirt with shortened sleeves that exposed biceps to die for. His shorts were khaki, revealing calves that I had to force my eyes from, lest I begin drooling.

"Krissy Hancock?" he asked, extending his hand. A mile-wide grin split his face. "I'm Lance Darby." I took his hand as if in a dream. His voice was deep and strong, as was his grip. "I'm Jules's live-in." He winked.

"I, uh." I cleared my throat. "Yeah."

He let go of my hand and planted his hands on his hips as he looked toward my house. "I can't believe they are able to just come waltzing in like that. They should have waited until you got home."

"They had a warrant."

He glanced at me. "And? That still doesn't give them the right to invade your privacy like that. Jules has assured me you could have had nothing to do with that young man's death."

"You're too good of a person to do something like that," Jules put in. Maestro gave a little bark of agreement.

"Thanks." I heaved a sigh and covered my face. I felt as if I was going to cry, and I wasn't even sure whether it was because of their kind words or how I felt violated by the police. I took a shuddering breath that ended in a hiccup.

A strong arm wrapped around me and I was pulled in close to tight, hard muscles. I could smell expensive cologne, and it was all I could do not to bury my face in Lance's chest and breathe it in for the next hour.

"It'll be okay," he soothed. "This sort of thing will blow over eventually."

"I wish I could believe that." It seemed like with every passing minute, things only got worse. What if David *had* been killed before I got to Death by Coffee? He could have been whacked beside the cutout, splattered blood on it, blood I'd somehow overlooked, and then been dragged upstairs to be stashed behind a bookshelf. If that was the case, I'd have a heck of a time talking my way out of a murder charge.

I thought frantically back to when Misfit had clawed me during the Flossing Incident. Had I gone into my bedroom before Paul took me away? What about after? Had I still been bleeding? Or could Misfit have had my blood on his claws, which he shook off onto the cutout? If so, my goose surely would be cooked.

"I still can't believe this has happened," Jules said. "I didn't know this David fellow all that well, but I had seen him at Ted and Bettfast. He seemed nice enough."

I looked up, brow furrowed. "Ted and whatfast?"

Jules waved a flippant hand. "Ted and Bettfast. It's a little bed-and-breakfast down on Elm. Ted and Betty Bunford own it. She goes by Bett, by the way."

"Oh." Why wasn't I surprised?

"The Cherry Valley folk always stay with Ted and Bett during the book club week when we have it here in Pine Hills. We saw David out by the pool with Sara Huffington all over him, didn't we, Lance?"

Lance nodded and squeezed my shoulder. "They looked very close, if you know what I mean." I could almost feel his wink without having to see it.

I pulled out of Lance's grip and wiped my eyes. "Were they together, then?"

Jules shrugged. "I can only assume so. None of the others were around, and I do believe I saw her kiss him, but that could have been a friendly peck on the cheek for all I know. We lost sight of them before I could tell for sure."

My mind started whirring to life. "Do you know if Sara has a boyfriend, or maybe a husband back home?" Maybe if she was snuggling up close to David Smith, her significant other found out and killed him. That would make my life a whole lot easier, especially if I could prove it.

"Not that I know of." Jules looked to Lance, who shrugged.

"She has something of a prickly personality," he said.

"It's a wonder they let her stay in the book club. It wouldn't surprise me in the slightest if she has never, well, you know." He mimed a crude finger gesture that involved making an "O" with one hand and poking at it with the other.

"Lance!" Jules giggled and slapped Lance's arm. They both grinned. "He is such a perv sometimes."

I forced a smile, thinking back to Vicki's balls comment at the alley. "Aren't we all?" That earned me a chuckle.

"Well, we best get home," Jules said. "It's getting late and we have yet to eat dinner." Maestro was also starting to squirm in his arms, but he refused to let the little dog down. "You could always come over if you'd like. Lance makes a mean lemon drop martini if you're interested."

As tempting as it was, I wasn't in much of a mood for company, no matter how pleasant it might be. "I should probably get inside and see what kind of damage Buchannan has done."

Jules nodded and stroked Maestro. "Well, if you change your mind . . ."

"I'll come right over."

Lance patted my shoulder and then took Jules's arm. Maestro's tail wagged about a million miles per second as they walked away, talking quietly.

I felt depressingly alone now that they were gone, and I almost took off after them. I'd never had a martini before, lemon drop or otherwise. It would be something new, and maybe, just maybe, it would get my mind off the horror my life had become.

But I still felt violated and could feel Eleanor's eyes on my back. I had half a mind to storm over there and yell at her for a solid hour about respecting other people's privacy. If it wasn't for her vigil, I wouldn't be in this mess and the police would be searching for the real murderer instead of harassing me.

With a sigh, I gathered my bags from the backseat of the car, suddenly wishing I hadn't spent so much money. What if I had to make bail? I didn't have enough in the bank to cover even a small one. Death by Coffee seemed to be sucking up nearly as much money as we were earning, and I had no idea how that was happening or if it would ever stop.

I refused to look toward the Winthrow place as I pushed through the front door. Misfit was nowhere in sight, which might have worried me if I hadn't known Buchannan had been there. The cat could smell bad people and would hide long after they'd left. And if there was one thing I knew, Officer John Buchannan qualified as a bad person.

"Here, kitty, kitty," I called, dropping the bags onto the table. I rounded the island counter and came to a sudden halt.

Cupboards were left hanging open. A few pans lay on the floor from where Buchannan had apparently tossed them in his search. Misfit was busy crunching away at a bag of treats that hadn't quite sealed right. The floor was a mess of crumbs.

"Are you kidding me?" I groaned, snatching the bag from the cat before he managed to eat them all. I sealed it and shoved it back where it belonged, which did little good considering the mess. Misfit made a mad dash for the open cupboard, but I slammed it closed in time. He huffed and sauntered away.

I turned and wandered into the living room. Pillows were tossed onto the floor and the couch cushions were pulled up, exposing the springs that were starting to show through. At least nothing else in here appeared to have been moved.

Anger built. Buchannan had no right to go through my things like that. They were searching for a cardboard cutout, which in no way would have fit in any of the places he'd checked out here. They already had the murder weapon, so Cardboard Dad was the only thing he could have possibly been after. One peek in my bedroom and he would have found the darn thing.

A groan escaped my lips.

My bedroom.

I turned and ran from the living room, down the short hall, and into my bedroom. The bed was still a mess from when I'd fallen out of it, so that was my fault, but the open drawers were definitely new. I walked angrily across the room and peered down into the top drawer, staring at what was once neatly folded underwear. It was now a jumbled mess.

"He didn't." My fists clenched at my sides. Buchannan had actually come in here and rifled through my underwear drawer!

I pawed through the mess and tried to determine if anything was missing. It was hard to tell, since most of my panties were either white or black, with only a couple of other colors thrown in. I didn't have anything fancy or too embarrassing, which I supposed was a good thing. But still, I wouldn't put it past Buchannan to have stolen a few choice pieces.

"I need a warrant for his house," I muttered. We'd see how he liked having someone go through his private things then. It might have been perfectly legal for him to look around, but that didn't make it right.

The underwear drawer wasn't the only drawer left open. He'd gone through everything, my entire life practically.

I ground my teeth together and counted slowly to ten. I really wanted to go find him and yell at him, but that would only make things worse. He already had it out for me. I needed to control myself until they found the real murderer. If I started accusing him of things now, he would only come after me that much harder. Not to mention the fact it would make me look as if I was deflecting.

But when this whole mess was over with, I wasn't going to hold back; Buchannan was dead meat!

I looked around at the open drawers, thought about the mess in the kitchen, and realized I wasn't going to be able to deal with it, not tonight, not after a day that wasn't half bad. I refused to let him ruin it for me.

I turned and walked out of my bedroom, down the hall, and to the front door. I paused there and looked back at my house. At least he hadn't overturned the furniture. Misfit watched me from the other room.

"A martini sounds good right about now," I told him. He cocked his head to the side, and then lay down, putting his back to me.

With one last look around, I opened the front door and headed for Jules and Lance's place, intent on taking them up on their offer.

8

"I'm so glad you decided to join us," Jules said, leading me toward the kitchen, Maestro yapping at his heels. "Have you eaten? We were just about to sit down and have a late dinner."

"Oh, I don't want to be a bother." I tried to back toward the door, suddenly feeling out of place, like an unwelcome third wheel, but Jules stopped me with a hand on my wrist.

"You're no bother, is she, Lance?" He turned to where Lance was standing in front of the stove, apron around his waist.

"Not at all."

I allowed myself to be led to the table, knowing that now that I was there, I wasn't going to be getting out of it. I should have stayed at home, had my own light dinner, and then cleaned up Buchannan's mess before bed.

But to do that would be to let him win. The man wanted to drive me crazy, and if I let his rifling bother me, then he'd get exactly what he wanted.

"I'll take that," Jules said, rushing over to the stove and taking a wooden spoon from Lance. "You get the martinis."

I watched them prep for dinner, and a vague sadness came over me. Sure, I *could* have sat at home and eaten a microwaved dinner, alone and vulnerable. But sitting here, watching how well they worked together, made me realize how much I really didn't want to be doing that again. I didn't know if it was because of Will's recent flirting or the way Paul had looked at me the last time I'd seen him.

And really, I wasn't sure it mattered.

"By the way," I said, suddenly remembering the couple's earlier kindness. "Thank you for the cookies. They were delicious."

"I'm so glad you liked them," Jules said, glancing back at me as he stirred something that smelled fabulous. "I was worried, since you make them for a living. I hope they lived up to your standards."

"Surpassed them," I said.

Jules grinned in a way that told me I'd just made his day before he turned back to the stove.

"Here you are," Lance said, handing me a glass. "One lemon drop martini." He stepped back and eyed me worriedly as I picked up the martini glass. I guess I shouldn't have been surprised they had the right kind of glassware, but I was.

I raised the glass to my lips and took a sip. I winced, not because it was bad but rather because I didn't know what to expect. I wasn't a drinker, so alcohol often hit me funny, especially the kind that didn't come out of a can.

"Is it bad?" Lance said, clearly worried he'd done it wrong.

"Actually, no," I said, taking another sip. This time my face didn't pucker. "I'm just not used to it. It's really good."

He looked pleased as he went back to make another. "I'm glad to hear it," he said. "But if you would prefer something else, feel free to let me know. We have pretty much anything you could ask for."

"Lance loves his mixed drinks," Jules said with a playful swipe at Lance with his spoon. "Whenever he travels, he comes back with something new for us to try."

Lance shrugged. "What would life be if you didn't try new things?"

"Boring," Jules filled in, and they both laughed.

I felt warmer after only a few small sips, and after taking one more, I started to get comfortable. Watching Jules and Lance wasn't depressing. In fact, it helped restore some of my faith in humanity. Not everyone had an agenda.

Speaking of which . . . there was one man whose agenda I really was curious about.

"Have either of you heard of a man named Will Foster?" I asked, taking another, longer sip of my martini. If all of Lance's mixed drinks tasted like this, I was going to have to start coming over more often. Then again, did I really want to risk turning into a lush?

Both men turned to me with identical knowing smiles on their faces.

"William Foster?" Jules asked, voice pitched in intrigue.

"I suppose." I shrugged. "He gave his name as Will. We met at the bowling alley."

Lance and Jules shared a look.

"You talked to him?" Lance asked.

"Yeah." I was suddenly worried. "Shouldn't I have? He wasn't wearing a ring." Had he taken off his wedding band and come on to me as some sort of joke? Could he be one of those guys who cheated on his wife every time he went out? It would be just my luck to talk to the one guy who was an unfaithful jerk.

Jules chuckled and went back to stirring as Lance answered. "It's not that," he said. "He's not married, and isn't planning on it anytime soon as far as I know. He's just so . . ." He looked to Jules for help.

"Dreamy?"

Lance pointed at me. "Dreamy."

That he was. I cleared my throat, feeling not just warm but absolutely roasting. I fanned myself off. "He offered to show me how to bowl sometime."

Jules's eyes just about popped from his head as he glanced back at me. "Please tell me you accepted."

I blushed as I answered with, "I did. Sorta. I guess."

Lance laughed. "I can see he has his hooks into you."

"He does not!" *Did he?* I'd just met the guy and knew almost nothing about him.

But those dark eyes, the skin that was the color of creamer-rich coffee. I shuddered, taking a sip of my martini to cover it.

"What about Officer Dalton?" Jules asked, putting the hand holding the spoon on his hip. "Weren't you two starting to become an item?"

"Not really," I said. "We went on a date."

"Just the one?"

I nodded, feeling stupid. "It didn't end well, and after I solved the murder, we just never had a reason to talk. We didn't go our separate ways or anything, but I think we both got busy—he had cop stuff, and I had to make sure Death by Coffee didn't go under."

It sounded as if I was making up excuses, but really it was the truth.

"Well, he doesn't know what he's missing," Lance said, setting a new martini down in front of me and scooping up my near-empty glass. "You look as if you could use a refill."

I nodded my thanks and started in on the fresh drink.

"I don't know what to think," I said. "I like Paul a lot. He's cute and smart, and has an important job."

Jules nodded along as I spoke, stirring away at the pot. I was dying to know what he was cooking. My stomach was grumbling nonstop, which probably wasn't such a good thing since I was drinking. If I didn't eat something soon, I'd end up drunker than a skunk.

"But?" Lance prodded, knowing there was more.

"But . . ." I shrugged a shoulder. "I don't know. I think he's not sure I didn't have anything to do with David's murder. He acted funny the last time I talked to him." I looked down at my drink and considered downing it. "Maybe I'm just reading too much into it."

"Maybe," Lance said. "But I'd trust your instincts. Don't let your feelings for Paul interfere with your feelings for Mr. Foster. You aren't tied down, so don't act like it. Maybe Officer Dalton isn't right for you. My dad was a cop and I saw how it affected my mother. He was always gone, always on duty, even when he was supposed to be relaxing at home."

"I don't know. I feel so . . ." I spread my hands, completely at a loss for words.

"Trust me, Krissy, we all feel that way sometimes," Jules said from his place by the stove.

"At least you two found each other," I said, not bitter in the least. Maybe a little envious, but definitely not bitter. "I feel like I'm wasting my time." I sighed and rubbed at my face. I felt suddenly tired. "I probably shouldn't even be worrying about men. After the murder, and now with Buchannan rifling through my things . . ."

Lance's eyebrows rose. "I thought he was looking for that cardboard thing I saw him with."

"He was," I said. "And he found it right away. But he went ahead and searched through my drawers, including my private stuff. I feel violated." My bad mood was slowly coming back, so I took a long drink from my martini.

There, that felt a little better.

"Maybe he was just being thorough," Jules said, though it didn't sound like he believed it.

"Maybe."

Lance placed a hand on my own and squeezed. "Don't let it get to you," he said. "You're here now, amongst friends. You shouldn't ruin it by thinking about things you can't control."

"I guess you're right."

"I know I'm right." He winked when I looked up at him. "Now, let me finish making the drinks, and then we can eat."

Lance rose and finished up two more martinis as Jules continued stirring. Every now and again he'd check the oven, filling the kitchen with pleasant aromas.

Maybe they were right. I was letting things get to me too much. The police were only doing their jobs, though I still didn't appreciate Buchannan treating me like a murderer and going through my things. Once they'd investigated a little more, I was sure they'd realize I could have had nothing to do with the murder, despite the evidence to the contrary.

What I needed to do was focus on Death by Coffee and my own business. I didn't know if Paul Dalton cared about me as much as I thought I did about him. It was time I found out where he stood once and for all. Maybe then I could move on.

I plopped my chin into my palms and watched Lance and Jules together. It was the definition of domestic bliss. Even when Lance bumped into Jules as he was reaching into the oven to remove what I thought was a pair of

Cornish hens, they took it in stride, laughing and nudging each other.

That was what I wanted.

And I wouldn't let David Smith's murder stop me from getting it, even if it meant I would have to solve the case on my own, without the help of the police.

"Dinner is served!" Jules said a moment later, carrying a plate over to the table. He set it in front of me and I just about melted into my seat, it smelled that good.

I waited for them both to take their seats, despite the fact I was practically drooling down my chin, before picking up my fork.

"Dig in," Lance said.

He didn't have to tell me twice.

9

The idea of going in to work the next morning was enough to make me sick. After I got home from the fabulous dinner Lance and Jules had prepared, I'd spent the rest of the night cleaning up after Buchannan. Even though I'd promised myself I'd stop worrying about things I couldn't control, I kept thinking about how he'd gone through my house, through my things, without me being there to make sure he didn't take anything. And to top it all off, I'd actually had the object he was searching for, the cutout the police had erroneously linked with the murder, thanks to Rita. And with all of the martinis I'd had, I was in no shape to sleep, let alone get up in the morning and spend all day working.

I staggered out of bed, hand to my pounding head. I dragged myself into the bathroom, where I took a couple of aspirin before stepping into the shower. There was no way I was going to survive work today. I wasn't even sure I could make it in without collapsing.

The one thing I *was* sure of, however, was that I didn't regret the previous day. I'd met someone new, and even if it didn't go anywhere, it had gotten me out of the house and made me feel better about myself. I'd spent a nice evening with a pair of great people, and while I'd spent the last hour before crashing cleaning up after Buchannan, it hadn't been all bad.

As I stepped out of the shower, I realized sitting around the house and moping would do me no good. I'd dwell on Buchannan, on how the murderer might have been inches away from me when I'd stolen Cardboard Dad. I'd completely forget about the good things that had happened, and that was something I wouldn't allow.

I left the bathroom, got dressed for work, and then with a determined if not shaky walk, I headed for my car. There'd be no slouching for me today.

Death by Coffee was mostly empty as I walked through the door, a strained smile plastered across my face. Vicki had opened up alone and was happily ringing up a sale upstairs. I gave her a short wave and a yawn before heading back into the office for my apron. When I came back out, she was waiting for me by the downstairs register.

"How are you doing?" she asked, resting a hand on my shoulder. "You look beat."

"I am." I proceeded to tell her all about what happened after I'd left her last night. Her brow furrows increased the longer I talked. By the time I was done, she looked ready to break someone.

"What a jerk!" she said with an angry shake of her head. Blond hair bounced around her face in a way that made me think of all those slow-motion videos of women shaking raindrops from their hair, or slowly emerging from the ocean, water spraying from them provocatively. "Something should be done about it."

"I just want to put it behind me." Buchannan wasn't worth all of the energy I was putting into hating him.

"Well, if you need to take some time off, I can handle this until Mike gets in."

I shook my head and winced when it made my headache worse. The thought of going home to Misfit now wasn't appealing in the slightest. Here, I could focus on the monotony of my workday. At home, I'd drive myself insane thinking about all the things I could do nothing about.

"I'll be fine. I need something to do."

Vicki nodded in understanding. "If you change your mind, just let me know."

"Yeah, thanks."

Vicki wandered back up into the bookstore to help a young couple who'd just come in. As I watched her go, I caught a glimpse of yellow tape in the far back of the stacks upstairs. I walked around the counter, eyes never leaving the incriminating flare of yellow, and moved so I could get a better look. A small section of floor was cordoned off with police tape—something I'd be happy to never see again. There appeared to be no blood, though I wasn't about to get close enough to be sure. A couple of people hovered near the area, pretending to look at books, though their eyes constantly strayed to the sectioned-off area.

I wondered whether the store cat, Trouble, was in today, or whether Vicki was keeping him at home until the excitement blew over. I hadn't seen him anywhere. He normally liked to perch atop one of the four-foot-tall bookshelves, watching customers until he decided to make a nuisance of himself. The black-and-white cat lived up to his name just as much as Misfit did. There were probably rules against letting a feline around a crime scene, so he probably was pouting back at Vicki's place, which was fine by me. I didn't think I could deal with his hijinks today.

"Excuse me, miss."

I just about jumped out of my shoes. I turned to find a short, balding man in a tweed jacket standing behind me,

hand over his nose. His eyes were watering as they darted
from side to side, presumably looking for the very same
cat I'd just been thinking about. He'd come in a few times
before, and each and every time he complained about
Trouble. The last time I'd seen him, he'd just about been
killed by the cat, so I was surprised to see him now.

"Yes?" I asked, swallowing my heart. If people kept
sneaking up on me, I was going to have a heart attack.

"Could I get a cup of coffee, to go?" He licked his lips
and his eyes scrunched up. He held the pose for a solid ten
seconds before letting out a strained sneeze. "Quickly," he
added, eyes watering all the more.

I went back behind the counter to get the man his
coffee. He claimed he was allergic to cats, and I for one
wasn't going to call him a liar, but Trouble was nowhere
to be seen and the man was acting as if the cat had just finished rubbing all over his face. Either Trouble's dander
was floating heavily on the wind, or the guy had more
than one allergy he was dealing with. I almost felt sorry
for him.

I passed the coffee across the counter and took his
money. He looked worried as he waited for his change.

"There you go, Mr. . . ." All these months in town and
I had yet to learn the guy's name. It wasn't very sociable
of me.

"Melville. Todd Melville." It came out nasally, as if he
was holding back another sneeze.

"Well, Mr. Melville, I hope we see you again." I handed
him his change.

He took it with a quick nod before darting out the door.
As soon as he was outside, his entire demeanor changed.
He took a deep breath of fresh air, wiped his eyes, and
then strode down the sidewalk as if he hadn't just been

gushing from the eyes and about to have the largest sneezing fit ever witnessed by man.

Go figure.

I spent the next two hours filling orders and pretending like my life hadn't been turned on its ear. At least half of the customers paid me sidelong glances as they sat at their tables, and nearly everyone stared openly at me as I went to fetch their coffee. One woman actually had the audacity to ask me if someone had truly died upstairs and if I had anything to do with it. I'll admit, the woman ended up with one less sugar in her coffee than she asked for. It was the only way I could get back at her without Buchannan all over me.

My eyes strayed to the window. I half expected Officer Underwear Rifler to come striding through the door, badge waving in the air. I couldn't see his cruiser, but that meant little if he was in his own personal car. Besides, the man had to sleep sometime, didn't he? He couldn't be watching me all of the time. He had Eleanor Winthrow for that, apparently.

I sighed and leaned against the counter. A few tables needed to be wiped down, but I didn't have the energy for it. I planted my chin in my palms and watched the world go by, doing my best to pretend that everything was peachy keen, though I did keep sneaking glances toward the door every few minutes in the hopes Will Foster would saunter in and proceed to make me feel better about myself again.

Sadly, I waited in vain.

At promptly noon, the door opened and Mike Green walked in. "Yo," he said, striding past me. He went straight to the office, where he tied back his hair and slapped on a hat to keep the wild strands out of the coffee. He returned five minutes later, looking about as ready for work as he could manage.

I frowned at a tear in his jeans that was high enough on the back of his leg to expose a portion of his faded blue boxer shorts. If it had been anyone else, I might have said something, but from what I gathered, Mike was living paycheck to paycheck and a good portion of what he earned was going out to his ex in child support. His tennis shoes were dirty, and the back end of one of them flapped at the heel where it was coming loose.

Mike smiled at me as he leaned on the counter next to me. "Crazy week, right?"

"Right." I sighed. "I could use a little less crazy around here right about now."

"You got that right, chica." His smile slipped and his eyes grew haunted as he looked toward where the yellow tape could just be seen. "Hard to believe, isn't it?"

"Sure is." I paused and frowned. "Hey, weren't you here the night he died?"

Mike looked at me and nodded. "Yeah, I was."

"Did anything happen that might tell us who could have killed him? Were there any big fights or anything? Vicki said you closed up after she left."

"I did." He wiped his hand over his mouth as if it had just gone sour. "There were some arguments, you know? About stupid stuff mostly. That Rita lady gets worked up pretty easily."

No kidding. "What about David?" When his eyebrows rose, I added, "The dead guy."

"What about him?"

"Did he fight with anyone?"

Mike's face scrunched up as he thought. "He spent most of the night with that stuck-up chick. He didn't say much as far as I can remember." He shrugged. "That's really all I can tell you."

"What about afterward?" I asked.

Mike's eyes narrowed. "What do you mean?"

"Are you sure everyone was out of the store before you locked up? Could someone have stayed behind, hiding in the stacks perhaps?"

Mike straightened and actually looked offended. "I'm positive; everyone was gone. I did a head count. That Dave dude was the last to leave. I specifically remember it because the rich chick walked out before him, looking pissed."

"Did they leave together? As in, did they get into the same car?"

"How am I supposed to know?" Mike was looking annoyed by all of the questions. "They left and I cleaned up and then closed up. That's all there is to it. They were gone by the time I left."

Well, that wasn't what I'd wanted to hear. I was kind of hoping Mike would have seen someone hanging around afterward, or perhaps a fight had broken out in the parking lot. Even if he would have said that he couldn't remember whether everyone had left, it would have helped. It would have given me direction.

As it was, I had no more to go on than I did before. "Thanks," I said. "You've been a great help."

"Sure, sure. Glad I could be." He turned to the register as an elderly woman came up to it. His smile looked genuine, which was something I could never pull off when taking orders. "Welcome to Death by Coffee. We've got some killer java in the pot."

I cringed and mentally reminded myself to have a talk with Mike about the lingo. This wasn't the '90s anymore.

Come to think of it, he couldn't have been more than five in the '90s. How he'd picked up the dated phrases was anyone's guess.

I wandered over to the front door and looked it up and down. No one had said anything about forced entry, but I thought it wise to at least give it a look. I opened the door enough so I could lean down and peer closely at the lock. There were no more scrapes than what you'd normally expect to find around a keyhole. There were no telltale crowbar marks—not that I knew what those would look like—or bent metal to be found.

"Thinking of changing your locks?"

A yelp escaped my lips and I clunked my forehead against the side of the door as I shot upright. I turned, rubbing at my throbbing head, to find Mason Lawyer smiling at me.

"What are you doing here?" I asked, sore from being startled yet again. What I needed were eyes in the back of my head.

Mason only smiled at my grumpy tone. His brother had been murdered a few months back, and while I didn't exactly dislike the guy, he hadn't made my life any easier during the investigation. He didn't interfere per se, but he hadn't been too happy about my asking questions. Really, I couldn't blame him, especially since I'd thought he might have slept with his brother's wife.

He ran his fingers through his hair, which was darn near black. He'd been letting it grow out recently, which looked good on him. Not that I was looking. I already had enough men in my life I didn't know what to do with.

"How are you holding up?" he asked, his demeanor suddenly changing to concern. "Vicki told me about that police officer following you around."

"She what? When?"

"Last night." His head popped up and a wide smile split his face.

"Mason!" Vicki rushed over and gave him a quick hug. "I'm glad you came."

I stared at them for a long time, unable to speak. Mason and Vicki? It not only didn't compute, it caused my stomach to do these strange little flips that made my legs wobbly.

I stepped back from the doorway as Vicki led Mason inside. She was babbling at him practically nonstop, pointing to where the yellow tape blocked off a small section of the bookstore. The door swung closed behind me, nearly catching me on the butt as I stared after them, still completely unable to process what I'd just seen. Mike sauntered over with a sly grin.

"What just happened?" I asked.

"Looks like sexy Miss Patterson found herself a disc jockey."

That was enough to distract me from the two of them. I turned a perplexed look to Mike. "What?"

He grinned, winked, and then shot a finger gun at me before walking away.

I shook my head in wonder. And I thought my week couldn't get any weirder. I went back behind the counter and looked out over the customers drinking their coffees. My stomach grumbled, which wasn't a good thing considering what I'd just seen, but it did give me a good excuse for what I was about to do.

"I'm going to take a break," I said, balling up my apron. "Call me if you need me. I'll have my cell."

Mike nodded. "Sure thing."

I grabbed a cookie, tossed my apron into the office, and headed out the door. I might not have learned much from

Mike about what happened the night David Smith was murdered, but thanks to Jules and Lance, I thought I knew where I could go to do just that. I'd never been to a bed-and-breakfast before, and now seemed like the perfect time to see what it was all about.

10

Ted and Bettfast was one of those old mansions turned bed-and-breakfast that had started popping up across the country over the last few years. The building was nestled halfway up one of the hills in which Pine Hills sits. The driveway slithered upward, turning back in on itself repeatedly. Hedge animals sat in the little half ovals created by the meandering drive. It made me feel as if I had transported to another time and place where only the rich and famous lived. *The Great Gatsby* maybe?

The illusion was diminished somewhat when the house came into view. While it was big and had all the makings of a mansion from the '20s, the house had deteriorated over time. Much of the once-white brick was stained an ugly brown. Ivy that might have at one time been decoration and character now spread over most of the place like a rash. One of the windows upstairs was boarded up, though the rest of them were curtained and looked mostly clean. A handful of cars were parked in the parking lot to the side. I pulled in next to an old red Ford pickup that had seen better days.

My best guess was that Ted and Bett Bunford had bought the mansion on the cheap and refurbished it, though it was entirely possible it had been inherited by one of them. There were definite signs of work speckled around the property, especially on the lower floors, where the windows looked new and the brick was scrubbed and painted to near its original white. It was evident the work had slowed recently because the ivy and grime were slowly taking back over. Before long, it would have the run of the place once again.

I entered through the front door, smile in position. A young woman met me just inside. She was smiling too, but it slipped just a little when she saw me. For a moment, she looked indecisive before raising her hand and miming wiping the corner of her mouth.

"Sorry," I said as I ran my finger over my lips. It came back chocolaty. "I ate a cookie on the way here."

"Totally understandable." She cleared her throat. "Welcome to Ted and Bettfast. Are you looking for a room? We have quite a few still available. My name is Jo, and I can help you with anything you need." The entire spiel sounded rehearsed. I wondered if I sounded that bad when greeting customers at Death by Coffee; perish the thought.

"Actually, no," I said. "I'm here to talk to a few people." I strained my memory to come up with some names. "Do you know if Albert, uh . . ." Did he give me his last name? I couldn't remember. I forced a smile in the hopes it would cover my gaff. "Is Albert here?"

"Do you mean Albert Elmore?"

I shrugged apologetically. "Not sure. He came with a book club."

Jo nodded. "He's here with the others." She turned sideways and indicated a door to the back. "They are out by the pool."

I thanked Jo, thinking I'd find my own way, but she

took the lead as I started forward. She led me through the foyer, through the dining area, to a large glass back door. She turned away as soon as I was delivered and headed back to wherever she spent her mornings. I wondered if she was related to one of the Bunfords or if she just worked here. At a place like this, I couldn't imagine them having enough business to hire many people. Then again, what did I know? The place could be packed most of the year.

The glass doors opened up on a surprisingly large patio dominated by a belowground pool. Lounge chairs surrounded the pool, which held a small volleyball net on one end and an inflatable raft on the other. Tables stood at regular intervals between the chairs. Near the doors and to my right was a small bar, but no one was manning it. My best guess was that drinks were served only when there was a party or well-paying customers.

The only people outside were the book club members. Albert glanced up as I stepped out onto the patio. He was sitting in one of the lounge chairs, next to a crying Sara Huffington. Vivian and Orville were seated across from one another, a chessboard between them. Orville was leaning in so close to the pieces, it was a wonder he didn't knock a few over with his nose. He started to make a move, reconsidered, and then moved a pawn instead of the knight he'd touched. Vivian cackled madly.

"Now I've got you!" She moved her own knight. "Checkmate!"

Orville sighed and then smiled. "You got me again." His eyes sparkled as he said it. Somehow, I was pretty sure he was letting her win.

Albert stood as I crossed the patio, bringing Sara's eyes up with him. She quickly wiped away her tears and grabbed a glass sitting beside her. The liquid inside was a light pink. I wasn't sure if it was pink lemonade or something stronger. I wouldn't have begrudged her an early afternoon drink to steady her nerves, especially if she was as close to David as Jules and Lance assumed.

"Ms. Hancock, right?" Albert asked, extending a hand. I took it and he gave a quick shake before retracting his hand and wiping it on the leg of his shorts. "I didn't expect to see you here."

"Call me Krissy," I told him. "I was in the area so I thought I'd drop by." I turned to Sara. "How are you holding up?"

She gulped from her glass, and by the way she broke out into an instant sweat, it was obvious it wasn't lemonade.

"As best as I can, I suppose."

I took a seat across from her, hoping she wouldn't mind my intrusion. Albert's jaw clenched momentarily before he retook his seat next to Sara. Both Orville and Vivian watched me from their places at the chessboard. Neither looked like they wanted to get involved in the conversation, though eavesdropping wasn't beyond them.

"How well did you know David?" I asked. "He wasn't with the group for long, was he?"

Sara's eyes brimmed with tears. She wiped them away with a hand that shook. "He was the love of my life, dear." She looked longingly at her glass, raised her hand like she might reach for it, but instead moved it to her neck as if wanting to fondle the pearls that were no longer there.

"Oh, Sara," Albert said, resting a hand on her wrist. "The man was practically a stranger."

She turned a sharp glare his way. "He was the greatest man I'd ever met, and I will not stand for anyone speaking against him."

That seemed kind of heavy for someone she had known

for such a short time. Basing my guess on what Rita had said about book club members needing to have lived in the town for at least a year, she couldn't have known him for that long. Then again, what was to say they hadn't been high school sweethearts reunited after years apart? There was really only one way to find out.

"How long have you been together?" I asked as gently as I could.

Sara sighed and looked away from Albert to stare into her lap. "Two weeks yesterday. He blew into my life so suddenly, I swear it was fate. Our love was magnificent!" She glanced up at me. "And I won't let anyone tell you otherwise."

"It was his voice you were in love with," Albert said, sounding bitter.

"I'll admit, that was what originally drew me to him." Sara sat up and pointed an accusing finger at Albert. "But you know it went beyond that. Just because you were jealous of him doesn't mean he was a bad person." The tears started falling again, and she buried her face into her hands.

Albert gave me a helpless shrug and stood. He jerked his head to the side, away from everyone else, a clear indication he wanted to talk alone. He patted Sara on the shoulder and then led me to the other side of the pool. I followed, hoping he had something important he could tell me, like perhaps he'd killed David Smith in a jealous rage.

If only it was that easy.

"I'm not jealous of that man," he said as soon as we came to a stop. "I never was. I could see through his act. He was using her. She was just so desperate to find someone willing to put up with her attitude, she couldn't see it."

"I take it you weren't fond of David."

"I'm not sure any of us were." He glanced back to

where Orville and Vivian sat, watching us. "Except for Sara, of course."

"If you didn't like him, then why let him into the book club?"

Albert spread his hands. "Sara wanted it, and what she wants, she gets. That's how it has always been." He frowned. "What we should have done was kicked *her* out instead of poor old Dan."

"Was he a member of the group before David?"

Albert nodded and started fidgeting with his shirttails. "He was never all that good at the club stuff, but at least he liked books. I'm not sure David even read. He had eyes for Sara and she for him, and that was the end of the story. Dan warned us this would happen." He paused. "Well, not the murder itself, but that it would end in disaster."

Interesting. A premonition, or a plan? "Dan wasn't a big David fan either, I take it?"

"Of course not." Albert gave a bitter chuckle. "Good old David Smith struts in from England and promptly sweeps all of the women off their feet. Dan took it as an affront, claiming David had waltzed in on his territory, as if Dan himself had girls hanging all over him." He shook his head at the memory.

If Dan was kicked out of the book club to make room for David, then he had to have been angry. Add to that how David was popular with the ladies, and you had a pretty nasty combination.

"Have you seen Dan around here in Pine Hills lately?" If he'd been spotted, I'd have a viable suspect, and likely the killer.

"I haven't seen him. As far as I know, he's still back in Cherry Valley. I have half a mind to head back there now. If it wasn't for the police asking us to stick around, I think

I very well might have left already, competition be damned."
He glanced over his shoulder and sighed. "I best get back
to Sara and apologize for upsetting her. She can hold something of a grudge when she wants to."

"Okay. Thanks for talking to me. You've been a big
help."

Albert gave me a strained smile before he turned and
walked off.

I thought I had a pretty good lead already, but I wanted
to know more. I walked across the patio to where Orville
and Vivian were still sitting. Before I was halfway there,
Orville stood and excused himself. He hurried off as
quickly as his old legs could carry him, leaving Vivian to
face me alone. She must have seen the curious look on my
face, because she chuckled.

"He has an overactive bladder, especially when he gets
nervous. Too much tea, I tell him, but he never listens."

"Why would he be nervous?"

"Doesn't like talking to strangers." She shrugged.
"Can't say I blame him."

"Ah." It would make talking to him next to impossible
unless I trapped him in a bathroom somewhere. It did
make me wonder how he could stand in front of an audi-
ence to talk about a book, though. I turned my full attention to Vivian. "Do you mind if I ask you a few questions
about David Smith?"

Her mouth puckered. "I really don't wish to speak of
the dead, ill or otherwise."

"What about Dan? What can you tell me about him?"

Vivian frowned and refused to meet my eyes. "He
couldn't have hurt David, if that is what you are implying.
Dan Jacobson is a fine young man." A blush ran up her neck.
I wasn't sure how to interpret that.

"Do you have any idea who might have killed Mr. Smith?"

Vivian looked up, eyes focused at my chin. "Don't you think you should ask Rita and her little flock that? They were jealous of David, I tell you. He could sweet-talk just about anyone out of their knickers, and they knew they were in trouble the moment they heard him speak. He could have recited the pledge and won the teapot for us." Her voice hardened. "If you are looking for a murderer, you best look in your own backyard." She turned pointedly toward the chessboard.

I took it as a dismissal and wandered back into the bed-and-breakfast without another word. I couldn't bring myself to believe that Rita or one of the Pine Hills people could have killed David Smith, but then again, how well did I know all of them? Jimmy and his wife, Cindy, were complete strangers to me. And I'd only sat in on meetings with Andi and Georgina. Could Rita have finally flown off the handle and killed David over some stupid teapot? It didn't seem likely.

I didn't see Orville as I worked my way to the front of the old mansion. Jo was waiting for me there, smile painted on. I was about to thank her and go on my way, but I had a thought that brought me up short.

"Do you think it would be okay if I saw David Smith's room?"

Jo gave me a quizzical look. "Now, why on earth would you want to do that?"

I scrambled to come up with an excuse that didn't make it seem like I was being nosy, which, of course, was exactly what I was being. I needed to see if David left a clue in his room, a journal hidden where no one could find it perhaps, detailing his worry that someone was trying to kill him. Maybe he kept notes on the other members of the group and something there would point to his killer.

I knew trying to sweet-talk Jo wouldn't work. And telling her I was just curious would only make her push me out the door.

I scooted up closer to Jo, who promptly took an alarmed step back, as if she thought I might hurt her. "I investigate murders for the police," I said at a near whisper. "Do you remember the Brendon Lawyer case?"

Her eyes widened. Brendon's murder had been all over the news a few months back. I'd figured out who killed him before the police did, and even had a hand in apprehending the murderer. Even if Jo didn't watch the news, I was positive she would have heard something about it from someone.

"That was you?"

I nodded.

Her hands flew to her mouth. "Do you think you . . . ?" She didn't need to finish the thought. She was watching me with wide-eyed wonder. I had her.

"I just want to take a look around," I said. "There's no need to tell anyone. Just let me in for a few minutes. I'll poke around, see what I can see, and then will be on my way."

Jo nodded as I spoke. "Of course. But the police have already been inside the room. They've taken most everything that could be important, so I'm not sure what you can learn."

I winked. "We'll just have to see, now, won't we."

She actually giggled before waving me to follow her. We went up a set of sturdy wooden stairs. They'd been varnished once, which would have scared me half to death back when it was new, but time and countless footfalls had worn away most of the shine, leaving the middle rough and faded. The upstairs hall was carpeted, muffling our footfalls as we headed to the third door on the left.

"This was his room," she whispered, glancing around as if someone might come along and discover us. "I'll keep everyone busy." She scurried off before I could respond.

With a shrug, I tried the door and was surprised to find it unlocked. I stepped inside, closed the door behind me, and then turned to scan the room.

There wasn't much to see. The bed was big enough for two people to sleep comfortably without touching. It was piled high with pillows that looked as if they'd been tossed there carelessly, more than likely by the police. Heavy curtains covered all but a sliver of the windows, leaving the room gloomy. It gave me the heebie-jeebies to be standing in a room where a dead man once slept. I flipped on the light by the door, but it barely helped.

A TV hung from the wall in the corner. A desk sat by the window. A padded wooden chair was pushed all the way in beneath the desk. There were no incriminating papers sitting atop it like I'd hoped. A wardrobe sat to my right, in the corner, next to what I assumed was a closet.

Unsure where to start, I wandered aimlessly around the room. David's suitcase lay open on the far side of the bed. Clothes lay rumpled inside it, but little else. I used the toe of my shoe to move the shirts and underwear around, but nothing seemed hidden inside. I turned toward the dresser.

The drawers were empty. When I went to the closet, I found it much the same. A robe embroidered with the Ted and Bettfast logo hung inside. When I checked the wardrobe, it was likewise empty of clues.

I grunted in frustration. Apparently, David was living out of his suitcase rather than settling in. If I was going to stay somewhere for a week, especially in a place like this, I would have wanted to settle in more, unpack my things, and try to make it as homey as possible. I moved to the desk, not really expecting to find anything. I opened the drawers and found them empty.

Either the police had taken everything but David's dirty clothes, or he hadn't brought much to begin with. I turned back to his suitcase and eyed it. There didn't seem to be enough clothing there for a weeklong stay. It didn't mean much, since there was probably a laundry room here or the police could have taken some of his things. And if Sara and David were as cozy as they seemed, he might have left a few things in her room.

I walked over to the window by the desk and opened the curtains with the intention of looking out at the view. There was a strange, almost papery sound as the curtain swept behind the desk. I leaned over the wooden surface and peered down into the crevice, thinking I'd find a directory or a pamphlet of some kind.

Instead, I found a photograph.

I had to stretch to reach it, but I managed to snag it with my fingertips. It was one of those old Polaroid photos you never see anymore since everything has gone digital. I hadn't seen a camera, so either he'd brought the photo with him or the police had taken the camera when they'd swept the room.

When I straightened, I was holding the photo so I was looking at the back. "Sara H. 13" was scrawled across it in white. I flipped the photo over and gasped at what I saw.

Sara was lounging by the pool, dim lights illuminating her as if she was sitting on a stage in a nightclub some-where. She was looking sultrily into the camera, one leg demurely crossed over the other. Her hair was loose and hung around her bare shoulders.

It was the only thing covering her.

I quickly dropped the photo onto the desk, where it landed facedown. If I had any questions as to whether Sara and David were an item, I knew now. I stared at the back of the photo, not wanting to touch it again, no matter how important it might be. I'd seen it; that was good enough for me.

Should I tell Paul? I frowned. I wasn't sure how a nude photograph would lead to David's murder, but I suppose it was possible.

And yet, did I really want to drag Sara's name through the mud? She was already suffering enough as it was. If I were to take the photograph to the police, they'd have to ask her about it, might even make it public. Could I really do that to her?

No, I decided. If it became important later, I could tell Paul. Until then, I'd let her have her peace. As far as I was concerned, the only thing the photograph proved was that David and Sara were intimate. Unless a jealous ex came along, I doubted it would be of importance.

Using my fingernail, I pushed the photo to the back of the desk, and it fell to where I'd found it. I closed the curtain, checked to make sure everything else was where it should be, and hurried out of the room, still uncertain if what I'd found meant anything more than the obvious.

Jo stood at the bottom of the stairs, a curious expression on her face. "Find anything?"

I hurried past with a "Nope. Nothing at all. I gotta get to work." I could still feel my embarrassment on my face.

I got into my car and started it up without another look at Ted and Bettfast. I could still see Sara in all her glory, under those dim patio lights, water droplets speckled across her bare flesh as if she'd just been splashed. How they managed to take the photo without anyone else seeing was beyond me. I wasn't even sure they could have.

As I sped back to work, knowing I'd stayed out well past my lunch hour, I wondered if someone might have seen them, watched them as they cavorted openly, and resented it.

And then, somehow, it led to David's murder.

11

The bell above the door jingled and Rita, flanked by the rest of the Pine Hills book club, poured in. Georgina and Andi were tittering with each other, looking around Death by Coffee as if they were in awe of the place. Jimmy and Cindy came in, one after the other, and hurried to the stairs without a word between them. Vicki greeted them all with a smile.

I'd hoped to get through the rest of the day without doing much more than working and thinking about what I'd learned so far about David and his murder. I also was doing my best not to stare at every arriving customer in the hopes Will would show. I'd said only a few words to the man, yet it appeared Lance was right and he *did* have his hooks in me.

Rita made a beeline my way the moment she saw me. She was wearing one of those hats that looked as if it belonged on a doll rather than a real person. It looked too small for her and was clipped to her hair by pins. The hat was a shade of teal anyone should find embarrassing, yet she didn't seem to care one bit. I don't think Rita ever considered that someone else might actually talk about her behind her back. With most of the town's gossips on her side, why worry?

"Lordy Lou," she said, waving a hand in front of her face. "It sure is a hot one today."

I shrugged. "It's not too bad." I noted her heavy, flowered teal dress and decided that the heat probably had more to do with her swaddling herself in enough fabric to cover a car than with the air temperature. A bead of sweat rolled down my forehead and I wiped it away. "Though it can get pretty hot back behind the counter with all of the coffee and baking."

Rita patted my hand. "I'm sure you'll get through it. I don't know how anyone could handle working like you do."

That made me wonder what Rita did for a living. As far as I could tell, she didn't work, wasn't married. She must have had a job somewhere at some point, yet outside of maybe a quilt shop, I couldn't see her working much anywhere. Rita was one of those people who would never get a bit of work done. She'd be too busy spreading gossip to actually, you know, sell something.

Of course, that was what made Rita great. If there was one thing a gossip was good for, it was to gossip. Not only don't they mind, they relish the opportunity to talk about anything and everything and rarely hold anything back.

"Are you having the book club meeting today?" I asked, glancing toward where the other four were sitting upstairs. "Even after what happened?"

Rita waved a hand in front of her face as if shooing the thought away. "I don't want to hear it. Cindy was all but beside herself about that man's death and tried to back out of the meeting because of it. Can you believe she would even consider such a thing?"

"Well, a guy did die."

"This is too important for something like that to get in the way."

I gave her an incredulous stare, which she missed because her eyes were on the menu behind my head. I mean, I understand that David was new and all, but to outright disregard his death was cruel, even for Rita.

"I think I might have an iced coffee," she said, fanning herself off. She was oblivious to my shock. "If you wouldn't mind."

I nodded absently and went back to get her coffee. If I didn't know her so well, I might have thought Rita could have had something to do with David's death. She seemed so unemotional about it, it was frightening. I carried the coffee back to the counter and set it down. Rita paid with exact change and then leaned up against the counter, eyes gleaming.

"The silver teapot is ours this year." She said it with such force, I actually took a step away from her. "I won't let Albert wiggle out of this one just because he no longer has an unfair advantage."

I winced. We were talking about a person here. "Has Albert tried to cheat before?"

Rita snorted in a very unladylike way. "When hasn't he? I swear, that man only cares about the bottom line. He never stops to consider about the *fairness* of the thing! It's downright undignified. I wouldn't put it past him to kill someone if he thought it would help him win."

My eyebrows rose at that. Could Albert be so against reading *Murder in Lovetown* that he killed David just to get out of it? It seemed a tad excessive, if not insane. It was apparent both Rita and Albert took the book club competition seriously, but to kill over it? I just couldn't see it.

"I think that's why Albert's wife left him."

"Excuse me?" I returned my attention back to Rita, not quite sure I'd heard her right. "His wife left him?"

Rita nodded sagely. "She was part of the book club years ago but left right before she dumped him for some exotic dancer she met in Florida while on vacation with her girlfriends. If Albert had paid more attention to her, instead of his own petty concerns, then perhaps she wouldn't have looked for someone more exciting."

I tried to come up with a way that Albert's wife leaving him could be relevant to the case now, but I came up blank. Maybe if David was hitting on a woman who was already taken, it might make him think of his ex and cause him to react poorly, but to kill? I seriously doubted it. I mean, I wouldn't blame him for getting angry. Every time I thought of my ex, Robert, my blood pressure rose and I wanted to break something. I just never acted on the impulse.

"What about the others in the Cherry Valley group?" I asked. The more I knew about them, the better handle I'd have on their motives. "Are they as bad?"

Rita sipped at her coffee thoughtfully a moment before answering. "Not really. Orville and Vivian keep to themselves mostly. Honestly, I think they have something for each other, but they'll never admit it. I can see it in their eyes, you know?" She leaned in close, pressing her breasts against the counter. The dress barely contained them, and I wondered how she wasn't wincing in pain. "It wouldn't surprise me in the slightest if they had a room together at the bed-and-breakfast."

I tried to scrub that image from my brain, and instead found myself thinking of the photograph I'd found. "What about Sara?"

"What about her?" Rita frowned. "I normally don't like to speak ill of anyone, but that woman had it coming."

"How's that?" I asked, ignoring the first part. When doesn't she speak ill of people?

"Well, she is the reason Dan was kicked out of the competition. She almost broke the group up over it. She was so insistent that David be allowed admittance, they very nearly cancelled this year until it was worked out. I have the e-mails to prove it!"

"Don't you think everyone is being a bit too obsessive over such a simple thing as a book club?"

I knew I'd said the wrong thing the moment the words were out of my mouth. Rita's eyes widened and she clasped her free hand over her heart as she took a shocked step away from the counter. The flowers on her dress jumped up and down with the motion of her settling bosom.

"Simple?" she asked. "There's nothing simple about this. If we don't win, the teapot will be in Cherry Valley for another whole year. I don't think I could take it." She shook her head and gave me a pained look. "I can't believe you said something like that." She took a deep breath and let it out slowly. "But I can find it in my heart to forgive you." She glanced over her shoulder. "I best go."

And before I could get in another word, apology or not, Rita was hurrying up the stairs to where the others waited.

I wasn't sure how much I'd learned from our little chat. Albert could have jealousy issues, but I just couldn't see him killing David over a little flirting—or a nude photograph. Orville and Vivian seemed outright incapable of killing anyone, so I wasn't even considering either of them as a suspect. And Sara seemed just as unlikely after what I'd seen at the pool.

My gaze ran over the Pine Hills group. If it wasn't someone from the Cherry Valley group, wouldn't that mean it had to be someone from our side?

Rita sat down between Jimmy and Cindy and immediately started talking. Copies of *Murder in Lovetown* sat between them, though no one had yet to open the book. I watched them for a good five minutes and noted that Jimmy and Cindy weren't looking at each other, let alone speaking. Could something have happened between them?

I decided it might be a good idea to find out. I waited another five minutes so I could fill a couple of orders, and then I handed the register over to Lena, who'd been focused on cleaning the tables and helping Vicki with the bookstore while I'd talked to Rita. I took off my apron, tossed it on the shelf beneath the counter, and then headed upstairs.

"Sorry to bother you," I said as I approached. "But could I speak to Jimmy for a minute? It's about the library," I added quickly. They'd all given me narrow-eyed looks.

"Can't it wait, dear?" Rita said in a "You're interrupting something extremely important" tone of voice.

"It will only take a second."

Rita sighed and then nodded, as if giving Jimmy permission. He looked around at the rest of the group, looking far more nervous than he should. Even his size seemed to diminish as he followed me across the room, between a pair of bookshelves that did nothing to conceal us from the others. I'd chosen it simply because Trouble was lying atop the shelf and would hide most of my face, just in case someone was good at reading lips.

"Is there something you needed?" Jimmy asked with a frown. "If you have an issue with something at the library, you could come in any time and we can discuss it there."

"It's nothing like that," I said before biting my lip. Now that we were alone, I wasn't so sure of myself. I didn't know how he would react to my questions, and if he flew into a sudden rage it was unlikely anyone could get to us before he strangled me to death. "Is everything okay between you and Cindy?" I asked, figuring I'd best spit it out and get straight to the point.

Jimmy straightened to his full six feet. "I don't see how that is any of your business."

"It's not," I admitted. "But I could feel the tension between you." I felt stupid, but added, "I'm afraid it might interfere with the chemistry of the book club. I wouldn't want something to hurt your chances at victory if it can be prevented somehow."

His frown deepened before his shoulders sagged. Once again, he seemed diminished. "We had a fight." His eyes flickered past Trouble's tail to where Cindy was sitting, trying hard to pretend as if she wasn't watching us. "A small one."

"Yet you aren't talking to each other."

He shrugged. "It's stupid, really. And I feel bad about what I said, considering what happened." This time, his gaze moved to the sectioned-off portion of the store where David's body had been found.

Things started clicking into place. "Was the fight about David?"

Jimmy reached up and absently stroked Trouble. The black-and-white cat looked surprised at first but quickly settled in, enjoying the unexpected attention. I gave him a glare. If I would have tried that, the feline would have promptly tried to remove my hand from my wrist.

Finally, Jimmy nodded. "Cindy just about hyperventilated when that man spoke. She's always had a thing for the British. She watches BBC almost constantly. And with the way David looked on top of his accent . . ." He shrugged. "It was all she could talk about the other night. When we went to bed later, she asked me to, well . . ." His face reddened. I didn't have to think hard about what she'd asked him to do.

"So you were jealous?"

"Of course I was jealous. You saw the guy. What woman would want someone like me when she could have something like that?"

Jimmy might have been wearing another sweater vest and slacks, yet I could still see the muscles moving beneath the thick cloth. Despite Rita's insistence it was a hot day, he barely seemed to have broken a sweat with the extra layer. David might have been nice to look at and listen to, but Jimmy wasn't half bad either.

"She married *you*," I reminded him unnecessarily.

"I know." Jimmy sighed. "I felt insecure. I was dumb. And now, with this . . ." He gestured toward the corner of the room. "I feel bad."

I eyed him. Jimmy was big and strong enough to kill someone with his bare hands. It would take someone strong to kill with a silver teapot. If I'd tried it, I might have dented the thing, but not killed anyone. I'd have only agitated whomever I was attacking.

"What time did you leave the night of the murder?" I asked, hoping I didn't sound like I was accusing him of anything. I plastered on a smile to help my cause.

Jimmy squinted his eyes as he thought about it. "I don't know the time exactly. I left with everyone else."

"Did David fight with anyone during or after the meeting?"

"Outside of Rita? Not that I recall. It was mostly Albert and Rita who were arguing, which is the norm."

"What about later, when you got back to the bed-and-breakfast?"

Jimmy shrugged. "I really didn't pay all that much attention. I went straight to my room with my wife where, well . . ." Oh yeah, I knew.

"Okay, thank you for talking to me." I couldn't think of anything else to ask him. "I should probably get back to work."

Jimmy turned and walked away without another word. He sat down and said something brief to Rita, who looked my way. There was a curiosity in those eyes, one I knew she would need to sate before she was satisfied. I had a feeling Jimmy wouldn't get a moment's peace until he told her what we'd talked about.

I reached up to pet Trouble. His ears pinned back and I jerked my hand away before he could swipe at me. "Traitor," I grumbled before turning toward the stairs.

"You're not off of the hook."

I screamed and jumped about a foot into the air.

Officer John Buchannan stood a few feet away, blocking the stairs, finger leveled at me. His glare was hot enough to melt steel.

"Excuse me?" I started forward, hoping he'd get out of my way and get out of earshot of Rita before throwing around more accusations. Of course, he didn't move and I was brought up short.

"Chief Dalton might think you are innocent, but I'm not fooled." He was speaking loudly enough that everyone in the entire store must have heard what he was saying. "You killed him."

"I did no such thing!"

Buchannan grinned. "I'll prove it."

"Yeah?" I asked, cocking a hip. "And how do you plan on doing that when I had nothing at all to do with it?"

"I'll find a way." He took a step closer to me, pressing out his chest in a way that made his badge catch the light and nearly blind me. "Just because there was no blood on that cardboard cutout doesn't mean we can't use it as evidence."

"You found him?" Rita was up and across the room so fast, she very well might have teleported there. "You found my James?"

Buchannan's eyes gleamed with a sinister light. "We did." He nodded to me. "Miss Hancock here had it in her house." His grin widened. "In her bedroom, no less."

Rita's eyes just about popped from her head as she turned a hurt gaze on me. "You . . . you stole James?"

"I didn't do it on purpose." That didn't come out right, so I tried again. "I mean, I did, but I didn't kill anyone. And I was going to give it back."

"How could you?" Rita looked as if she might cry. "He's your *father*." There was far more implied in that last comment than I cared to deal with. She turned to Buchannan. "When can I have him back?"

"After the case is closed," he told her, adopting a concerned tone I didn't buy for an instant, though Rita seemed to melt into it. "It's currently being held as evidence."

Rita nodded and wiped at her eyes. "Is he . . . damaged?"

Buchannan hesitated, causing me to wonder if he'd bent it getting in or out of his car. "He is as we found him. I can't tell you anything more."

Liar, I thought, but I didn't say it out loud. I was sure if I did, Buchannan would be all over me. He'd probably drag me down to the station on some trumped-up charge. It wouldn't be the first time.

Rita spun on me and just about punched me on the nose as she wagged a finger in front of my face. "I'm very disappointed in you. What would your father think?" And then she turned and stormed back to the group, presumably to tell them of my theft.

"Thanks a lot," I grumbled as Buchannan turned back to me.

"You brought it on yourself," he said. "I'll be watching you."

"How about you try to find the real killer instead of harassing me?" I said it with something of a snarl. I usually didn't let people get under my skin so much, but Buchannan was pushing all the right buttons. Everyone in the store was watching me, judging me. Their eyes practically burned with curiosity.

And it was all Buchannan's fault.

"I am," he said before turning and walking down the stairs. I hoped he would keep on walking right out the door, but instead he found a seat in the corner and sat down. His eyes never left me as I sulked my way behind the counter.

Vicki was there with Lena. They both stopped talking as soon as I came around the counter. I knew they'd been talking about me, which hurt. The cloud hovering over my head got just a little bit heavier.

"You okay?" Vicki asked. The concern in her voice was real, which was something I sorely needed. I suppose if anyone was going to talk about me behind my back, Vicki was the one I wanted to do it. She would defend me, no matter how bad I looked.

"Not really." I picked up my apron but didn't put it on. It seemed to weigh a ton. If I were to put it around my neck, I'd be on the floor, crying my eyes out, in seconds. I didn't know why Buchannan had it out for me so much. Sure, I'd made a mistake when I'd first gotten to town, and I went on a date with his work rival, yet it seemed to go deeper than that. I'm not sure there was much I could ever do to repair the relationship.

"Do you want to go?" she asked. "We can handle this. Right, Lena?"

Lena nodded, purple hair bouncing around her ears. "It's no problem at all. I can help close up."

The door jingled and the Cherry Valley group came in. How they could even think of a stupid book club after David's murder was beyond me, yet here they were.

I so didn't want to deal with them tonight.

"Yeah," I said, tossing the apron back behind the counter. "If you're both sure . . ."

Lena and Vicki nodded in unison.

"Get some rest," Vicki said.

"Thanks." I turned and headed for the door. Albert hesitated in the process of going up the stairs and looked as if he might come over to talk to me, so I hurried my pace just a bit. I couldn't handle him tonight, not with Buchannan sitting right there.

I stepped outside with a sigh of relief. All of my troubles were locked away in Death by Coffee, at least for the moment. Once back home, I could sort through everything I'd learned and hopefully figure out who killed David Smith before the pressure killed me.

I walked over to my car, opened the door, and slid

inside. Just as I started the engine, Officer Buchannan stepped out of the coffee shop. His eyes immediately found me and he smiled. I pointedly ignored him and then backed out, hoping against hope he wouldn't follow me home.

12

The car was parked across the street with its two right tires sitting in the neighbor's yard, the other two on the road. The engine was off and no light came from inside it, yet I knew who was out there; he'd been sitting there since I'd gotten home a couple of hours before.

Buchannan.

His name resounded in my head like a gong strike. He was positive I'd had something to do with David Smith's death and was going to do anything he could to prove it, even if it meant sitting outside my house all night. Even if I had killed David, what made him think I'd sneak out and kill someone else? He was wasting his time.

I let the curtain fall back into place and left the window. Staring at him wasn't going to make him go away. I could only imagine him sitting there, a stupid grin on his face, while he watched me watch him. He had to be out there on his own volition, because I couldn't see Chief Dalton sending him. Didn't he have other duties, like saving cats from trees or making sure no one else got killed?

I ground my teeth together, getting angry despite myself. I didn't do anything. There was nothing he could do to me. As long as I played it safe and didn't do something stupid, he could wait out there forever and it would get him nowhere.

I sat down at my island counter where a smattering of puzzle pieces lay in the upturned lid. The puzzle was of a pair of kittens sitting in a field of daisies, silly kitty grins on their faces. Misfit lounged next to the partially completed puzzle, eyeing each piece as I laid it down. The moment a stray came anywhere close to his immediate vicinity, he would snatch it up and run, hence the lid. I had more than a few puzzle pieces come up missing because I wasn't paying close enough attention.

"We're just going to have a nice quiet evening together, right?" I asked the orange furball. "Just the two of us."

He huffed and watched my hand carefully as I placed the corner of a kitten's ear.

Puzzles were normally my way of relaxing, yet tonight it wasn't helping. My back ached with tension that seeped down from my shoulders, which were trying to close up beneath my neck. I rubbed at a sore spot with a grimace. Sitting on the tall stool at the counter wasn't helping matters any. David's murder was stressing me out far more than I liked.

Then again, it wasn't the murder so much as it was Buchannan's insistence I had something to do with it. If he wasn't following me around, hounding me like I was some common criminal, I might be handling things far better. In fact, I might have already come up with the real murderer by now! He was hindering *my* investigation with his lurking. If I would have done the same to him, he'd nail me with obstruction.

I heaved myself up and headed for the window again. The car was still sitting there, but now the overhead dome light was on, illuminating his grinning face as he accepted a mug of what I assumed was hot tea from Eleanor Winthrow.

Eleanor was wearing a tattered blue bathrobe that was parting in the front, though she didn't seem to mind, not with Buchannan looking at her like she was the most precious thing ever. Big, fuzzy pink slippers adorned her feet. Her hair was done up in rollers, and it looked as if she might have dyed it recently, though it was hard to tell; it might only be wet.

As one, both Buchannan and Eleanor looked toward my house, matching grins splashed across their faces. They watched me for a long moment before Eleanor turned back to talk to Officer Annoying.

"Argh!" I let the curtain flop back and stormed across the room. Eleanor was part of the reason I was a suspect in the murder at all. If she hadn't been sitting at her window, watching me in the middle of the night, no one would have even considered that I had anything to do with the murder. In fact, I steadfastly believed that nearly all of my troubles as of late were her fault.

I paced the room, steaming. Misfit watched me with interest from his perch. His tail swished a few times and then his eye darted to the upturned lid.

"Oh, no, you don't," I said, hurrying across the room. I closed the box and then gently moved the puzzle away from the devious cat before setting the box on top of it. There was no way I was going to be able to focus on finishing the puzzle tonight, and I wasn't about to let the cat destroy what progress I'd already made.

I scooped Misfit up and deposited him on the couch before throwing myself down next to him. He gave me an indignant look, flipped his tail into my face, and then jumped down. He strode halfway across the room, turned to face me, and then sat down. He gave me a look that quite clearly said, "Come over here and pet me."

Cats. Always have to be in command of every situation.

I ignored his silent pleas and dug out my phone. If I wasn't going to relax, I might as well do some research. The more I knew about David Smith, the better chance I'd have of figuring out why someone would have wanted to kill him.

I started with the Facebook app, which was quickly becoming my favorite investigative tool. I typed in David's name, and about a zillion David Smiths popped up. I spent five minutes going through them before giving up. There were far too many of them, and since he wasn't from around here, no one I knew would be his friend.

But I *did* know a few names of people who had known him, and one especially closely.

"Sara Huffington." I spoke her name out loud as I typed it. If anyone was David's friend on Facebook, it would be her.

I found her almost immediately. Her profile pic made her look like a millionaire. She was wearing a black dress, hair pulled up off her neck in one of those stylish hairdos I could never pull off in a million years but was common enough with celebrities. Her heels were so tall, it was a wonder she didn't pitch face-first into the pavement. Her pearls were around her neck, and she was wearing a diamond bracelet and ring. She was giving the camera one of those holier-than-thou smiles.

"Geesh," I grumbled. My pic was just a basic one of me sitting on the couch from a few years back, looking as boring as could be. She'd really gone all out for this one.

I skimmed her basic info, learning little, before moving on to her friends. I used the search there to find any Davids and found none. I tried Smith next. Still nothing. From there, I scrolled down through the list of names and faces, hoping something would catch my eye, but found no one that looked like our favorite dead Brit.

"Huh," I said, closing the app. Apparently David didn't use Facebook, or he hadn't told Sara about his page. If he hadn't told her, then I seriously doubted he would have told Albert or any of the others. I wasn't sure whether that was important or not.

I rose from the couch and headed for my laptop. I sat down at the little desk, opened the lid, and brought up the Internet browser. From there, I Googled "David Smith" in the vain hope I'd find something. I much preferred to do my Googling on a computer rather than on the tiny screen of my phone.

My first search brought up nothing, so I added "Cherry Valley" to the search. Still, not a single thing about the murdered man appeared. It was as if he'd never existed, or at least kept his online profile to a bare minimum. It was frustrating to say the least.

A paw reached up and whacked me on the elbow as I brought up Facebook again. I absently reached down and stroked Misfit's ears as I considered who to look up next. There had to be someone out there who would know something, someone whose profile might give me insight into David's life outside of the book club.

A ping brought my eyes to the lower right of my screen where a message from Old Birnhul waited. It simply stated, *Hey.*

I frowned at the message. I didn't recall having a friend named Old Birnhul, and thought it a rather strange name. I quickly checked my friend list, thinking it might be some sort of glitch, but sure enough it was right there. The person could very well be someone I used to play Facebook games with, back when I was addicted to them, who had recently changed their screen name. I clicked on the message box, curious, and replied with a *Hey* of my own.

What are you doing tonight?

My frown deepened. Who would ask that, especially if it was someone I didn't know personally? For a moment, I thought that maybe Paul Dalton might have changed his name for some reason, but it made no sense. The letters didn't match up. This had to be someone else.

Who is this? I typed, and hit send.

I've been thinking about you. I want to smell you, to taste you. It's all I can think about.

My eyes bugged out at that message, and my heart started to beat a little faster. I knew of absolutely no one on my friend list who would talk to me like that. Had I somehow gained a stalker due to my minor celebrity status around town? I suppose anything is possible, but that didn't make it any better. In fact, it made it worse.

I typed in, *I don't know what you are talking about,* before picking up my phone and dialing Paul's number. It rang a good five times before his voice mail picked up. I stared at the laptop screen the entire time, dreading the next reply. I clicked off my phone without leaving a message and set it aside just as the reply popped up.

I know more about you than anyone else in the world. You know you want me just as much as I want you. Don't deny it.

So you think. I sat back, trembling. I racked my brain, trying to come up with someone in Pine Hills who would send such horribly invasive messages. Rita was a bit strange, but I doubted she'd stoop to this level, even if she was still mad at me about stealing Cardboard Dad. Vicki would never do something like this, and I'd never added Lena or anyone else at Death by Coffee to my friend list. And since I knew it wasn't Paul, there was really no one else I could think of.

I still have a pair of your underwear. It's the silk ones with the little pink bow on the front.

"Ew!" I just about puked as realization set in.

Old Birnhul. I took a quick moment to move the letters around in my head. It was a puzzle, so it came pretty easily. Rob Dunhill.

As in, Robert, my ex.

You're sick in the head, Robert. I typed it in a fury. *Leave me alone, perv!*

Before he could reply, I found his name in my friend's list and removed it. I then changed my password, figuring that was how he'd managed to get himself added. After that, I went through my friend list one more time and removed any names I didn't recognize, just in case.

It was pretty obvious what had happened. That cheating jerk, Robert, had my Facebook password from when we were dating. He'd gone in, added a few names, ones I wouldn't immediately recognize as his, though like a dope, he used anagrams rather than coming up with something completely new. He'd probably been stalking me all this time, reading everything I ever posted. It gave me the heebie-jeebies to think of him sitting there, my underwear balled in his fist as he scoured my Facebook posts and pictures like some loony in his mom's basement.

There was a reason I'd broken up with the man. Now I was beginning to wonder why I'd ever started dating him in the first place. Could I really have been *that* desperate?

Satisfied I'd excised Robert from my Facebook life, I closed my laptop and moved to the window. Officer Buchannan was still sitting out there, more than likely sipping his tea. Eleanor was gone.

My house sat on a road that ended in a cul-de-sac, so there was little to no traffic this late at night. Buchannan could sit just off the road all he wanted, and the only people who'd know it would be my neighbors.

And, well, anyone Eleanor Winthrow told, of course. I

had no doubts that she was already on the phone, talking to her bestie, Judith Banyon, about me.

With a sigh, I closed the curtain and went about turning out the lights. There was no way I was going to get back onto my computer tonight. I was tired and had to work in the morning, so turning in a little early wouldn't hurt. I carried my phone into the bedroom, where I tried to call Paul one more time, only to hang up before it could even go to voice mail. I didn't know whether he was avoiding me because I was a suspect or was mad at me for some other reason. Either way, it hurt, and right then I was too tired to care.

I began stripping out of my clothes, dropping them into the hamper beside the bathroom door. Misfit jumped up on the bed and made himself at home. I was reaching for my pj's when a brief flare of light caused me to freeze.

I was standing in my underwear—all black, without a pink bow anywhere, thank you very much—and there was something outside my window. My hand moved toward my bathrobe, which was hanging off the back of the bathroom door. I put it on slowly, afraid if I moved too fast something awful would happen. I cinched the robe at the waist, eyes never leaving the reflection coming from somewhere outside.

It was dark enough out that I couldn't see much from clear across the bedroom. My curtains were parted in a way that told me Misfit had been lounging up there while I'd been out. Normally, I kept them firmly closed. I crept across the room, all kinds of horrible thoughts going through my head.

What if it was the murderer come to kill me before I learned his or her identity? What if it was Buchannan, watching me with his own handful of my underwear clutched in his sweaty fist? What about Robert? If he could find my phone number and infiltrate my Facebook profile, then he could just as easily find out where I lived.

It wasn't until I got near the window that I realized what I was seeing.

There were actually two small circles. The light from my bedroom was reflecting off them.

And they were coming from the parted curtains in the house next to mine.

Frustration and anger welled up inside me like a live wire. Eleanor Winthrow was spying on me while I was changing! How many nights had I forgotten to make sure the curtains were closed and she'd sat there in her room, watching me as I strutted about half-naked? What about after a shower, when I left my clothes on the bed, thinking I was safe and secure in my own house? What kind of horrible woman was she?

I couldn't let her get away with it.

I slipped my feet into a pair of plain blue slippers and stormed out of my bedroom, down the hall, and into the living room, turning lights on as I went. I was breathing hard and very near tears. I couldn't believe someone would spy on their neighbors this way, even though I'd seen her do just that many times before. I should have taken more seriously the warning Jules Phan gave me about Eleanor the day I moved in.

I unlocked the front door and stepped outside. The night was hot and humid. My hair instantly plastered itself to my face as I pointedly turned away from Buchannan's parked car and headed for the Winthrow place.

A faint, repeated *ping* tried to tear its way through the haze of anger that was clouding not just my vision but my thoughts. I was going to have words with the old woman and nothing short of a nuclear bomb was going to stop me. I felt violated, mostly thanks to Robert's icky messages, and maybe a bit because of Buchannan's lurking and rifling through my stuff.

I beat on the front door of the small house, fist hitting with a resounding boom as I shouted, "Eleanor! Get out here!"

She didn't answer right away, so I pounded harder. "I know you're in there! I saw you watching me!" The old woman had probably watched me cross the yard.

I glanced at the windows at the front of her house, fully expecting to see her watching me from one of them, yet the curtains remained closed and all of the indoor lights were off.

"Eleanor!"

Lights in the neighborhood began to click on. Faces appeared at many of the windows, just not in the one I was concerned with.

"Miss Hancock. Step away from the door."

I turned to find Officer Buchannan standing about two yards away. His hand was near the gun in his holster like he thought I was going to do something stupid and attack him.

Maybe I was. I wasn't sure yet. And then there's the fact I was wearing nothing but a robe, with my hair a mess, plastered around my face, and my eyes bugging out in my rage. I probably looked like a banshee from a horror movie.

Or, well, maybe a reject from one. I wasn't in good-enough shape to be in a movie, villain or not.

The thought only made me angrier.

"She was spying on me!" I shouted at him, gesturing toward Eleanor's house. "I saw her while I was getting dressed."

Buchannan's eyes moved from my face, slowly down my body, and lingered lower and longer than they should. Something snapped in me as Buchannan finally met my eyes again. I closed the distance between us in two strides and raised both of my hands at once. Something in the back of my mind screamed at me to stop, but I was beyond listening, even to what reasonable part of me remained.

"Don't. You. Stare. At. Me!" I punctuated each word with a pair of ham-fisted blows on Buchannan's shoulders.

He seemed stunned for a moment, letting me beat at him with punches that were so weak, they probably didn't even hurt, before he took a quick step back. He caught both of my arms in mid-down-stroke and spun me around in one fluid motion.

"Miss Kristina Hancock," he said, his voice filled with anger. "You're under arrest for assaulting a police officer."

I thrashed against him, so angry I could just spit. He held me tight, refusing to let me go.

And then, slowly, reason returned. All of the fight went out of me at once and I sagged to my knees.

Buchannan didn't hesitate. He zip-stripped me just as Eleanor's front door opened. She stepped outside, looking the part of an innocent old woman. I didn't even have the energy to be mad at her anymore. I was too embarrassed for much of anything.

Buchannan jerked me to my feet and spun me around. He marched me to his cruiser, hand on my bicep, and shoved me into his car. I went without a struggle. I'd lost control. This was my fault.

He slammed the door closed and said something softly to Eleanor, who nodded, eyes watching me from her stoop. A moment later, he got into the car, started the engine, and then we were zooming down the road, heading for the Pine Hills police station.

13

I ran my finger through the dust lining the bunk. I gave it a long look before sitting down. A plume of dust and stale air wafted up, sending me to my feet, hacking, which only caused me to suck in more dirty air. I staggered over to the sink and tried it, desperate for water, but only a trickle of brown water dribbled from the faucet before petering out. I turned to the toilet, not sure I was quite that desperate yet, to find that there wasn't even water inside it, and the seat was hanging on by a sliver of plastic.

"Really?" I croaked, turning to Buchannan, who was leaning on a desk that was covered in just about as much dust as my cell. It was obvious no one had spent any time down here for quite a while. There were two other cells, both closer to the stairs out of here. I had a feeling they had working water and a less cloying atmosphere, yet I got the crappy one.

Buchannan only grinned at me and crossed his arms as he leaned. He was enjoying watching me squirm. It was probably the highlight of his month.

"Look," I said, opting for diplomatic. I walked to the front of my cell, batting at my robe to knock off some of the dust. "I didn't mean to hit you. I was just so upset, I lost control. Eleanor was peeping in my window and I lost it. Can you let me out of here so we can at least talk about it like civilized adults?"

"Peeping in your window? From her house?" He said it like he thought it was the most ludicrous thing he'd ever heard.

"She was!" I bit back the shouted insults I wanted to throw at him and forced a smile. "She was using binoculars. I saw the reflection while I was getting changed for bed."

"Have you ever heard of blinds? I understand they are quite useful."

"Argh!" I threw myself back down onto my bunk, sending another plume of dust flying into the air. It looked like I'd sat on an atomic bomb.

I couldn't believe Buchannan was actually sticking me in a cell like I'd gone and tried to murder him. I mean, I didn't actually hurt him with my pathetic punches. I might have surprised him, sure, but hurt him? I don't even think it was possible. The man seemed made out of stone—his brain included.

What I really wanted was for Paul Dalton to come waltzing down the stairs to my rescue. I hadn't seen him since he'd taken me home the night of the murder, and I was starting to worry he really did think I was responsible. He hadn't taken my calls, which could be because he was working. Or it could be because he doesn't want to talk to me anymore.

I heaved a sigh and crossed my arms, mirroring Buchannan's stance. His grin slipped a little at that, and he narrowed his eyes at me, but said nothing. Nor did he move like I'd hoped.

Time ticked slowly past. I was afraid Buchannan was going to stand there all night and watch me rot. At least he'd taken the zip strips off this time. I wouldn't have put it past him to cuff me to the cell and bind my ankles together, just so I'd suffer that much more. What did I ever do to him to deserve being treated like this?

"Can I have some water?" I asked. My throat and mouth were dry from all of the dust. It felt like I'd been sitting there for hours, but I had a feeling only twenty minutes or so had gone by. "I'm really thirsty."

Buchannan gestured toward the sink.

"Jerk," I grumbled, moving my hand in front of my mouth as I did so he wouldn't see or hear. He'd probably cite me for the insult. "What did I ever do to you?"

"What do you mean?" he asked.

"Why do you hate me so much? What did I do to make you angry with me?"

He was looking at me as if he had no idea what I was talking about. "I don't hate you," he said. It came out as if it surprised him to say it.

"Then why this?" I gestured toward the crappy cell full of dust.

His brow furrowed. Could he really not know why he antagonized me so much? Was it just a natural reaction for him? Could it go deeper somehow? Was there something in his past that made him automatically distrust anyone new until they were able to prove themselves to him?

I didn't get a chance to hear what he would come up with because just then Chief Dalton came in. She strode meaningfully down the short hall, eyes never leaving Buchannan. She was glaring so hard, it was a wonder he didn't burst into flames.

She stopped a foot away from him and eyed him angrily. "Why is Ms. Hancock down here?" she asked. "You know we only use these cells for overflow."

I rose and moved toward the cell doors so I could hear

better. Before Buchannan could answer, Chief Dalton spun on me and released her wrath. "Sit down!" Her shout echoed off the walls.

I scurried back so fast, I very nearly missed the bunk in my haste to sit. My heart was suddenly pounding in my ears, and a warm flush was rising up my neck. I'd been so sure she would round on Buchannan, I didn't know what to do now that she was staring at me with fire in her eyes.

The chief started pacing in front of my cell. "I don't know what to do with you anymore," she said, aiming the words at me, though she didn't look my way. "You repeatedly put yourself into situations you have no right being in." She darted a glance at me. "What were you thinking? Attacking an officer? Krissy . . ." She shook her head in disappointment. It forcibly reminded me of all the times my dad acted that same way when I was younger and had done something stupid.

"I wasn't thinking." I said it as meekly as I could. "Eleanor was spying on me, and my ex was sending me lewd messages. I sort of snapped."

"Well, sort of snapped is no excuse. You could have hurt someone, yourself included. What would you have done if Mrs. Winthrow had opened the door?"

I shrugged. "Yelled at her?"

"And would it have stopped there?" Chief Dalton finally approached my cell. Her eyes were hard, angry. I had the distinct impression she was reconsidering her view of me. "We can't let this sort of thing slide around here."

I felt all of the blood drain from my face. Could she really mean what I thought she meant?

"I'm sorry," I said, words spilling out of me in a rush. I couldn't imagine staying in that dusty cell for very much longer. "I've apologized to Officer Buchannan repeatedly. I'm much better now. I won't yell at anyone ever again."

Chief Dalton stared at me for a long time before giving me a helpless shrug. "There's nothing I can do. You assaulted Officer Buchannan. You inflicted bodily harm upon him. We have strict rules against that, in case you were ignorant of the fact that throwing wild punches at an officer of the law is illegal. We might play it loose with a lot of things around here, but attacking one of my men isn't something I'm going to let go." She turned as if to leave.

"No, wait!" I leapt from my bunk and ran to the cell doors. "You can't leave me in here!"

She paused and looked back at me. "Oh, I can," she said. "And I will." She took another step before stopping again. She didn't look back at me when she said, "I'm starting to wonder if I was wrong about you."

And then she walked away.

She actually walked away.

I was stunned. I mean, this was the same woman who had given me, a virtual stranger, her son's phone number in order to hook us up. She'd ignored our breaking and entering, and my other little misdemeanors and misadventures, yet this time she was leaving me down here to rot with Buchannan.

That couldn't be good.

I turned to face him.

"This is your fault."

He actually looked surprised. "Me? I'm not the one who was throwing punches."

"If you hadn't been following me around, then none of this would have happened." I wanted to shake my finger at him through the bars, but I was afraid he might bite it off if I did. "You put too much pressure on me and I lost it."

Buchannan didn't look the least bit sorry. He yawned and checked his watch as if I was keeping him from an important meeting.

I glanced back at the bunk and decided I didn't want to take another dust shower. I started pacing my cell, hoping against hope that Chief Dalton would come back down and tell me she'd only been testing me before letting me go. Or at least move me to one of the other cells. From what she'd said, I was thinking there were better cells somewhere else in the building.

And if the chief didn't show, I'd be just as happy to see anyone who wasn't Buchannan. Even Paul would do, despite the fact he'd been ignoring me lately. At least then I could ask him if he truly thought I could be the killer. If that was the case, then I would know where I stood and could move forward with my life.

Pacing was getting me nowhere, and sitting and sulking just wasn't my style.

But what could I do? It wasn't like Buchannan was suddenly going to get chatty. I could ask him about David Smith or his antagonism toward me all I wanted and I wouldn't get a damn thing out of him.

"I didn't kill anyone," I said, sulkily. Saying it made me feel better, though it didn't seem to move Buchannan.

"We'll see."

"I still don't get why you think I did it. Why would I kill someone I just met? In fact, I'd only said a few words to him before I left. Don't you think I would have been smarter about it if I killed him? Leaving him in my own store would be pretty stupid."

Buchannan's eyes narrowed, as if he thought I was trying to trick him somehow.

"I didn't kill him," I repeated in the vain hope I would get through to him. "I didn't even know the guy."

Buchannan shrugged and looked away. No matter what I said, he wasn't going to listen.

"Maybe *you* killed him and are framing me because you don't like me," I said, mostly under my breath but loud enough so he heard.

Buchannan took a step toward me, face going hard. "I am an officer of the law. I do not kill people. I keep people who do in cells like these." He jerked a thumb at the empty cells. "Tread lightly, Ms. Hancock, or you'll be spending a lot more time down here than any of us would like."

"It doesn't feel too good when people accuse you of things you didn't do, does it?" I grumbled.

"I know you are sticking your nose in this business like you did before. If you didn't kill the guy, then you need to stay as far away from it as possible. I don't want you interfering. If I catch you snooping around, I'm going to stick you back down here and keep you here until the murderer is caught."

I wanted to keep pushing, keep denying, but it was getting me nowhere. And if I kept at it, I'd inevitably spend the next week sitting behind bars, breathing in the ancient dust. I had no illusions that Buchannan wouldn't stay true to his word. He was practically begging me to make a bigger nuisance out of myself so he'd have a reason.

"Can I have my call?" I asked, keeping my voice as steady as I could. I wasn't sure if I wanted to scream and yell or if I wanted to cry. In all my life, I'd never spent more than a few minutes in a jail cell. The first and only time had been for one of those high school scare tactics where they take kids to a local jail, shove them into a cell, and then leave them there for a few minutes. The other inmates would heckle and jeer at you, and then it would all be over.

That had been a terrifying couple of minutes. This was simply embarrassing.

Buchannan looked like he might deny me my right out of sheer spite, but relented. He walked over, unlocked my cell door, and then took me by the arm, as if he thought I might make a run for it. He led me a dozen feet to the rotary phone sitting on the desk. I stared at it incomprehensively for a moment, not quite believing one of those things still existed, let alone worked, before picking up the receiver. I waited for Buchannan to take a couple of steps back before dialing Vicki's number.

I was worried she might not be home—with the way my luck had been going lately, it felt a near certainty—but she answered on the second ring with a cheery "Hello?"

"Vicki." I practically sobbed her name, I was so relieved.

"Krissy? Is everything okay? You sound . . . weird. Are you calling me from a tunnel?"

"No, just using an old phone."

"Ah."

"So, uh . . ." This wasn't going to be easy. How do you tell your best friend you've been arrested and that the cop had a good reason for doing it? It wasn't like I'd gotten drunk and accidentally flashed the neighbors or ran a red light. I'd actually *hit* a police officer. Never mind that it was Buchannan. The reality of the situation was finally sinking in, and I was quickly realizing I was the one who was a bonehead.

"Krissy?"

I sighed. What else could I do but tell her?

"I sort of got arrested."

"Again?" I could hear the incredulous tone to her voice, tinny as it was coming through the old phone. "Please tell me you didn't go snooping around and get yourself caught somewhere."

"If only," I said. "This time, I might have taken a few swings at a police officer."

There was silence from the other end of the line.

"Vicki? Are you still there?"

"Yeah," she said. "I'm just trying to take it in."

"It was Officer Buchannan. He was sitting outside my house when I caught Eleanor looking in my window with binoculars. When I went out to yell at her, he sort of got in the way."

More silence. And then a faint sound. At first, I wasn't sure what I was hearing. And then it got louder.

"It's not funny!" She was actually laughing at me. Some best friend! "I'm stuck in a dirty jail cell and will probably have to stay here all night with the fleas and who knows what else." I looked down at my now filthy slippers. "And I'm wearing nothing but my underwear and a robe."

The giggles turned into loud laughter. Vicki managed to choke out "I bet you're a sight to look at" between guffaws.

"It's not funny," I grumbled.

"You're right, it's not." I imagined her wiping her eyes as she composed herself. "So you think you'll be there overnight, then?"

I glanced at Buchannan. "Yeah. I don't think they're going to let me go until tomorrow."

Buchannan nodded.

"I'll head over to your place tonight and feed Misfit for you if you need me to?" She made it a question.

"Would you, please?" I didn't want to think about what the terrible orange feline would do to my house if I wasn't around to feed him. "And lock up, too. I wasn't given the chance."

"Will do." She paused. "Will I see you tomorrow at work? You can take the day off if you need it."

"I'll be in." I stared hard at Buchannan, daring him to try to stop me. There was no way I was going to stay trapped in that cell longer than I had to. If he tried to keep me past sunrise, I was going to claw my way through the concrete.

"Okay," Vicki said, still sniffing from her laughing fit. "I'll see you then."

I hung up and let Buchannan lead me back to my cell. As soon as I stepped inside, he closed the door behind me and locked it. I trudged over to the bunk, eyed it with distrust, and then decided I couldn't get any dirtier, so I sat down. With one last glare Buchannan's way, I leaned back and closed my eyes, knowing that no matter how hard I tried, I wasn't going to be able to sleep.

14

By morning, I was stiff, tired, and just about willing to do anything to be allowed to go home. The bunk was the most uncomfortable thing I'd ever had the displeasure of sleeping on. It felt like the mattress was full of rocks and razors. Every twist and turn sent stabbing pains shooting through my body. At one point, I seriously considered moving to the floor, but decided against it because, well, ew. Who knew what was down there.

Buchannan didn't stay all night, thank God. He gave me some water in a rare act of mercy and then left about an hour after Chief Dalton had abandoned me. I kept hoping someone would come and rescue me, but all I got were a few polite check-ins throughout the night. I think it had less to do with making sure I was okay and more with gawping at what was probably the first inmate in a few months. Pine Hills was normally a low-crime area, at least until I got here.

Lucky me.

Footfalls echoed through the empty cells at first light. A female officer whose name tag read GARRISON opened the cell and stepped aside without a word. She wasn't smiling and didn't so much as soften when I gave her my sappiest "Good morning."

She took me by the arm and led me back out into the harsh light of the station. Two police officers were at work, busily typing up reports or whatever they typed up. I didn't know any of them, which was disheartening. I glanced toward Chief Dalton's office; the door was closed, and I couldn't tell if she was inside. The lights were off, so I was guessing no.

I didn't have any personal belongings to pick up. My poor robe was grungy from my night in the cell, and my slippers were practically black now. I didn't even want to know what my hair looked like, let alone my face.

Garrison kept ahold of my arm as she led me out to her cruiser. "Get in," she said in a husky voice that hinted at years of smoking. I slid into the backseat—I apparently didn't qualify for a comfortable front seat ride after my incarceration—and she closed the door firmly.

I didn't bother with small talk. I doubted Garrison had much to say to me. I was just thankful Buchannan hadn't been assigned to take me home. I think I would have rather stayed locked up alone than to listen to any more of his accusations.

As we rode toward my place, all I really could think of was Paul. Why hadn't he come to see me? I was positive either Buchannan or the chief would have let him know about my predicament. If not, someone else would have called him to tell him. In this town, everyone knew just about everything that happened almost as soon as it did. The accuracy of the rumors were debatable, of course.

I was afraid I'd scared off Paul for good. He never came to see me, hadn't been taking my calls. I'm sure he was busy with cop things, like trying to solve David Smith's murder, but how much effort would it have taken to pick up the phone to give me a quick ring hello?

Will would have come to see me, I was sure. We might have just met, and barely spoken much more than a hand-ful of words to one another, but he seemed the type not to let a girl suffer alone. Even if the chief warned him off me, I doubted he would listen. I wasn't sure I could say the same about Paul.

Man, when did my love life get so complicated?

We pulled up in front of my house. Garrison got out of the cruiser, walked around to open my door, and slammed the door closed behind me as soon as I was out. She gave me a curt nod before getting back into her car and leaving.

"Thanks," I grumbled. I turned for my front door, stead-fastly refusing to look at the neighbors. If I saw Eleanor Winthrow today, I was going to throttle her.

I didn't have my keys on me and was worried for a minute that I wouldn't be able to get into my own house, but when I opened the screen door, an envelope was tucked by the doorknob. My key was inside. "You're a saint, Vicki," I said as I dumped the key into my palm. I unlocked the door, feeling somewhat better, and stepped into a disaster zone.

My mouth fell open in shock. An orange blur darted my way, and I just barely managed to close the door behind me in time. Misfit slammed into my legs, arched his back, and then took off running the other way. I barely saw him go.

I was almost afraid to step inside any farther. From where I stood, I could see more than enough damage. One of the dining room chairs was lying on its side. Everything on the table had been knocked to the floor, including a candle I'd purchased just in case Paul had wanted to come over for dinner some night. It lay broken in two halfway across the room. There were chunks missing from it where Misfit must have used it as a chew toy.

The living room was no better. The curtains were hanging crookedly, the screws that held the rods in place having come most of the way out of the wall. The arm of the couch was in shreds. Stuffing littered the floor from one end of the room to the other. Like the dining room table, the coffee table had been swept clear of items. A magazine lay in hundreds of pieces on the floor.

"Misfit!" I shouted, frustration growing. I kicked off my filthy slippers, determined not to make the house any dirtier than it already was, and stalked farther into the room. The kitchen was in disarray. The cabinet where I kept his treats was hanging open. Catnip and little chunks of kitty treats lay everywhere. His bowl was filled, as if he hadn't bothered to touch it all night, and his water dish had little green specks floating in it.

I stepped into the hall. "I'm going to string you up!" I turned toward the bedroom. "Misfi-ugh!" I jerked back. A spot about a foot wide was soaking wet in the hall. One sniff told me what had happened.

I closed my eyes and counted to ten. *I won't kill my cat. I won't kill my cat.* I stepped over the wet spot and went into my bedroom. One of the pillows was on the floor, but otherwise the room seemed undamaged. Misfit lay on the middle of the bed, curled up as if he'd been sleeping there all day. He yawned, stretched, and gave me an innocent kitty blink. What kind of fool did he take me for?

I snatched him off the bed, turned, and carried him right back down the hall. I stepped in the wet spot again, which just about caused me to drop the squirming feline. I turned to the laundry room, intending to throw him into his litter box, but why bother? The room was covered in litter. It was as if he'd stood in the box and purposefully kicked every last bit of litter out onto the floor. It was in my clean clothes basket that was currently full of washed clothing I had yet to carry to my bedroom.

Misfit squirmed his way free, and I let him go. What good would punishing him do? It was me he was mad at, and really, he had a good reason. I'd abandoned him all night, left him alone to fend for himself. He'd gotten into the catnip, which often turned him into a whirling dervish, especially when I wasn't there to monitor how much he consumed.

"I'm sorry," I said, leaning against the wall. Misfit watched me from the edge of the bedroom as if unsure. "I'll make it up to you."

He watched me warily as I walked down the hall and past him, into my bedroom. I had a lot of cleaning up to do, but I didn't have the energy or time for it. I had to be at work in less than an hour, and I was determined not to be late.

I stripped out of my dirty robe and underwear, considered dumping them into the trash, and instead dropped them onto the floor. I stepped into the shower and cranked up the heat. I scrubbed myself ragged, dried off, and then got dressed for work. I carefully stepped over the wet spot in the hall, grabbed some paper towels, and then dropped them on top of the spot to be cleaned up later. With one last glance at the ruins of my house, I grabbed my purse and headed for work.

Vicki was already there when I arrived. Steaming cookies sat in the display case and the smell of percolating coffee filled my nose as I stepped through the door. I drifted over, drool already trailing down my chin, as I poured myself a cup.

"How are you doing?" Vicki asked, joining me at the counter.

I shrugged and slurred something inarticulate. Boy, how

I managed to get this far into the day without my jolt, I'll never know. I felt half dead.

"Did your night in jail go okay?"

I glanced at her grin. "It went awesome."

"I can tell. You look like something out of a zombie movie."

I mimed coming at her, arms outstretched and with a not entirely fake moan, before slouching back against the counter. "It was awful."

"I can only imagine." Trouble came down the stairs to rub up against her leg, and she picked him up. "Why would they keep you overnight like that? Couldn't Officer Stud convince them to let you go?"

"He never even came to see me!"

"What a jerk!"

I sighed. "Maybe he was too busy."

"A real gentleman would never leave his damsel in distress."

"Maybe he wasn't allowed," I said. "There could be some sort of rule against talking to the accused."

Vicki gave me a flat look. "It wasn't like you killed anyone."

I winced, eyes flickering toward where David had indeed been murdered. "I don't know," I said with another sigh, this one heavier than the last. "I felt abandoned."

"You'll be okay," she said, a concerned look on her face. It cleared and she grinned at me. "Maybe your new guy will end up making it all better."

I blushed. "He's not my new guy. We haven't even talked outside the bowling alley yet."

"Uh-huh." Her grin only widened as she shoved Trouble into my arms. "Customers," she said. "Can't leave them waiting." She hurried to the door to open.

I carried the black-and-white cat at arm's length, up

into the bookstore. He was related to Misfit, so I knew what he could do to me if I wasn't mindful of his claws. Maybe, despite how I thought of myself, I wasn't really a cat person. I liked them most of the time, but they sure didn't seem to like me.

As I went back downstairs, I passed Vicki. She was grinning her head off and winked at me as she went by. I didn't understand her reaction until I reached the counter and looked at the man standing there for the first time.

"Will!" I said, just about shouting his name. "I wasn't expecting you."

He smiled. "You told me to come see you at work, and here I am." He was wearing a nice button-up shirt and a pair of black slacks that fit him perfectly. It was all I could do not to stare.

"Oh, yeah, I did say that." I felt my face flame and cleared my throat. "I'm glad you came."

His smile widened. "I just wish I could stay longer." He glanced at his watch and then tapped it. "Got to get to work." His eyes strayed to the menu above my head. "How about a hazelnut coffee?"

"Sure thing!" I turned and scurried to get his drink, thinking I might die of embarrassment. Clearly, Will had an important job. His watch wasn't a cheapo, and his clothes were just as nice. I should have told him to meet me somewhere else, somewhere where he wouldn't see me at work with my apron on and messy hair.

I carried the coffee back to him and plastered on a smile. "This one is on me. Consider it early payment for anything you can teach me."

His eyebrows rose and one corner of his mouth quirked upward. "Now I'm going to have to come up with something interesting," he said, taking his coffee. "Thank you."

"No problem." It came out as a squeak.

Will looked like he wanted to stay, but a line was starting to form behind him. "I'll talk to you again soon," he said.

"I hope so." I mentally smacked myself upside the head. God, I'd sounded desperate.

He only chuckled and sipped his coffee as he headed for the door.

I spent the next hour and a half serving coffee and cookies to a steady stream of customers, mind completely elsewhere. I was shocked Will had actually come to see me, and he hadn't even looked bothered by my job, or how I looked. Could he truly be interested? I just about giggled every time I thought about it.

Time passed, and Vicki helped out whenever she could. The bookstore was just as busy as I was, meaning we were both run just about ragged. My entire body ached as I got coffee after coffee. By the time Lena came in for her shift, skateboard tucked under her freshly scraped arm, I was pooped. I handed serving duties over to her and went about cleaning tables.

Throughout the morning, I hoped Will would return, knowing it was unlikely, but couldn't stop my heart from racing every time the door opened. What I needed was a distraction, something to take my mind off the one good thing that seemed to be happening to me, lest I forget that a man was murdered. A part of me hoped the Cherry Valley group would come in so I could talk to them, or at least one of the Pine Hills book club members. At one point, I thought Rita had come in with some juicy bit of gossip, but the screeching sound I'd heard was only a chair scraping over the floor.

An hour later, things were finally under control and I took a quick break. I was sweating horribly and my feet felt like they were three sizes too big for my shoes. I wanted to rub them in the worst way, but I settled on putting them up onto a chair in the office instead. I just started relaxing when there was a knock at the door.

"Can I talk to you for a minute?" Vicki asked, almost shyly. I don't know why, but my heart leapt into my throat at her tone.

I put my feet back on the floor to brace myself. "Sure."

She closed the door quietly behind her and sat down in the chair my feet had so recently occupied. "Lena is covering for us for a minute. This won't take long."

I nodded, worried. Was she going to tell me she has given up on me and was going to move elsewhere, away from my bad influence? Or could she be firing me from my own business? I mean, all I ever really did these days was come in late and cause trouble. Lena and Mike could do my job, and were probably a lot better at it than I was, especially since I couldn't seem to focus on what I was doing.

I knew my fears were an overreaction, but with how things were going, I couldn't help but worry. I wouldn't have been surprised if she would have told me that the coffee I'd drank was laced with poison and I only had a few minutes to live.

"Do you think you could close for me tonight?" she asked. "I know you just spent a horrible night locked up and are scheduled to work only until three, but the auditions for that play I was telling you about are tonight. I really want to go, but if you don't feel up to it, I can skip it."

"No," I said. "You should go. I can handle this."

"Are you sure?" She gave me a sympathetic look. "I tried to call Mike in, but he already has plans. And you know how I like having one of us here at close. . . ."

"It's okay." I gave me a genuine smile. I was glad Vicki was finding her footing here in Pine Hills and was getting involved in something that didn't involve dead people. I could learn a lot from her. "I'll be fine."

She stood and gave me a quick hug. "Thank you. Lena will be here, and she does a great job closing up. You won't have to do much if you don't want to." She started for the door.

"Hey, wait," I said, standing. "I have a question for you."

Vicki turned and gave me a curious look. "Hmm?"

"Well . . ." I felt stupid for what I was about to ask, but I really needed to know. "So, you and Mason?"

Vicki beamed. "I know! Isn't it amazing? He's such a great person, and we have so much more in common than I thought we ever would." Her hand absently rose to smooth down her hair, as if she thought he might walk through the door at any moment and wanted to look her best.

"But he's Brendon's brother." And Brendon had been a no-good cheat who was murdered because of it.

Vicki cocked an eyebrow at me. "So?"

"So, do you think it's safe?" I regretted the words the moment they were out of my mouth.

Vicki stared at me a moment, her always pleasant demeanor slipping just a little. "He's not his brother."

"I know, but . . ."

"No," she said. "There are no buts here, unless you count you, you butthead." She gave me a faint smile, as if telling me the last was a joke. Something in her eyes said that my doubts had actually hurt her, so maybe it wasn't so far from the truth. "I like him and he likes me. That's all that matters."

And really, wasn't it? As long as he treated her better than his brother treated women, what was wrong with Vicki finding happiness? With all the craziness lately, we all deserved some of that.

I knew I was projecting my own frustrations. Between

Paul's seeming indifference and my fear of saying or doing the wrong thing around Will, who was I to judge someone else's love life?

"I'm sorry," I said. "I'm just worried about you."

This time her smile was genuine. "There is absolutely no reason to be." She opened the office door. "We best get back to work."

I followed her out, feeling oddly lighter. Maybe it was knowing that at least someone I knew was having a good day that did it. Maybe it was Vicki's bubbly personality. Whatever it was, I felt just about as good as I could get considering the circumstances.

Lena was busy cleaning the tables, so I went about brewing some fresh coffee. Things weren't as bad as they seemed. I had a job, a business even. I had friends here, and maybe, if I could figure out what was going on with both Paul and Will, a possible boyfriend.

And tonight, when the book clubs arrived for their meeting, I would have someone to talk to. I might not have a hot date, but my life wasn't completely empty. I could talk to them, learn more about David and his murder.

And if I came up with some new clue, well then, maybe, despite how it started, it wouldn't be such a bad day after all.

15

The Pine Hills book club was the first to arrive. Rita came through the doors of Death by Coffee like a queen returning to her palace. Her chin was held high, even as she nearly tripped over her own two feet stepping over the threshold. The other members of the group came in behind her, as if they were her court.

I was standing by the table near the door, rag in my hand, when they came in. Rita's eyes fell on me immediately, and I had just enough time to think, "Oh crap," before she was hurrying over to where I stood.

"I'll be right up," she called over her shoulder as she took me by the arm and led me to the back of the store where no one was currently sitting. "Oh, my Lordy!" she said a little louder than necessary. "I've heard a rumor that you were arrested! How can that be?"

Apparently, Rita had gotten over my stealing Cardboard Dad, because she was looking at me in a way that said she couldn't believe anyone would dare arrest the daughter of her beloved favorite author. I was simply an extension of my dad, and if anyone laid a hand on me, it was a crime committed against him.

"It was nothing," I said. "I got angry. Officer Buchannan didn't like it." I shrugged helplessly. "I got arrested."

Her eyes widened and her mouth opened into an "O" that would have been comical if it hadn't been expected. "Did he hurt you? If so, you could get him on police brutality. I know of a lawyer who would take your case like *that*." She snapped her fingers before leaning in closer. "I hear John Buchannan likes to drink down at Beers and Rears when he's off duty."

I stared at her blankly before managing a weak, "Beers and Rears?"

"Oh yes." She waved a hand in my face. "It's one of those bars where the girls wiggle their booties in front of men's faces while they get drunk. The men get drunk, not the women." She chuckled.

I couldn't imagine a town like Pine Hills having something like that. This wasn't a big city. It wasn't even a medium city, to be honest. Back home in California, there were more than enough nudie bars or strip clubs to satisfy all the men in the world, but here? I could hardly imagine it.

Then again, with how most of the men were treating me lately, I had no problem thinking of them all as pigs. Maybe it wasn't so far-fetched after all.

"I see," I said, already plotting how I might use this information against Buchannan the next time he accused me of something. He wasn't the saint he pretended to be; not by a long shot.

"He's been known to take his wife, too," Rita added, hand placed beside her mouth as if sharing a deep, dark secret. "I don't think she enjoys the shows themselves, but she likes what it earns her afterward, if you know what I mean."

I took a step back and shook my head, trying to dislodge the thought. I didn't even want to think about Buchannan with a woman, his wife or otherwise. Ever. Never, ever.

"But it's just a rumor," Rita said with a flippant wave of her hand. She just about clipped me on the nose. "It's probably why he has such a thing for you, really."

"Wait? What? What thing?"

"You are the closest thing we have to a celebrity here. I've seen the way he looks at you. Like most men, he undresses you with those eyes of his."

I'd seen Buchannan looking at me before, and he sure wasn't undressing me with his eyes; not unless he was replacing what I was wearing with an orange jumpsuit. But he *had* gone through my underwear drawer when the object of his search was right there.

"It's all blown out of proportion," I said. "And I'm sorry about taking the cardboard cutout." I hoped bringing up Cardboard Dad might deflect the subject away from Buchannan and anyone else I'd rather not see losing their clothes.

"That's old news," Rita said. "I just hope I get him back soon." She heaved a sigh of longing. "I never should have loaned him to you in the first place. The bedroom does get lonely at night without him."

I was *so* done with this conversation. "I best get back to work." I quickly extracted myself before she could reply.

Rita didn't seem to mind. She patted me on the arm as I walked past before she headed up the stairs to where the rest of the group waited. I joined Lena at the counter and watched them, both of us with frowns on our faces.

"Crazy, isn't it?" she asked.

"What do you mean?" Death by Coffee had died down

to just a trickle of customers here and there, meaning there would be a lot of standing around and waiting until close, which was only an hour away. The book club would stay an hour after that, meaning I'd be forced to hover until they finally left and I could lock up.

"Having the meetings still." Lena shook her head. She ran her hand through her purple hair, pushing it back from her face. "A guy died. I just can't imagine going on like nothing happened the way they are. It's almost obscene."

I watched as Rita giggled at something Cindy said. Andi, as was her custom, gasped and covered her mouth with her hand as if shocked by whatever she'd heard.

"They don't seem too upset by it, do they?"

"Neither do they."

I followed Lena's nod toward the door, where the Cherry Valley book club was coming through. Albert paid me only a cursory glance before heading for the stairs with Vivian, Orville, and Sara close behind. The door started to swing closed but was caught at the last minute by a man I didn't know. He was about five seven, one hundred sixty pounds or so, and his hair was combed to the side. It seemed to bounce as he walked, like it was fused together. I couldn't tell if it was real or glued on.

I was prepared for him to come over and place an order, but instead he followed the group up the stairs to where Rita and the others waited.

"Huh," I said, watching him. He seemed at ease with the others. He put a hand on Sara's back as he talked to the group, gently rubbing in comfort, before they all took a seat.

Dan perhaps? It was the only thing that made sense. If they were indeed going to go through with the book club competition, then it seemed reasonable that they'd call in someone who knew the rules to fill in the empty spot.

I immediately became suspicious. The man I believed

to be Dan was smiling and talking with the others as if nothing had happened. I noted him glance toward where the police tape still hung, but outside a slight tightening of his smile, he didn't seem fazed by it.

Maybe because he's the reason it's there.

If this man was who I thought he was, I really needed to get him alone to talk to him.

A couple of customers came in over the next hour. Lena and I served them, though I did so distractedly. I kept finding my gaze traveling to the meeting. Each group remained separate, despite how close they were sitting, talking amongst themselves. Many had my dad's book in hand, though I didn't see anyone open their copy. Eyes darted suspiciously around, as if each member was afraid someone from the other group would overhear what they were saying and use it against them somehow.

I couldn't understand why they didn't have separate meetings in different places. Why sit so close together if you're only going to whisper to your own group?

Then again, why did Rita and her crew do anything? I was quickly learning not to question her motives too much, lest I drive myself bonkers trying to make sense of them.

I really wanted to go up and eavesdrop on the conversations, but I held off until the last customer walked out the door. I cleaned off all the tables as Lena switched the sign on the door over to CLOSED.

"I'm going to see how everyone is doing," I told her. "Go ahead and clean up the kitchen. You can leave after that. I'll finish up with the tables and deal with the money later."

"Got ya," Lena said with a wink. She knew what I was doing, always seemed to. She was perceptive like that, something I hoped to take advantage of someday.

As I ascended the stairs, the two groups turned their

chairs to face one another. Rita started to speak to the group as a whole, but I cut her off before she could start.

"Can I speak with Dan a moment?"

All eyes turned my way, and for an instant I thought that maybe I was wrong about who the new guy was. No one said anything at first. They just stared at me, and then almost in unison they turned to Rita. It was actually pretty creepy.

"Oh, well, I suppose you can," she said. "But hurry. We have important matters to discuss, and Dan needs to catch up."

Dan rose, looking mildly worried.

"I just want to introduce myself and get to know you," I told him as I led him to the same aisle between the shelves where I'd talked to Jimmy the other day. "I hope that is okay, Mr. Jacobson."

"Just Dan," he said, crossing his arms. He looked annoyed to be singled out.

"I'm Krissy Hancock," I said, holding out my hand. He took it and gave it a weak pump before crossing his arms again. "I was wondering if you are David's replacement in the book club."

The look that rose in Dan's eyes was enough to melt steel. "I am," he said.

I might be slow on the uptake sometimes, but I catch on to some cues quickly enough. "Not a fan, were you?" I asked, thinking back to what I was told about Dan and David's relationship.

"No, I was not." He licked his lips. "David Smith was a foul human being. I didn't trust him and his 'oh, I'm so sexy' voice." He tried to mock a British accent at the last but failed miserably.

"He took your place in the group. They kicked you out, just so he could replace you. Why come back now?"

Dan shrugged. "It wasn't like I had anything else to do with my time."

"How well do you know the group?" I asked. If he wasn't the killer, then perhaps he knew someone who might be. "Do you think any of them could have hurt David?"

Dan snorted. "I'm sure any of them could have for the right reason." He sighed and seemed to sag in on himself. "Look, I'm not sure why I came back here after what happened. I was never truly liked by anyone. There's a reason they didn't want me back, even if I was their best asset in these things. David comes in, pretends to be interested, and I got kicked out. That's really all there is to it. I don't know anything else about any of this."

I was surprised at how honest he was being. Few people admit to not being liked, especially when someone else has recently died. It is the undesirable who is often the first to be accused.

"If they didn't like you, then why come back at all?" I asked.

He smiled. "They needed me."

There was something in his smile that put me off. I couldn't put my finger on what it was. I just didn't like it.

"Do you have any idea who might have wanted to kill David?"

Dan laughed and shook his head. "Look at you, acting the part of a detective. You know, I heard about you, about how you investigated some crime in your free time and solved the case with little in the way of help. Rita made sure to include it in the e-mail she sent everyone before this year's event."

"Did she, now?" I felt my face grow warm.

"I didn't believe it at first. I even followed the links, yet I couldn't imagine some little coffee girl chasing after a killer." He took a step closer to me. "But standing here, listening to you question me, I think I might have changed my mind." Another step, followed by a deep breath. "It's intriguing."

I cleared my throat. Standing this close, I could smell Dan's cologne and could see down the front of his shirt. There were muscles down there, muscles that flexed even as I watched.

I took a hasty step back, face flaming. At first glance, Dan Jacobson wasn't much to look at. With that hair, and the way he dressed, he could be just about any man, really. But up close, with his cologne washing over you, those muscles flexing, the knowing smile, and wild eyes, there was an animal magnetism to him. It wasn't something you could ever admit to anyone, let alone yourself, but it was there.

"I don't care what you think!"

Rita's shout saved me from having to cover my embarrassment with some mumbled words that would have only made things worse. Both Dan and I turned to find Rita and Albert on their feet, facing each other as if they were about to go ten rounds.

"This book isn't worth the paper it's printed on!" Albert fired back. "You are forcing us into reading it because you have the advantage here. It's no secret that you are going to use her to win!" His hand jerked back my way.

"Uh-oh," Dan said with a grin.

"Great." I hurried over to where the two were arguing. The rest of the group looked on with eagerness, as if this was the kind of thing they lived for.

"You know it's not like that," Rita said. "The book was chosen ahead of time, agreed upon, and as you know is an important piece of crime fiction. Just because you are too dense to understand it doesn't mean it isn't worth reading!"

She looked close to tears, as if anyone putting down a James Hancock novel was enough to break her heart.

Of course, I knew *Murder in Lovetown* well enough to know Albert had a point. Even my dad would rather forget the book existed. It wasn't one of his best works.

Albert shook his copy in her face. "I have half a mind to call this competition forfeit. Not only did you take advantage of resources the rest of us couldn't acquire, you made sure to remove one of our members in a vain attempt to cripple us!"

"What?" Rita's hand flew to her chest. "Well, I never!"

"Please," I said, stepping between them. "Can we all just calm down for a minute? There's no need to fight."

"He started it!" Rita's hand slapped me upside the head as she pointed at Albert. "He's accusing us of cheating."

"You are!"

"I don't want to have to kick you both out," I said in as reasonable a tone as I could manage. Lena was standing on the stairs, dish soap on her hands, looking as if she was willing to jump in and break up a fight if fists started flying. Her presence made me feel a little better.

"You wouldn't," Rita said, taken aback. "After all I've done for you."

"I can't have you fighting in here, even after hours."

"We're just having a heated discussion," she said. "This sort of thing happens all the time, doesn't it, Albert?"

He grunted and looked away.

"Maybe we should call it a night," Jimmy put in. "I think we've all had just about as much stress as we can handle."

That was met with a mild round of agreement.

I slowly stepped out from between Rita and Albert, afraid they'd start going at it again the moment I was out of the way. Dan was watching me with a smile. When he saw me glance his way, he gave me a thumbs-up before moving to help Sara up. There were tears in her eyes, and I felt bad for her. She'd just lost the man she loved, and here the others were, fighting over a stupid book. It was downright rude, if you asked me.

Rita huffed, gathered her book, and headed straight for the stairs, clearly put out. Everyone else was quick to follow.

I watched them go. Tempers were definitely flaring, yet I couldn't seem to figure out which one of the angry readers might have reason enough to kill David Smith. None of them seemed capable of it, really. I mean, when was the last time you saw a bookworm bash someone's head in? It just didn't add up.

But one of them did it; I was sure of it. Beneath all of the anger and accusations, someone knew the truth. I was determined to figure out who it was.

I needed to learn more about the Cherry Valley group, Dan Jacobson especially. Why was he the one who was kicked out and not someone else? And could he have come to Pine Hills early, before they asked him to join the group again? I needed to sit down and talk to him alone, without the others around, distracting me.

As the last of them left, I latched the door to Death by Coffee behind them, my mind a million miles away, and began the slow process of closing down for the night.

16

The house was still a mess when I got home. A part of me had hoped that it would all magically repair itself while I was gone. I felt that I deserved a break after everything that Buchannan had done to me lately. Why couldn't some well-meaning neighbor have come in, picked up the mess for me, and then left me with a freshly baked batch of chocolate chip cookies and hot coffee so I could sit back and relax and enjoy the evening for once?

I closed the front door with a sigh. Misfit was sleeping on the island counter instead of rushing the door. He looked as beat as I felt. I wondered what other mischief he'd gotten himself into while I was at work, and then decided I really didn't want to know. It would only mean more cleanup.

I dropped my purse onto the table, dug out my cell phone, and then headed into the living room to plop down on the partially shredded couch. Plumes of stuffing shot out of the cushion, to join the rest of it on the floor. I waved my hand in front of my face a few times to waft the remnants away before focusing on the little device in my hand.

What I really wanted to do was call Paul Dalton and ask him to come over. I didn't care if he helped me clean or if he simply sat down amid the mess and comforted me while I cried my eyes out. I was so exhausted, I could hardly think straight.

But Paul hadn't returned any of my previous calls, nor had he stopped by to make sure I was okay. I mostly wanted him to come over so I could talk to him. I didn't like leaving things hanging like that. If he was told to stay away from me, well then, he should have told me.

Yes, I was probably being overly sensitive, but I was in desperate need of someone to talk to. If I had Will's number, I might have called him instead. I knew where I could find it, but for some reason it felt invasive. *Let him give it to you, Krissy,* I told myself. *Guys like that. And it will show you he's truly interested.*

I considered the phone for a good five minutes before dialing. It rang three times before someone picked up and answered.

"Krissy?"

The sound of the gravely voice just about had me in tears. "Dad."

"What's wrong, Buttercup?"

I hadn't said a thing, yet my dad already knew something was wrong. When I'd spoken, I hadn't sobbed the word. I didn't even speak in a way that would give away my feelings, outside of my voice being a little lifeless. But dads pick up on things like that. It is one of the best things about them.

"Oh, you know, murder and mayhem. The usual."

I could hear the frown in his voice when he said, "Tell me."

I let it all spill out of me in a rush. I told him about the book clubs, about the weird competition between the two towns. I told him about David Smith and the people of Cherry Valley, and how no one but Sara Huffington seemed to be upset the guy was dead. I left out the details about the cardboard cutout and Rita because, well, yuck. I didn't want him thinking that a cardboard version of him was keeping someone company during the night, even if it was true.

Dad listened like he always did. Any time I had any problems at all, I just needed to call him up and he would let me regurgitate all of the details without interruption. He was good like that, always had been. Without Dad, I probably would have needed professional help long ago.

"And there was no indication of a break-in," I said.

"Has a key come up missing?" Dad asked.

I paused, a frown slowly creeping over my features. "No one said anything about a missing key," I said. Could it be that easy? Had the killer stolen one of the store keys? It would explain a lot.

And what if that wasn't the case? Could the killer be someone who worked for me? I hoped not. I so didn't want to have to start accusing my friends and employees of killing someone. If I felt lonely now, just wait and see how I'd feel once I'd alienated everyone I knew.

I sighed in frustration. "I'm sure none of this would have happened if they hadn't been reading *Murder in Lovetown.*"

"They're reading my book?"

Oh crap. "Well, yeah," I said, feeling dumber than ever. I mean, I love my dad and all, but there's a point where you have to draw the line. Pine Hills was my getaway, my chance to start my own life, yet I was still living in my dad's shadow. Everything from Death by Coffee, to the books we sold, to the book the stupid book club was reading, all went right back to him.

I needed to be my own person. I didn't want to drag him into this more than he already was by my dumping on him.

"Well, I'll be," Dad said. I could hear the pride in his

voice. "It might not be one of my best works, but to have them read it together . . ." He actually sniffed as if he was tearing up. "Maybe I should come down and talk to the group about the novel."

"No!" I reined back the shout so it didn't quite rattle the phone. I swallowed back my panic and went on in a calmer voice. "That's not necessary. Besides, the Cherry Valley group would continue to complain that it is an unfair advantage to have you come here. They've already tried to weasel out of it because of me."

"I see." He sounded disappointed.

"Maybe next time," I promised him, though the thought of him in town terrified me. If Rita saw him, I had no doubts that she would be all over him, possibly even go as far as to try to drag him back home with her. I didn't want to have to beat her off with a dishrag, but I'd do it if I had to.

"Maybe." He sighed. "I guess it probably wouldn't be a good idea, especially since someone has died. You'd think they'd just cancel the thing and try again next year."

"I know, right?" I still was struggling with that myself. "But if you knew these people, you'd understand. I'm not sure there is a sane one amongst them."

"Hmm."

I frowned into the phone. "Hmm?" I echoed, making it a question. It wasn't like my dad to make inarticulate sounds.

"Are you sure sanity comes into this?"

My frown deepened. "What do you mean?"

"I know you don't understand these people very well, Buttercup, but from the sound of things, they mean well."

"Outside of whoever killed David Smith."

"Of course." He groaned as he settled in, telling me he was getting ready to lay on the wisdom. "But what about those who had nothing to do with the man's death? They love books and are willing to take the time to discuss them each and every year. You might not understand their methods, but I'm sure this has been developed over the years to where both sides agree with how it works. Perhaps you should consider joining yourself. Then perhaps you could see things from their point of view."

"Uh . . ." The thought of joining the Pine Hills book club was enough to put me off my dinner. It was bad enough I spent time at the writers' group, listening to Rita prattle on about everything but her writing. Most of the time, the women would gossip for a good hour before spending the last thirty minutes reading their work. I could only imagine what it would be like at a book club meeting, especially now with David's death. The gossip would never end. "I'll think about it."

"You do that." There was a slight pause before, "How has work been?"

"Better," I said, happy to be off the murder and the possibility of him coming down. "Business has been steady for the last few months."

"I detect a 'but' in there."

I smiled. Of course he did. He noticed everything. James Hancock was a mystery writer for a reason. "But it feels like we aren't making enough money based on the amount of customers coming in."

"How's that?"

"I don't know." Frustration was trying to set it. We should have been skating by easily, and yet it seemed as if something was holding us back. "Maybe we need to raise prices or something. We have two new hires, so that could be it, too. Before, it was just Vicki and me."

"Maybe," Dad said. "Or perhaps you need to look harder at everything and see where the money is leaking from. If you believe you should be doing better, then I'd bet you are. Check the bills and make sure you aren't being overcharged for something."

"I will."

"And Buttercup?"

"Yeah, Dad?"

"Be safe. I know this man's death has nothing to do with you, but I don't want you taking any risks. You don't have to try to be a hero. You are already one."

"Thanks, Dad," I said with a blush.

We said our good-byes and I hung up, feeling only marginally better. Normally, a talk with my dad made me feel lighter, made everything seem to line up properly, yet this time I felt as if I were walking through a hazy cloud that blocked all of my senses. I was confused, lost, and saw no way out of it. We'd barely talked about David Smith, which was sort of the entire point of my call, yet what else could he have said? It wasn't like he could tell me who killed him.

I heaved myself off the couch and looked around the disaster of the room. I needed to clean in the worst way, yet I didn't want to do it alone. I bit my lip, considered the phone a moment longer, and then finally made the call— the one I should have made from the start.

It rang only twice before Paul answered with a sharp "Yeah?"

"Hi, Paul, it's me."

There was a pause. "Krissy?"

"Yeah."

"Oh." He cleared his throat. "I'm kind of busy right now."

"That's okay." I felt stupid for calling, but what else was I supposed to do? I couldn't keep wondering why he was avoiding me. It was bogging me down, adding to my already cluttered mind. "What time do you get off?" I asked, determined to see this through. Despite everything, I still wanted to see him. And besides, if nothing else, I could tell him about the photograph I'd found at Ted and Bettfast. I didn't want to drag Sara's name through the mud, but it might be the only way I could show him I was helping.

There was an even longer pause before, "Tonight wouldn't be good," he said, knowing what I was going to ask before I said it. "I have a ton of work to do here and I need to get home to the dogs." Paul had a pair of huskies I'd never seen with my own two eyes. "Let me call you tomorrow sometime, okay? We can figure out something then."

"Okay." I frowned. I couldn't tell if he was blowing me off or was legitimately too busy to see me tonight.

"It might be late. Is that still okay?"

"Sure."

I fought back an urge to cry or scream or do something to vent my frustrations. A part of me did understand why Paul was keeping his distance, but come on, I was suffering here. If only he'd say something kind, ask me if I was okay, then I could forgive him. As it stood now, I was starting to wonder if Buchannan's disdain for me was affecting Paul's own judgment.

If my own actions haven't been doing the same already.

"Krissy? Are you still there?" Paul sounded annoyed. I must have been off in my own little world for longer than I thought.

"Yeah, I'm here."

"I have to go. I'll call you tomorrow."

"Okay," I said, but he never heard it. I was listening to an empty line.

I shoved my phone into my pocket and considered what to do. Tonight, I had to clean; there was no getting around it. If I left the house a mess now, chances were good it would remain that way up until the moment I was smothered in it. There was no way I was going to let that happen, especially if Paul might come over tomorrow night. I doubted he'd want to sweep me off my feet even if he could find them in the mess. And there was no way I was going to have him sweep the floor for me.

I began picking up the worst of the mess, mind elsewhere. If I was cleaning tonight and not talking to Paul—and I hoped seeing him—until later tomorrow night, I needed to find something to do to fill the hours in between. I wasn't about to sit at home and sulk, that was for sure.

As far as I could tell, there were no clues on who could have killed David at Death by Coffee. If there were, the police had already taken them. When I talked to Paul, I'd have to ask him if they'd found anything, though I'd need to do it in a way that wouldn't make him suspect that I was prying information out of him. I had a feeling he wouldn't look positively on that, and I was already on thin ice with him as it was.

I'd already talked to the members of the Cherry Valley group and had even gone into David's room at the bed-and-breakfast, but outside the provocative—to say the least—photograph of Sara, I'd learned nothing.

But there was one member of the group I really hadn't had a chance to talk to. Dan was new in town, and while I'd asked him a few questions I hadn't gotten all the answers I needed. I was certain he knew more about the death than he was letting on.

I carried the torn-up magazines and couch fluff to the trash, where I threw them away with a sigh. Misfit watched me lazily, though I did think I detected a mischievous grin beneath all of that fur.

"This is your fault, you know?" I scolded him before heading to the hall closet for the vacuum. Misfit took one look at it and bolted down the hall, where he would hide beneath the bed until the loud sounds stopped.

I hardly paid him any attention. I had only one thing on my mind. Tomorrow, I was going to ask Dan more about David Smith. Nothing would stop me from learning everything he knew, not even Buchannan or the fact I might very well be going to interrogate a murderer.

17

I was up early the next morning, fully determined to learn something new about David's murder. I dressed in one of my better outfits—a light blue summer top with spaghetti straps, and white shorts with sandals to match. I topped it off with a floppy hat and sunglasses. I looked like I was heading to the beach, which was precisely the point. How could you not relax around someone dressed so causally?

I left the house with a spring in my step. I wished I had a convertible I could drive with the top down instead of my small black car. With the way I was dressed, I felt as if I were back in California, and a convertible would only enhance the feeling. I didn't want to go back there for more than a visit, but I did miss the breeze and California sun.

I arrived at Ted and Bettfast just past nine. It was probably a bit too early to interrogate someone, especially if they'd talked about the book some more after they'd gotten back and had gone to sleep late. I didn't know how these things worked, so it was entirely possible.

I parked in the lot, got out of my car, and then just stood there, soaking in the morning sun. There was a cool breeze that would have been cold if it wasn't for the heat pounding down from the cloudless sky. Today was going to be a scorcher, and I couldn't be happier. Maybe once all of this was over with, I'd take some time to lay out. It had been forever since I'd tanned. One look at my bone-white legs was enough to tell you that, just before they blinded you.

I headed for the front doors, purse thrown over one arm, feeling oddly like a movie star arriving on set for the first time. Maybe it was the clothes. Maybe it was the atmosphere of the bed-and-breakfast that did it. The place might be crumbling around the edges, but it still held a magnificence to it that seemed to enliven everything around it. One of these days, I'd have to stay for a weekend, just to see if the feeling lasted past the first day.

An older couple stood talking to one another just outside the front door. The discussion wasn't quite heated, but I could tell neither of them was happy about whatever it was they were talking about. I slowed my pace, hoping they wouldn't notice my approach so I could catch a hint of their conversation, but as soon as I was out of the parking lot, they both clammed up and turned my way.

"Looking for a room?" the woman asked with a smile. She had dyed black hair and wore huge hoop earrings in ears that were starting to sag from all of the weight. Fine lines wrinkled the corners of her eyes and mouth when she smiled. Her hands, which were folded demurely above her navel, were spotted with age yet looked strong enough to work for long hours tending a garden.

The man next to her had black hair as well, though his wasn't dyed. Gray streaked his temples, adding character to a face that was already full of it. He had a pair of reading glasses on a chain around his neck, and one of those Burt Reynolds mustaches rested above his lip.

"Not today," I said. "I'm here about one of your previous guests, David Smith. Did you know him?"

The couple looked at each other and frowned in unison.

"We did," the man said. His voice was surprisingly soft, almost feminine. "He stayed with us for a night or two."

I noticed the "us" and took a stab in the dark. "Are you Ted and Bett Bunford, by chance?"

Bett nodded. "We are. I don't know why you would want to know anything about that man. He sure could sweet-talk the ladies, but there was just something about him I didn't care for."

"Really?" I asked, interested. "Did he do or say anything that roused your suspicions?"

"Well, no, not exactly." Bett looked at her husband.

"He was too much of a smooth talker," he said. "You could tell he was trying too hard. I don't know what that girl saw in him. I think everyone else saw through the act." He heaved a sigh. "It truly is a shame what happened to him, of course. I don't want you to get the wrong idea."

I took another stab in the dark. With the way they were opening up, I had a feeling I knew what they'd just been talking about. "Was that what you were discussing when I pulled up?"

I was rewarded with a pair of nods.

"It's just not right that they are still having the book club competition so soon after his death," Bett said.

"We were considering asking them to leave," Ted added.

"*You* were considering," Bett retorted, turning on him. "*I* was thinking we should at least have a memorial or something in his honor."

"We didn't even know the man well enough to know if he had any honor!" Ted threw his hands up into the air and looked at me. "See what I have to deal with? She doesn't like the guy and then wants to honor him like a damn fallen hero."

"It's not that," Bett said. "But he *did* stay here with us, you know?"

"Is it okay if I go in and have a look around?" I asked, cutting in before they could get too deep into their argument and drag me into it. "I won't disturb anyone."

Ted frowned at me. "Well, I don't know about that. . . ."

Bett's eyebrows rose. "Who did you say you were again?"

"Krissy Hancock," I said with a smile. "I'm looking into David's death." I paused, inwardly wincing at the coming lie. "I'm working with the police."

"Oh, well, why didn't you say so," Bett said. "Go right in. If you need anything, Justin is inside, helping the guests."

"Thank you." I turned away, hoping they wouldn't call the police to verify my story. They didn't seem the type, but as I was quickly learning, you can never quite tell with some people. They might appear to be a sweet older couple, but deep down they might be as cynical as the old man who sat on his front stoop screaming at kids to get off his lawn.

I entered the bed-and-breakfast and found my gaze landing on a young man who stood just inside, wringing his hands worriedly as he looked past me to where the Bunfords were arguing again. He quickly looked away when he saw me watching him but didn't move as I approached. I saw by his name tag that I was looking at Justin.

"They aren't talking about you," I said with a smile, hoping to win him over.

Justin glanced at me with only one eye. He kept the other averted by the downward angle of his head. Shoulder-length hair hung down, concealing half of his face. Acne covered his chin and cheeks, and I imagine if I were to be able to see it, his forehead as well. His clothes were probably a size too big for him, making him seem smaller than he really was. Soaking wet, I bet he didn't weigh much more than 130 pounds, though he was near six feet.

"That's good," he said, shooting a quick glance to the door. "Is there something I can help you with? Do you need a room?"

"No thanks." I kept my smile firmly in place. The poor guy looked ready to bolt at the first provocation. I put his age at seventeen, and that might even be generous. "I'm here about someone who recently stayed here. Did you happen to know David Smith?"

Justin's eyes darted around me, as if he was afraid to look me in the eye. "Yeah, I guess. He's the guy that died, right?"

"Right."

I was hoping Justin would take the lead and suddenly start filling my head with previously unknown facts about our mysterious British guest. Instead, he just stood there, looking everywhere but at me.

"Do you happen to know anything about him?" I asked after it was evident he wouldn't speak on his own volition.

"No."

"Did he have any visitors to his room while he was here?"

He shrugged and looked at his feet.

"Did he pay any of the other guests a visit late at night? Did he fight with anyone? Did he do or say anything that you found odd?"

Justin shrugged again. "I just work here. I don't pay much attention to what the guests do."

Something about the statement seemed off to me, like he'd rehearsed the line, but I didn't push. Justin looked ready to flee, and if I kept nagging at him, he might never open up and tell me what it was that was bothering him so much.

Sure, he could naturally be like this—a lot of awkward young men were—but there was something about him that told me he was hiding something. I couldn't ask him now, not without scaring him off, though I intended on coming back later to try again.

"Okay," I said. "Thank you." I started to walk away, but paused. "Do you know if any of the other guests from Cherry Valley are up yet?"

His face brightened from miserably sober to only mildly depressed. "Two of the women are out back. The guys are still up in their rooms."

"Thanks." I turned and headed for the back, figuring that I could talk to Sara again and see if she had anything new to add. Now that more time had elapsed since David's death, she might remember something that would help point to his killer. Without Albert hovering over her, she might open up more.

As I stepped through the back doors, my mind went to the photo I'd found. There was no way I could bring that up now, or like ever. I don't think Sara would appreciate it.

Sara was lying in a chair by the pool, wearing a bikini on a body that made me feel oafish by comparison. Her skin had already bronzed more than the last time I'd seen her. If I'd lain out that much, I'd have promptly turned blister red and would have spent the next three days sick as a dog. Vivian was in a chair on the other side of the pool, eyes closed and snoring softly.

I approached Sara's chair, passing right in front of her sun. She heaved a sigh and without opening her eyes barked, "What?"

"Excuse me," I said. "I was hoping I could ask you a few questions." That sounded diplomatic and police-like enough, didn't it?

Sara opened one eye and squinted up at me. "You're the coffee shop girl, aren't you?"

"I am."

"So why are you asking me anything?"

"I was hoping you could tell me more about David, who he was, what he did for a living."

Sara blinked at me, her face suddenly pale. She raised a finger and delicately wiped at her eye. "Why would you want to know about him?" she asked, a twinge of jealousy marring her words. "What is it to you?"

I winced at her tone. Clearly she wasn't ready to talk about him, and feared I was attracted to him. But if I wanted to get an accurate portrayal of who David was, Sara was the best option. She was the one who'd spent the most time with him, saw him at his most private. She was the one who had lost the most by his death. They were obviously more than just friends, if the photo I'd found was any indication, so she had to know more than the others.

"I only want to know more about him," I said. "It might help me figure out who killed him."

She sat up straighter. "Are you working with the police, then?"

"Well, not exactly."

"Then how could telling you anything possibly help?"

I bit my lip. Apparently she hadn't read Rita's e-mail that talked about my awesome detective skills. "I helped on another murder case," I said. "I solved it, in fact. And this murder happened in my store, so this time it's sort of personal."

Sara grew tight-lipped. "I really don't want to talk about it. I just want to spend a few minutes out here without someone reminding me of what happened. How would you like it if someone killed your boyfriend and then started poking at the wound while you were still suffering?"

Her voice rose as she spoke. I took a step back, worried she might come off her chair and take a swing at me. "I didn't mean anything by it," I said. "I just want to help. I'm sorry."

Vivian was sitting up in her chair, watching us with interest. Sara was breathing hard, barely able to contain her anger. Tears coursed down her cheeks and dripped onto her tanned chest. I felt like a royal jerk for asking her questions so soon after his death, but how else was I supposed to get answers? I suppose after the last murder investigation I should have learned my lesson; the wife hadn't taken it well then, either.

I turned and hurried away before I upset Sara any further. I didn't think she knew who killed David, or else she would have told the police about it already. Then again, I hadn't had contact with anyone about the case, so as far as I knew, she had and Paul was moving in on the killer even now. And if she turned out to be the murderer herself, well then, it wasn't like she was going to suddenly admit it in the middle of my not-so-official interrogation.

I threw open the door that led back into Ted and Bettfast, not really looking where I was going, and ran straight into the arms of the man I'd originally come here to meet.

"Whoa!" Dan said with a lopsided grin. He was wearing a Speedo suit with a towel draped over his shoulder. His body was hot where I pressed against him. His arms had reflexively gone around me when we'd bumped into one another—or at least, that's what I hoped.

"I'm sorry," I said, extracting myself from him. "I wasn't watching where I was going."

"That's okay." Dan let his hand fall away from me almost

reluctantly. He eyed me up and down, and his smile grew. "I should have seen you coming."

I kept my eyes planted firmly past his right ear. I'm sorry, but Speedos don't look good on any man. I don't care if you are built out of nothing but pure muscle—and Dan was a close thing—there is something obscene about them.

"I was hoping to see you, actually," I said. "Do you, uh, think you could get dressed and we could sit down and talk?"

Dan chuckled. "Do I make you uncomfortable?"

"Just a little." I blushed. Fool betrayer of a face.

"I was thinking of having a morning swim before breakfast, but I suppose I could take some time to talk to you."

"Great."

"But not here." Dan turned his head so his neck cracked. "I feel too confined here, too stuffy. It's the atmosphere, I think. Would you mind if we talked somewhere else?"

"No, that would be okay," I said, probably a little too quickly. If we left, Dan would have to put on some clothes and would stop flexing his shoulders and pecs every time he moved. I could just make out the motion out of the corner of my eye, and it only served to make me blush that much harder.

"How about you give me an hour?" he asked. "I can get cleaned up and we can have a late breakfast together. Have you eaten?"

"No," I said. "And that would be great."

"Good, good." Dan smiled and leaned back on his heel. "So, I'll see you in an hour. I've heard there is a place in town that is supposed to be really good. Do you mind if we meet there? I think it is called the Banyon Tree."

"J&E's Banyon Tree?" I asked, dreading it even as it came out of my mouth.

"That's the one."

I considered saying no, but somehow I knew this might be my only real chance of talking to Dan alone. Albert could come strolling down the stairs at any moment, and I was positive he would want to talk, or at least eavesdrop on our conversation. I wasn't welcome in the Banyon Tree, and just because Judith and Eddie Banyon had been seen in the vicinity of Death by Coffee recently didn't mean they'd suddenly decided to like me.

But I couldn't let this opportunity pass.

"I'll see you there," I said, plastering on a fake smile.

Dan winked at me and pulled me into a one-armed hug. His finger slipped under a spaghetti strap and lifted it as if he might pull it from my shoulder before letting it fall back into place. He stepped back with a grin.

"I'll go make myself presentable," he said, before turning.

I couldn't help it; my eyes traveled down his backside as he strode away. I mean, the guy was practically naked, and well built to boot. You can't blame me for sneaking a peek.

The little blue Speedo suit left little to the imagination, and I felt my temperature rise. Dan paused at the bottom of the stairs and both of his cheeks tensed, springing up and then down. My eyes jerked up to see him grinning at me.

"In an hour," he said, before vanishing up the stairs.

My face felt hot to the touch, and I promptly decided I wasn't going to stand around and wait for someone to come ask me why I looked as if I'd been tanning next to Sara without sunscreen. I gathered whatever dignity I had left, pulled my hat down low over my eyes, and walked briskly to my car, hoping no one noticed my embarrassment.

18

I sat in the parking lot of J&E's Banyon Tree, wondering
if I should just turn around and leave. The usual smells
of diner food wafted into my partially lowered windows,
causing my stomach to rumble. I had nothing against
the food here. In fact, it was actually quite good. It was the
owner I had a problem with.

Judith Banyon had hated me from the moment Vicki
and I opened Death by Coffee. She claimed we were trying
to steal her customers, which in a way I guess we were.
Before we opened, the Banyon Tree was the only place you
could go for a good cup of coffee. Or at least that's what
Rita had told me. I'd never actually tasted it myself.

The parking lot was pretty full, and a vague part of me
hoped that there would be no seating left. I could then talk
to Dan in the parking lot, or perhaps convince him to go
somewhere where I wouldn't get chased from the premises the moment I was noticed. I wasn't looking forward to
Judith shouting into my ear.

I shut off the engine with a sigh. There was no sense sitting out in the heat when I could be inside in the cooler air.
I got out of my car, eyes scanning the front of the diner,

almost positive I was going to be assaulted the moment I came anywhere near J&E's.

Judith didn't come roaring out of the diner. Instead, an elderly couple walked slowly out, the man's hand on the woman's arm as if to steady her. They waved to me before easing into a battered Buick.

I hoisted my purse onto my shoulder and adjusted my sunglasses and hat. Maybe if Judith did see me, she'd fail to recognize me. I doubted I was the first person to wear sunglasses indoors at this time of day. If she thought I had a hangover, maybe she wouldn't bother coming over, even if she did recognize me.

Fat chance of that, I thought as I opened the doors and stepped inside. The rockabilly music that normally played over the speakers had been replaced by old country music turned down low so it wouldn't disrupt the morning customers. I cringed just a little inside—I abhor country music of any sort—and scanned the restaurant. Two waitresses were bussing tables and a college-aged girl stood at the counter, taking money from yet another elderly couple. There was no sign of Judith or Eddie Banyon, and I hoped it stayed that way.

A sign by the door told me to seat myself, so that's what I did. There was an open table back by the bathrooms, and I made for it. It put me out of the way, and around the corner from the counter, meaning it would be harder for Judith to spot me if she were indeed here and on the prowl.

I sat down, putting my back to the bathroom. It allowed me a view of the rest of the diner.

A harried-looking waitress hurried over to where I sat. She raised her voice to be heard over the voices and music permeating the air around us.

"What can I get ya?"

"Coffee, please," I said, figuring I might as well see what all of the fuss was about. "And some French toast."

The waitress scribbled the order on a pad before hurrying off without another word.

The Banyon Tree wasn't so bad, I decided, leaning back. Sure, Judith hated me, but the atmosphere and food more than made up for it. As long as I didn't do anything to draw attention, I could see myself eating here more. It sure beat cooking for myself, that was for sure.

I considered taking off my hat, but I left it on just in case Judith happened to make an appearance. The diner was bright enough that my sunglasses didn't feel too much out of place. Sure, no one else was wearing their shades, and most of the men had taken off their hats, but it didn't seem as my refusal to remove mine bothered anyone.

The waitress returned a moment later and quickly set down a coffee mug. Black coffee slopped out over the sides and onto the table as she spun and all but ran back to the counter. At least she'd left the sweetener and creamer.

I reached for the artificial milk and sugar. I poured enough in to choke a small animal, stirred, and then took a sip. It was okay, but nothing like coffee adorned with a chocolate chip cookie. Nothing could compare to that.

I drank slowly, watching the doors all the while. After about five minutes of that, I checked my watch to find that a good hour and fifteen minutes had passed since I'd left Dan at Ted and Bettfast. If he stood me up, I was so not going to be happy.

My French toast arrived a minute later. The bread was drowning in maple syrup and coated in a white layer of powdered sugar that pretty much turned it into candy. My mouth immediately started watering so that when I attempted to thank the waitress, all that came out was a line of drool. She didn't see it, of course; she was already halfway back to the front counter.

I dug in, figuring if Dan wasn't here by the time I finished, he wasn't worth another minute. I wasn't going to wait for him here. He'd eventually show at Death by Coffee for the book club meeting. I could talk to him then.

The door opened and, as if thinking about him had summoned him, Dan Jacobson walked in. He'd ditched the Speedo, thank God, and was wearing loose-fitting running shorts and a black T-shirt instead. His eyes landed on me almost immediately. A wide smile lit up his face as he crossed the room to take the seat across from me.

"Sorry I'm late," he said. "I needed to get in my morning jog lest I turn into a pile of jelly."

I was nearly done with my breakfast already. My teeth hated me, but my stomach was in so much love, I could almost see the little floaty hearts. There's something about sweets that can make even the worst situation worth it, and let me tell you, J&E's French toast qualified. I might be in seventh heaven now, but I'd be regretting it later in the day.

"Okay, then." Dan leaned back just as the waitress returned. "Can I get a water and egg whites?" he asked her, smiling.

She nodded and scurried off.

I looked down at the gooey mess on my plate, and for a moment I was embarrassed. Apparently, Dan was a health nut. I could only imagine what he thought of me with my high sugar and caffeine intake.

Then again, who cared? It wasn't like I was dating the guy. I swallowed a large lump of goo and decided I was happy being me. Besides, as far as I knew, Dan was a no-good murderer. No amount of egg white and water would save him from that.

"So," he said, eyes finally returning to look at me. He'd

watched the waitress walk away as if his eyes were glued to her backside. "What was it you wanted to talk to me about, exactly?"

"David Smith," I said. "What can you tell me about him?"

Dan shrugged. "What is there to say that I already haven't? He was new to town, came in acting like he was some big shot, and then promptly cozied up to the richest girl in all of Cherry Valley."

Richest girl? "Do you mean Sara?" I asked.

"The one and the same." He sighed. "She's the daughter of Joey Huffington." He said it like I was supposed to know who that was. I gave him a blank look. "CEO of Huffington Mulch?"

I raised my eyebrows at him. "A mulching company has a CEO?"

Dan chuckled. "If it is big business, it does. Big Joe has always had a nose for business, and when he realized we didn't have a quality mulch company in these parts, he decided to start up one of his own."

Quality mulch? I was beginning to wonder if Dan was putting me on. I mean, wasn't mulch just shredded trees or something? I couldn't imagine someone making a lot of money doing that, but I guess anything was possible.

I decided to move past Big Joe, mostly because I was more interested in Sara. I might have to come back to him, especially since his name sounded like something out of a gangster movie. If he'd earned his fortune that way and it had trickled down to his daughter, that put a whole new spin on who might have killed David.

"How much is Sara worth?" I asked, genuinely curious.

Dan lifted his hands, palms open and upward, and moved them as if they were weighing scales. "I'd say a million or two."

I just about choked on my coffee. "A million?" Or two? I was so in the wrong business.

"It's mostly inherited," Dan said. "But she also crafts jewelry and sells it online. Makes a pretty penny on that. Did you know that if you can manage to establish yourself, you can just about sell anything online and make some real money?" He shook his head. "I'm not creative enough to pull something like that off."

Neither was I, sadly. I'd tried my hand at writing recently, but I had rambled on with no clear direction and no clear end in mind. I promptly gave up without showing anybody. Rita was none too happy about that. She thought I was going to be the next James Hancock, but apparently his writing talent hadn't been passed down to me. I still went to her group for some reason I couldn't quite explain. Maybe eventually I'd try my hand at writing again, though I doubted the results would be any different.

"Okay," I said, composing myself. I still couldn't believe someone worth so much would hang around with people like Albert or Rita. You'd think she'd make rich friends and have wine-tasting parties instead of going to a book club. "So Sara is loaded. Do you think David was interested in the money more than the girl, then?"

"Hard to say." Dan paused as the waitress returned with both his water and egg whites. He shoved a forkful into his mouth before continuing. "But I wouldn't put it past him. It was the only thing that made sense, considering he knew jack about books."

Interesting. If David had moved in on Sara as a way to get close to her money, that brought up even more scenarios to consider. Sure, jealousy could still be involved. Dan was acting all nonchalant now, but what if he'd been upset about how David was not just moving in on his territory, but perhaps even the woman he had his own eye on? I had no proof he had interest in Sara, but it wasn't too far-fetched.

Dan's eyes roamed around the diner. They landed on each and every moderately attractive girl, and lingered on those who had the most to show. One woman bent over to pick up her toddler at a table close to the window. Before Dan turned back to me, he paid special attention to the way the top of her blouse opened up as she leaned forward.

Yeah, I could see it. Sara wasn't bad looking. Add in the money and she had to look that much more attractive to most men. Dan could have had eyes for her and then David swooped in and swept her out from under him. He'd have to be jealous and angry. And then to top it all off, David takes his spot on the book club team at Sara's request. That would have tweaked his anger even more.

But angry enough to kill?

I wasn't so sure. If you add the fact that David was found in Death by Coffee, behind a locked door, it didn't work out. How had they gotten in? Could Mike have accidently left the door unlocked when he closed that night? The killer could have come in, killed David, and then locked up when they left. I suppose it was possible, but didn't like the idea that one of my employees could have made such a fatal mistake.

"I'm tired of talking about David," Dan said. "He's dead, and I'm sure the police will figure out who did it soon enough. It wouldn't surprise me in the slightest if he slipped and fell after breaking in to rob the place. The man might have acted suave, but I'd seen him bumbling about when he didn't think anyone was looking. I'm sure his cool demeanor was all an act."

"Really?" I asked. "Why do you say that?" A lot of people acted differently when people weren't around to see them. I mean, who wanted anyone to know they picked at their toenails or danced in their underwear, singing oldies, while at home alone? It seemed natural, really.

"There was just something about him is all." Dan sighed. "He had those eyes that were always darting around him, like he was looking for something to steal, if you know what I mean. I saw him trip over his own two feet while walking down the street. The David everyone else knew would never do something like that." He shook his head. "I do wish people would just leave it be."

I was finding it hard to believe a little clumsiness was enough to rouse Dan's suspicions. Everyone misstepped every now and again. I shoved the last of my French toast into my mouth and contemplated Dan. If he was in love with Sara—something I was speculating with zero evidence— then he might have killed the one man who had gotten in his way, inventing reasons out of the blue. The worse he made David look, the more people would view his death as nothing to be concerned about.

Dan set his fork aside and leaned forward. He reached out and took one of my hands in his own. "What do you say we get out of here, huh?"

"Uh, what?" I asked, too surprised at the sudden gesture to jerk away.

"I know you are worried about what happened at your store, but that's not why you asked to see me."

"It's not?"

"Of course not." He smiled, teeth and eyes gleaming in the overhead lights. "It's obvious. I saw it the first time we met."

I wasn't quite sure I followed, but I went along with it. "Is it, now?"

Dan nodded. He picked up my other hand and leaned in even closer. "We should probably go to your place," he said at a near whisper. "We can be as loud and rambunctious as we please." He waggled his eyebrows at me.

My brain must have been on vacation, because it took me a good five seconds to realize what he was saying. The moment it hit me, I jerked out of his grip and stood, knocking over my chair in the process.

"What do you take me for?" I asked, angry. I mean, really?

Dan rose slowly, looking around as if worried everyone in the room was watching us. Hint: They were.

"I just thought . . ." he started, and then frowned. "Don't you want to have sex?"

I sputtered. "What? With you? I . . . No!"

His frown deepened. "You were just leading me on?"

"What? No!" Who did this guy think he was? He might be okay to look at, but his personality left a lot to be desired.

"I saw how you looked at me. I read desire in your eyes. You wanted to get me away from everyone else so that you could seduce me. I saw it." He shook his head angrily. "But that wasn't it at all! You led me on so you could pump me for information."

I grabbed my purse and threw it over my shoulder. "I don't think so," I said, blushing when I realized how the murmurs and chuckles were starting around the room. I really wished there was a way to keep my face from betraying my embarrassment every time something, well, embarrassing happened. "You're the one who wanted to come here. I was fine talking to you at the bed-and-breakfast where, you know, everyone was watching." And where he wouldn't take innocent actions the wrong way.

All eyes were on us and I felt exposed. The whispers were getting louder, the grins wider. A pair of middle-aged women had their cell phones up and were quite clearly recording my outburst. I'd have to do a YouTube search later to make sure it wasn't made public.

Dan didn't seem to care. Why would he? He was from out of town. He didn't have to live with these people, see them every day. "How about we sit down and talk about it," he said, trying on calm. "After you hear about what I can do, I'm sure you'll change your mind. No one has left me disappointed."

Ugh! Some men just didn't get it. I didn't even dignify the last with a response. I didn't have time to.

There was a loud crack as the door behind the counter swung open and slammed against the wall. I had moved in a way that gave me a partial view of the register. I looked up just in time to see Judith Banyon appear, chest heaving angrily as she looked out over the interested crowd. She was wearing one of her old schoolmarm outfits with an apron thrown on over top. The dress was sagging a bit in the back, as if she'd been heavier once but had lost some weight. Her hair was pulled up tight to her head, and it looked as if she had long spearlike needles holding it in place. They could easily serve as weapons.

She paused a moment to take in the staring eyes, the chuckles and giggled whispers, before following their gazes to where I stood.

"You!" she all but growled, pointing a trembling finger at me.

I turned away, but it was too late. Even with the hat and sunglasses, she'd recognized me.

Dan looked confused as he eyed the both of us. I didn't have time to explain, and even if I did, I wasn't about to do it for his benefit.

Judith started around the counter, narrowed eyes on me the entire way, as if she thought she could pin me to the spot with her glare. Before she could round the bend, I was on the move. I pushed my way through the diner and out the door. By the time I hit the pavement, I was moving at a near run, hand on my hat so it wouldn't blow away.

"Don't come back!" came Judith's shout as I jumped into my car. I looked up, half afraid I'd see her charging across the parking lot, needles in hand. Instead, she stood just outside the door, hands planted on her hips, a crowd of eager onlookers behind her.

I started the engine, slammed the car into gear, and tore out of there, unsure whether I was simply terrified by the ogre of a woman or mortified by what Dan had implied in front of everyone.

I had a feeling that by tomorrow it wouldn't matter either way. Both would be all over town soon enough.

19

Chocolate and sugar were calling to me after such a traumatic experience. Sure, Dan wasn't all that bad to look at, but add in the creepy assumption that I wanted to take him to bed with me when we'd just met a few days ago and you suddenly have one of those crazy stalkers who show up outside your window and stare at you while you sleep. I've had enough of those for one lifetime, thank you very much.

I drove straight downtown, a hankering for something that would make my teeth fall out pushing me onward. I didn't care what it might do to my hips, or my mouth, or, well, anything at all for that matter. If I could find a chocolate fountain to stick my head into, I'd do it.

Unfortunately, there were no chocolate fountains in Pine Hills as far as I was aware, so I headed for the next best thing: Phantastic Candies.

Even from the outside, you knew what you were getting into. The front door is decorated like the door to a gingerbread house, icing and all. The frosted windows and bright pink lettering above the door all but screamed candy shop.

I parked out front, thankful I wouldn't have to walk far for my fix. I was seriously jonesing for a chocolate-covered caramel. If someone were to get in my way before I reached my goal, I'd probably end up hurting them.

The door opened to the sound of a large piece of candy being unwrapped. Jules Phan stood behind the counter, wearing a loud yellow suit with red stripes running down it. He wore a matching hat and tie, and I bet his shoes and socks were the same. He looked like a giant piece of colorful taffy. Even his fingernails were painted yellow and red. My mouth watered just looking at him.

"Krissy!" he said as I entered. "I'm so glad you stopped by."

I barely paid him any mind. Chutes full of candy lined the walls. Bins of every sort of sweet you could imagine took up much of the available space. There were suckers as big as my head and jawbreakers that looked as if they could quite literally break your jaw if you tried to shove one of the massive things into your mouth. It was a candy lover's dream.

I went straight for the wrapped caramels. I snatched one up, unwrapped it right then and there, and shoved it into my mouth before finally turning to Jules, who was giving me a worried look. I walked over to the counter and leaned against it, chewing contentedly.

"Is everything okay?" he asked.

"Mut mrery." I chewed faster and swallowed. "Not really," I amended. Chocolate and caramel were stuck to my teeth. I sucked at it, knowing it would be hours before it all came away. I was okay with that.

"Care to talk about it?" Jules snatched a lollipop from

the bin next to him and handed it to me before picking up a rag. He started wiping down the counter.

I plopped the lollipop into my mouth and shrugged. "I don't know. I don't want to dump on you."

"It's perfectly fine." He gave me a winning smile, displaying his ultrawhite teeth. It's so unfair that a guy who works in a candy store has such good dental hygiene.

"If it would help to get something off your chest," Jules continued, "I'm your man."

"I guess it's just the whole David Smith thing," I said with a dramatic sigh. "I mean, Officer Buttface still thinks I'm involved in this somehow."

Jules raised his eyebrows at me.

"Officer John Buchannan." I practically spit his name. "He's following me. He ransacked my home. He even arrested me when I'd done nothing more than tap him on the shoulder a few times."

"I saw," Jules said, not bothering to call me on the white lie. I'd done a lot more than tap him.

"I just don't know what to do," I said. "I can't seem to find a better suspect to throw to the wolves. No matter how hard I try to fit someone into the role of the killer, there is always something that excludes them. I mean, how did they get into a locked store at night without actually breaking in?"

"A missing or copied key?" Jules asked.

"I suppose." I frowned. Dad had asked the same thing. As much as I didn't want to believe someone from the store could have killed him, it was looking like I might have to at least consider it a possibility. "I haven't lost mine. And if Vicki or Lena or Mike would have lost theirs, they would have said something." Unless, of course, one of them was the killer.

"Could the killer have picked the lock?"

I shrugged. "I always thought there would be signs of tampering if they did. I guess it is possible, but why go to all the trouble? I'm not worth framing, that's for sure. And if it has something to do with the book club competition, it didn't do anything but bring back one of the older members. They're determined to have the thing, despite the murder."

Jules was frowning. "Could it have been this old member? Maybe he killed David in order to reclaim his spot."

"Maybe." I really wanted Dan to be guilty after the way he treated me. "But why do it in Death by Coffee? As far as I know, he hadn't been there before yesterday. If he followed David there, that brings us right back to the question of how they got in, and why."

Jules finished wiping down the counter. The rag vanished as if it had never been there. I narrowed my eyes at him, which only caused him to smile.

"Magic!" he said, wiggling his fingers.

I didn't have a smile in me. I lowered my face into my hands, nearly shoving the lollipop into the back of my throat in the process. I removed it and tried again, wondering how I was going to get through this without going insane.

"Is this horrible murder business the only thing that is bothering you?" Jules asked. He patted my shoulder a few times before leaving his hand there, gently massaging. I was so tense, it actually hurt a bit, but despite the pain it still felt oh-so good.

"No," I admitted after a groan of contentment. "We're having a little money trouble at Death by Coffee."

"Really?" Jules sounded genuinely surprised. "I thought business had picked up recently."

"It has," I said. "But we also have two new employees

to pay and just added a Wi-Fi hot spot. Vicki doesn't want to talk about it, but I think we'll have to either raise prices or let one of our new hires go until we figure out where we are bleeding from."

"I've seen the place packed," Jules said, removing his hand. I think I whimpered just a little. "Unless you are paying those two younguns like kings, you shouldn't be having any problems. Your prices are fine."

I spread my hands. "I don't know what else we can do." If I took care of the money myself, maybe I'd spot something, but I doubted it. I was more likely to end up causing us more problems. Once I started looking at numbers like that, it all turned into a jumble. Give me a puzzle, I'm fine. But ask me to balance a checkbook . . . forget about it.

"It'll all work out," Jules assured me. "You just have to keep believing."

I plopped my lollipop back into my mouth and bit down. It shattered with a satisfying crunch. "I suppose." I extracted the remaining stick. Jules took it from me and tossed it into a trash can behind the counter.

While my troubles hadn't been solved by candy and a friendly ear, I did feel better. Maybe Jules was right; if I kept believing that things would eventually work out, the positive energy should help guide me in the right direction. Things didn't always have to be so doom and gloom.

My eyes strayed to the street just as a car shot down the road, going far faster than it should. Instant recognition buzzed through me. I knew who was driving the car, knew where they were going. In fact, I'd been *in* that car, scared out of my mind only a few months ago.

"Thanks for listening," I told Jules as I headed for the door.

"Anytime."

I pushed out onto the sidewalk and rushed over to my car. There was no way I was going to catch up to the other driver—he was going way too fast for that—but since I thought I knew where he was going, I didn't have to. I just needed to reach him before he got inside.

Thankfully, there was little traffic and I was able to push it a few miles per hour above the speed limit. I normally wouldn't have done it, knowing Buchannan was more than likely lurking around somewhere, but I really wanted to have a little chat with the driver before he got where he was going. This was going to be between us, and I didn't want anyone else to hear.

The car was sitting in front of Lawyer's Insurance, which was right across the street from Death by Coffee. For a moment, I was afraid I was too late. I pulled up behind the car, thinking I might have to wait until he came out again, but almost as soon as I shut off the engine the door opened and Mason Lawyer stepped out, looking mighty fine in a pair of dark blue slacks and a white polo. He looked both ways and was about to cross the street when I leapt out of my own car and called for him to wait.

He glanced my way, then started to frown, but it morphed into a resigned smile. He walked over to me.

"Sorry to bother you, Mason," I said, meaning it. I felt bad about what I was going to do, but I thought it needed to be said. "I want to talk to you alone for a few minutes, if that is okay."

The frown found his face this time. "This better not have to do with the murder," he said. "Like the last time, I had nothing to do with it."

"I never thought you did." I reddened slightly, thinking back to how I'd accused him of sleeping with his dead brother's wife. Boy, was I wrong on that one.

"Okay, then," he said. "What do you want to talk to me about?"

"It's about Vicki."

His face went carefully blank. "What about her?"

I took a deep breath. I'd just talked to Jules about the mess my life had become, and here I was, about to stick my nose where it didn't belong. It was as if I had some sort of sickness that caused me to do things I shouldn't. Eventually, someone was going to pop me a good one right in the eye for all my nosiness.

Still, I didn't let it stop me. "What are your plans for her?"

"Plans?" He looked genuinely confused.

"You know. *Plans.* If you're only talking to her because you are trying to get back at me for what I did to you before, I'm going to have to stop you right there. She's my best friend, and I won't see her hurt."

His frown slowly turned into a smile as I talked, making me feel stupid. When I finished, Mason rested a hand on my shoulder and squeezed. He looked directly into my eyes as he spoke.

"I'm not going to hurt her." There was a slight pause. "Not on purpose, anyway."

"Okay, so why are you here?"

He chuckled and lowered his hand. "I'm here because I like Vicki. We have a lot in common, and she's interesting and quite lovely. I came here now, at this very moment, because it is my break and I wanted to ask her if she got the part in the play. She should know by now. They don't have long to think about it."

"Oh," I said. I looked down at my feet. "So you aren't using her?"

"I'd never do such a thing."

And, of course, I believed him. I never should have

questioned him to begin with. We might have started off on the wrong foot all those months ago, but since then he'd been nothing but nice to me. I really needed to reevaluate how I viewed others. Distrust wasn't healthy.

"Let's head in together," he said. "I think Vicki would like that."

I nodded and followed Mason across the street. Death by Coffee was busy. Lena and Mike were both behind the counter. Mike took the orders while Lena filled them. They barely glanced up as Mason and I crossed the floor and headed for the stairs that led to the bookstore portion of the shop. I let Mason take the lead, which probably saved me from getting trampled, because the moment Vicki saw Mason, she rushed forward and threw her arms around his neck.

"I got the part!" She all but screamed it.

Then there was the kissing.

It was the icky, "it's not happening to me" sort of kissing that made me want to crawl into a hole and never come out until there was at least six feet of snow on the ground that could hide me. I took a step back, thinking I'd extract myself from the PDA before it spilled over onto my shoes, when Vicki came up for a breath and saw me.

"Krissy!" she squealed, relinquishing her hold on Mason. She threw her arms around me and squeezed. "I got the part!"

"I heard." I hugged her back, feeling a little better now that I was a part of the festivities. I wasn't as much of a third wheel after all.

Vicki let me go and stepped back. She was positively beaming. It reminded me of how natural she was when it came to acting, how much she liked it—as long as she wasn't being forced to stand in front of a camera while some director screamed at her. She liked it simple. I don't think you can get any simpler than a play in Pine Hills.

"Congratulations," I said, a split second after Mason said the same.

"You both are coming, right?" She barely waited for the nods before going on. "I can't wait for you to see my outfit!"

While Vicki was sharing the details, I realized, she was focusing on him more than me. I felt like an intruder again and gave them both a "I have to run" before quickly making my way out of Death by Coffee. I didn't want the storm clouds that had been hovering over my head the last few days to disrupt the celebration.

I crossed the street, got into my car, and then drove home, thinking warm thoughts about a tub of Rocky Road and an orange, fluffy furball. This was my day off. I was determined to enjoy it, even if it was the last thing I did.

20

A groan escaped my lips as I lay on the couch, empty tub of ice cream on the floor next to me. Misfit lay a few feet away, whiskers heavy and white from his own vanilla ice cream. My stomach felt as if I'd opened a bag of sugar and poured it straight down my throat. Apparently, candy plus an entire tub of Rocky Road for lunch isn't such a good combination.

The TV was on, turned to the Home Shopping Network. I wasn't actually watching it, mostly because I wouldn't be able to afford anything they were selling, but the voices were comforting. And let me tell you, I needed the comfort.

Misfit's paw twitched. My left foot jumped in sympathy. My stomach did yet another flip. In a way, it felt like my insides were trying to make cotton candy, slowly spinning all of the sugar I'd consumed around and around until it came out as a cheerful pink fluff.

A gurgle worked its way up my throat. No more spinning, even in thoughts, or I was going to end up having to throw out the couch.

I forced myself to sit up. Lying around in a sugar-induced coma wasn't going to get me anywhere. There were countless things I could be doing on my day off, not the least of which was laundry and cleaning. I might have gotten most of Misfit's mess cleaned up from the other day, but there were still spots I'd missed. It wasn't exactly the most enjoyable of chores, but it gave me something to do that would force me to stop worrying about my upset tummy.

And don't forget about the murder. How could I? It was all I thought about these days, and I *so* needed a vacation from it.

I made it to my feet, took two steps forward, followed by two quick steps back, and I sat right back down. The mess wasn't going anywhere. I could clean it up later. My head was spinning, and every motion made the cold knot in my stomach churn. Sitting was probably a better option right now.

Of course, the universe is cruel and a knock sounded at the door.

"Could you get that for me?" I asked Misfit, who gave me a one-eyed blink before rolling over, putting his back to me. "Jerk," I grumbled, working my way to my feet.

I felt pregnant as I waddled across the room. I don't think my stomach was actually bulging more than usual, but it was hard to tell. I couldn't look down to check without getting dizzy. It was no wonder I could never seem to get healthy and fit. Ice-cream binges might be great while they're happening, but the results afterward aren't pretty.

The knock came again just as I reached the door. I leaned against the doorframe, winded from such a short walk, and breathed in through my mouth. After a few steadying breaths, I opened the door, fully expecting to see Officer Buchannan standing there, zip strips in hand, ready to arrest me for assaulting a tub of ice cream.

Instead, I found myself staring at the kid from the

bed-and-breakfast, Justin, rocking from foot to foot outside my door.

"Uh, hi," I said. My brain was currently frozen, so it was a struggle thinking through why a guy I'd met once would come to my house. As a matter of fact, how did he even know where I lived?

Fear turned the ice cream in my gut sour. "How did you find me?" I asked before he could say anything. I clutched the doorframe, doing my best not to look as if I was about to fall over. If he came at me with a knife, I was so dead. There was no way I was running from anyone in the condition I was in, let alone from a young man who had yet to put on the postcollege poundage.

"Phone book," Justin said. He glanced past me into the house, which reminded me of Misfit. If the cat wasn't in his own ice-cream coma, he would have already bolted for the door.

"Is there something you need?" I asked, closing the door a little in preparation for the orange blur. It might take him a few minutes to work up to speed, but I had no doubts the cat was in the process of readying himself for his grand escape.

"Can we talk inside, Mrs. Hancock?" Justin asked, looking back over his shoulder. He was still prancing from foot to foot, looking to all the world as if he really had to pee. His eyes were round in his face, and he was still wearing his work uniform and name tag, as if he'd come straight from Ted and Bettfast to talk to me.

I wasn't keen on letting what was pretty much a total stranger into my house, but Justin did look rather harmless.

Of course, that was probably what all murdered girls think just before the psycho sticks the knife into their back.

"Sure." I stepped aside, letting Justin in, despite the

warning clanging in my head. I closed the door and turned
to find Misfit stalking slowly my way. As soon as the door
closed, he flopped over onto his side, resigned to his
indoor fate.

Justin was pacing back and forth in the dining room. I
watched him a moment, since he'd apparently forgotten
I was there in his nervousness. He kept glancing at my
purse, which I'd tossed onto the table when I'd come in
earlier. It made me even more worried about his motives
for seeking me out.

"So, how did you find me again?" I asked, walking into
the dining room.

Justin jumped at the sound of my voice. "I, uh . . ." He
cleared his throat. "You told everyone your name." He
spoke haltingly, as if unsure of his words. "So I just found
out who you were, looked you up, and here I am." He tried
on a smile, but still looked terrified before choosing to
scratch at his chin instead.

I walked past him and picked up my purse. As not to
make him feel as if I didn't trust him—which I didn't—I
rooted around in it for a tissue before carrying it to the
island counter in the kitchen. From there, I returned to the
dining room and pretended to blow my nose.

I watched him in an attempt to deduce why he would
come all the way to my house, unannounced, looking nervous enough that it was making me jittery. When I'd gone
to the bed-and-breakfast, I'd spent the entire time asking
about David Smith, so it seemed likely that David was
what he wanted to talk to me about. Was it something he'd
suddenly remembered? Were there new developments he
wanted to keep me apprised of? Or was this about something else entirely? It was hard to say as long as he didn't
speak up and explain himself.

"So," I said, drawing out the word. "What's up?"

Justin took a deep breath, glanced toward the door as if he was thinking about running, before finally turning toward me. There was definitely fear in his eye. I couldn't tell if it was because he was afraid of me or if it was something else. When he opened his mouth, nothing but a faint squeak came out.

"Is someone after you?" I asked, dreading the answer. If he came running here because the murderer was on his tail, I'd kill the kid myself. I so didn't need killers knowing where I lived, thank you very much.

"Nah," Justin said, trying to act cool despite the sweat running down his brow. "I, uh, just wanted to tell you something."

"Okay?"

"Well, um . . ." He looked all around me, as if looking directly at me might turn him to stone. "I work at Ted and Bettfast, as you know." He started pacing again. I wanted to grab him and hold him in one place. "I mostly just clean the rooms and stuff. I rarely interact with the guests, so I don't know much about them."

He paused and started running his fingers through his hair as he paced.

"Well, you see, while in the rooms, I come across a lot of stuff." He glanced at me out of the corner of his eye again before focusing on the comatose cat. "Some of it is valuable."

A lightbulb went on over my head. "You steal from the guests?" I quickly looked around to make sure nothing valuable was within Justin's reach.

"Not all of the time," he said. "But if they leave something out where anyone can see, it serves them right, you know? You gotta be more careful in this day and age." He cleared his throat. "What I take is usually stuff they won't miss too much, or could put off as simply lost. You know, earrings and stuff like that."

"I see." I touched my wrist where my watch resided. It wasn't expensive, and how Justin would have removed it from me without my knowledge I don't know, but it made me feel better to know that it was still there.

"So, you came asking about that Smith guy, right?" I nodded. "Well, he left some things lying around in a drawer. I didn't know the dude was dead until after I took them, I swear."

"Did you take these items to the police?"

His eyes got as big around as dinner plates. "No way." He shook his head so fast, it was a wonder he didn't break his neck. "I ain't going to the slammer over this."

Ain't ain't a word, I thought before saying, "I'm sure they'd understand."

Justin chewed on his lower lip before suddenly reaching into a back pocket. He removed a wallet and held it out to me. "Here."

I stared at it like it might be a bomb. The wallet was plain brown leather with nothing special about it from first glance. It wasn't faded like a normal wallet would be, telling me it was either rarely used or brand new.

Justin motioned for me to take the wallet, almost urgently, and I finally reached out for it. He held on for a moment and finally met my eye.

"Please don't tell anyone where you got this," he said. "I only take things because I have a little sister who needs providing for. Pay at the B&B isn't as good as you might think. Without this money, we'd have nothing."

He held onto the wallet until I gave him a nod and a "Okay, I won't tell."

Justin relinquished his hold and immediately stepped back, as if he was afraid I might throw it back at him. "I'd better go," he said. Before I could ask him anything further, he was out the door and into a pickup that had seen better days. It started up with a rumble that made me wonder how I'd missed it coming up the driveway, and then he backed out, leaving flakes of rust behind.

Misfit made it to his feet just as I closed the door. This time, he gave a kitty huff before working his way down the hall, toward the litter box. I carried the wallet over to the island counter and set it down for inspection.

As I'd first thought, the thing looked unused. It wasn't bulging, telling me there was little to no money in it. I didn't know if that meant there never had been any or if Justin had lifted it before bringing the wallet to me. It wasn't like anyone would know. The man it belonged to was dead.

A shudder ran through me as I thought about that. I was looking at something that someone who had been alive just a few days before had carried with him. But if this was his wallet, why hadn't it been on him when he was killed? I didn't know many men who left their wallets behind when they went out.

There had to be a reason why Justin thought it prudent to bring the thing to me. I was asking about David, sure, but that didn't mean I was an expert about these things. And I surely wasn't with the police—not with how they were treating me. I might have solved a murder in Pine Hills before, so there *was* that at least.

And if that was why he'd brought it to me, that could mean only one thing.

The wallet was a clue.

I snatched it up off the counter and opened it, fully expecting to see a note or a picture that would tell me everything I needed to know about who killed David Smith. Had he known who was going to kill him? Could he have left a message behind, one of those "in case of my death" sorts of letters? It was almost too much to ask for.

What I found when I opened the wallet didn't make sense at first. There were a handful of cards tucked into the slots and, like I expected, no money. David's face was smiling up at me from his driver's license, which was shoved into a plastic holder that allowed it to be shown without taking it out of the wallet.

I looked at David's face, and a sense of sadness washed over me. I glanced at his birth date and saw that he'd just turned twenty-eight a month and a half ago. It seemed too young to die.

And then I saw it.

My eyes focused on the words, not quite comprehending what I was seeing. It was David's face on the license, all right. The age and eye and hair color were all correct, from what I remembered of my brief meeting with him. All of that was just as it should be.

But the name on the card . . .

It wasn't David Smith.

21

"Caleb Jenkins." I said it out loud as I paced the room, hoping it would ring a bell. I didn't recognize the name on David's ID. No one had mentioned it as far as I was aware. And I wasn't sure whether Caleb was David's real name or if this was a fake ID of some sort. There hadn't been much online about David Smith that I could find, so if I did a little online research, there was a chance I could learn something about the murdered man. Caleb Jenkins wasn't nearly as common of a name as David Smith, and since the license listed his address in Idaho, it would give me one more thing to add to the search to narrow it down.

"No, Krissy," I reprimanded myself. "Wait for Paul."

I'd called him almost as soon as Justin left. He didn't answer, but I left him a voice mail message in the hopes he'd at least return my call. Even if he was avoiding me, surely he would check his voice mail. He wouldn't dismiss a prospective lead just because he was mad at me, would he? And besides, he'd promised he'd call me tonight.

Misfit was sitting on the arm of the couch, watching me. He'd woken from his ice-cream coma an hour ago and had stared at me ever since. Two hours had passed since

I'd made the call and I was getting antsy, which was making the overlarge cat nervous.

"Why hasn't he called back?" I asked Misfit. "This is important." I should have started my online research while I waited, but I hadn't thought Paul would take this long to get back with me. I had left out the exact reason for my call, mostly because I wanted to come up with a good excuse as to how I'd come across the wallet before Paul arrived. I didn't want to go back on my word to Justin about telling on him, but I also didn't want to get myself into trouble.

I was considering picking up the phone and calling Paul again when headlights lit up the front of my house.

"Oh, God," I said, suddenly worried. I hadn't come up with a good excuse yet. I so didn't want to spend more time in jail because I couldn't explain where I'd gotten the wallet.

I looked wildly around the room, nervous about how it looked. There was still something of a mess from the night of my arrest, and I hadn't even bothered to throw away my ice-cream tub yet. I should have started cleaning up the moment I'd made the call, but it hadn't even crossed my mind. I'd been too focused on what Justin had given me.

The car engine shut off, and a door clicked open. I sprang into motion. I shoved the wallet into my purse for safekeeping before I began to gather garbage. I couldn't let him see the results of my ice-cream binge, even if he was no longer interested in me. I crammed the tub deep into the trash can and then dropped the morning paper on top of it, despite the fact I had yet to do the crossword. I'd just replaced the trash can lid when a knock came at the door.

My palms started sweating as I crossed the room to answer it. I hesitated at the door long enough to smooth back my hair. I considered shouting at him to give me a minute or two so I could run to the bathroom to freshen up, but it was too late for that now. Besides, I asked him over to tell him about the ID, not to convince him to give me another chance. I was no longer sure I even wanted him to.

And what are you going to do if it isn't Paul out there?

I firmly clamped down on that line of thought. Why would it be anyone else? I plastered on a welcoming smile and opened the door.

And there he stood, the man who had once saved my life. He was wearing his tan police uniform, badge proudly displayed on his chest. His gun rested at his hip, though his hand was nowhere near it. He was wearing one of those stiff hats cops sometimes wore while on duty. He wasn't smiling.

My own smile slipped just a little at that. He didn't look like he was happy to see me. "Paul," I said. "I'm glad you could make it."

"Krissy." He nodded once. "You said it was important."

"It is." I glanced around the corner of the house, toward the Winthrow place. Sure enough, the curtain fluttered just a little bit as binocular lenses made an appearance. "Let's talk about it inside."

A frown flickered across Paul's face, but he stepped past me and into the house anyway. Despite my best efforts not to, I took a deep breath as he moved past, relishing the smell of his cologne. There was a hint of oiled leather beneath it, telling me he'd recently polished his shoes or belt.

I closed the door behind us and led him into the living room. He glanced around, as if expecting to find something incriminating sitting in the corner, before turning to me.

"So, what is it you want to talk to me about?"

"It's about David Smith," I said. My purse was still sitting on the counter. I could wait to show him the wallet and the ID it contained after I finished laying everything I knew on him. Besides, I was hoping to get a few things out of him first. Once I gave him the ID, there would be nothing keeping him here.

Paul sighed heavily. "Krissy . . ."

"I know you don't want me interfering." I spoke quickly before he could say anything. "But his murder *did* happen at Death by Coffee. I see these people every day."

Another sigh, followed by a nod. "Fine. Okay. I'll give you that."

"Thank you."

"But I still don't like you getting involved. You are a suspect in this thing, whether you like it or not. If you go making a scene, you'll only make yourself look worse."

I bristled a bit at that. I was *so* not a suspect, and he knew it.

Okay, I'll admit, one date and a confrontation with a murderer don't exactly make a steady relationship. And honestly, I doubted we would ever have anything more than that date. But he knew me better than that. We'd bonded, even if it was just a tiny bit. His comment hurt.

"Buchannan is doing that well enough all by himself, don't you think?" I said, biting off the words. "I swear that man has it out for me."

"He's only doing his job."

"Oh, so you're defending him now?"

"He might be a little overzealous at times, but John is a good cop when he wants to be."

"Really?" I said, growing angrier by the moment. This was *not* how I imagined our conversation going. "Does a good cop follow an innocent woman around? Does he go through her things and steal her underwear while she isn't home?"

"Wait, what?"

"I don't think so, Paul Dalton. And I can't believe you'd believe it, either." I stamped my foot for good measure. "You should be thanking me for all the hard work I've been doing."

"*Thank* you?" he said, an incredulous edge to his voice. "Krissy, you got yourself arrested for assaulting a police officer."

"He was antagonizing me!"

"That doesn't matter." He was speaking calmly, but I could hear the frustration growing in his voice. "You broke the law and you paid for it. Do you want it to happen again?"

"No," I said, lowering my eyes. A part of me felt ashamed, but that part was slowly getting pummeled to submission by my anger and annoyance. I was beyond frustrated and was taking it out on Paul simply because he was here. I was tired of people looking at me like I killed David.

I lifted my gaze and gave Paul a steady look. "Why didn't you come to visit me while I was locked up?" I knew the answer already, but I wanted to hear him say it. It might give me the closure I needed.

He actually flushed a little at that. "I was busy."

"Too busy to make sure I was being treated okay? Too busy to stop by for one minute to assure me everything would be all right?" Tears threatened, but I held them in check.

Paul cleared his throat and looked toward the window. "I wasn't allowed to see you," he said. "Chief made it clear I am not to go anywhere near you while this investigation is taking place. I am defying her orders coming here now."

He turned back to me, a pleading look in his eyes. "You have to understand, you *are* a suspect. I might not like it, and you might not like it, but it's true. I have to treat you as such until we can completely rule you out."

I knew he was right, knew he was doing exactly what he needed to do, but I couldn't help myself. I wanted to prove to him that I wasn't a killer, *or* a girl who was totally helpless. "Do you, now?" My hands found my hips. "Are you saying you can't give me the benefit of the doubt?"

"I'm not saying that at all."

"Really? Then why are you acting as if you think I could very well be guilty of killing a man I didn't even know? I haven't done anything to warrant this kind of treatment."

"Except when you stole the cardboard cutout."

"Yeah, but . . ."

"Or when you stormed over to the neighbor's and started beating on John."

"Yeah, but . . ."

"Or when you started sneaking around, talking to everyone involved in the case like you are some sort of detective working for the police."

I dropped my eyes at that. "You know about that, huh?"

"Of course I do." Paul took a step forward and rested a hand on my shoulder. "You can't keep doing this. If you snoop too much, you're only going to get yourself into more trouble. Do you really want that? I can't protect you if you end up burying yourself with your own actions."

I tried really hard to accept his comforting. I mean, he wasn't wrong. The last time I stuck my nose into a murder investigation, I very nearly got it blown off. That time, the murder had been an accident. There wasn't anything accidental about it this time, I was sure. There was a cold-blooded killer running around out there. If I kept asking questions, he or she could very well end up knocking on my door.

But if I didn't keep looking into it, the murderer might get away with it. I didn't doubt the police could handle it, but what was wrong with a little extra help?

"You can't stop me from talking to people," I grumbled.

"I can if you interfere with the investigation."

"Are you going to throw me in jail?"

"If I have to."

What could I say to that? I *was* interfering in a police investigation, though I wasn't hindering anything. I was trying to help. He had to see that. They all did.

"Look, Krissy," Paul said. His hand still rested on my shoulder, so I shrugged out of it and crossed my arms. He looked lost for a moment before shoving his thumbs into his belt. "I'm only trying to keep you safe. How about you tell me what it was you wanted to talk to me about and then drop this whole thing? I can take care of it."

I sighed. It *was* the reason I'd called him over. I might have wanted our conversation to, I don't know, blossom into something more. It would have been nice to have him tell me exactly how he felt so I could do the same. Standing here now, with Paul, I could almost forget Will existed.

Almost.

"Well, I . . ." I trailed off as his phone buzzed to life.

Paul frowned, hesitated, and then held up a finger as he grabbed his cell. He checked the ID, sighed, and then looked at me. "Give me a sec. I have to take this."

I nodded as he lifted the phone to his ear and walked into the other room. He kept his voice low so I couldn't hear what he was saying. I wasn't eavesdropping, per se. Maybe trying to see what the call was about, but not eavesdropping.

Paul's back was to me, so I couldn't see if he was

smiling or frowning, but with the way his shoulders tensed suddenly and his back straightened, I guessed what he was being told wasn't good.

"I'll be right there," he said before shoving the phone back into his pocket and turning to face me. "I have to run," he said. "Something important has come up." He started for the door, but stopped. "Can this wait until later?"

I winced inwardly but nodded. "Sure." If nothing else, it would give me more time to look into the name on the ID and how it related to David Smith before handing it over. "It can wait."

Paul didn't look convinced but nodded anyway. "We'll talk soon." He hurried out the door without a good-bye. It made me wonder how bad whatever he had to deal with was.

Could it be another murder? If so, it was all the more reason to get investigating immediately.

I waited until Paul sped away before closing the front door. I turned and found myself looking at my purse.

"Well," I said to the empty room. "It looks like I'll be taking care of this myself." I crossed the short distance to my purse and removed the wallet. After a moment's consideration, I plucked out the ID and turned to get started.

22

I started things off with a quick Google of Caleb Jenkins, hoping I'd hit pay dirt right away but knowing it was unlikely. Quite a few links popped up, but after only a couple of clicks, I moved on to the one place where I knew I could go to take a peek into someone's private life.

I'm not sure how people learned about each other without Facebook. In a way, it makes us all stalkers, which is sort of creepy. Not everyone locked their profiles up tight. Some left practically everything out in the open. And with the way things are always changing, even friendly responses to innocuous posts can be seen by people you know. It's not easy protecting yourself, especially these days.

Bad for your privacy.

Good if you want to do some snooping.

I hesitated before clicking the Facebook link. What if I hadn't excised my ex completely? If Robert messaged me now, I was going to hunt him down.

But I couldn't let him stop me. He'd interfered in my life enough already.

I opened the link, typed in Caleb Jenkins's name, and then sat back to let the magic happen. A list of names appeared, pictures and all. I scrolled past kids and old men,

and even a few guys that caused me to admire the view
before going on. I scrolled past name after name until my
eyes started to cross.

And then I found him.

David, or Caleb, or whatever you wanted to call him,
looked quite different in his Facebook photograph than he
did when I'd met him. His hair hung around his ears like
a rug that had been beaten to death, shredded, and then
turned into the worst toupee ever. He wore glasses with
thick brown frames that were broken in parts. He was
wearing, I swear to God, a pair of bright blue running
shorts with a long-sleeve button-up shirt beneath a black
sleeveless leather jacket. An American flag was proudly
displayed on the breast.

I blinked at the photo, trying my best to align what I
knew of David Smith with the Caleb Jenkins presented
here. I clicked on his name, feeling as if this was some
sort of joke, or perhaps an old Halloween photo. This
couldn't be the same suave Brit who'd caused nearly every
woman who saw or heard him to melt into a quivering pile
of sappy goo.

I went straight for his photos and found even more horrible pictures. They all seemed to have been taken at least
five years ago, if not longer, judging by how young he
looked. Caleb couldn't be any more than eighteen in the
pictures, perhaps younger. It was hard to tell with the unruly
hair and bad clothing.

A few of the pics showed him sitting astride a scooter
that had seen better days. The seat was torn in many places,
the tires looked so worn, it was a wonder they hadn't exploded. The handlebars looked crooked and bent, as if the
scooter had been wrecked a few too many times and re-
paired by someone who had no idea what they were doing.

I scanned the pictures in wonder. In each and every

one, hidden beneath the poor, dirty biker, David's face looked out at me.

"No way," I said, clicking through. It was like a train wreck, or maybe a ten-car pileup outside a bikini car wash. Each photograph seemed worse than the last one, yet I couldn't stop staring. My finger kept clicking over and over, mouth slowly falling open until my chin rested comfortably in my lap.

The horror culminated in a picture of Caleb, glasses and flat hair and all, grinning at the camera while wearing one of those awful one-piece swimsuits that was striped red and white. He was wearing combat boots, unlaced, of course.

I backed out of the photographs. I'm not sure what I'd learned exactly, other than David had once been a pretty sad excuse for a man. Not a single picture had shown him with a woman, and it was no wonder. It was as if he was trying to scare them away on purpose. No one dresses like that and thinks they look good.

So the question was, how did Caleb the dork transform into supersexy David Smith?

Or the better question, why?

I suppose he could have simply looked at himself and realized he was going down the wrong path. We all do it at some point in our lives. It was why I was living in Pine Hills, selling coffee, instead of working retail. It was why Vicki wasn't a high-paid actress whose name was known all across the world. Sometimes you just have to step back and see what it is you are doing wrong, and what it is you want out of life.

David had reinvented himself, changed his look, and more than likely his lifestyle. The change helped him with the ladies, which was probably pretty high on most men's wish list of things they would like to do. He became a man who women practically drooled over.

And then he was killed.

Could they be related somehow? If he ran with a scooter gang before his transformation, could they have gotten angry at him for abandoning them? It seemed a little unlikely, but you never knew. He could have gotten mixed up in drugs and had decided he wanted out. It could have triggered his need for change, forced him to come up with a new identity and flee to Cherry Valley.

It made sense, though if I'd been him, I would have taken my Facebook profile down with the rest of my life. It could only hurt him in the long run.

Then again, there was no more long run for David. I scrolled down through his posts, and like I'd assumed would be the case, none of the posts were recent. The last was posted sometime in 2010, and it was just a vague "Still alive and Kicking!" random capitalization and all. It wasn't much to go on.

There was little else listed in his profile that helped. He didn't list a place of employment, not that I thought he'd still work there. I was able to confirm that he did indeed once live in Idaho, but I wasn't about to drive all the way out there, chasing a man who no longer existed. What I needed was information on who he had been now.

At least at this point I had a little more to go on. I closed Facebook and went back to Google and tried again, this time adding "Idaho" to Caleb's name, like I should have done from the start. There were a few articles where he was mentioned, all old and all from his time on the swim team in high school. I was actually surprised he was involved in any sort of sport, what with the way he looked, but I guess you can't judge people solely by appearance. I was learning that firsthand.

I decided to make one more attempt at finding information on David, as Caleb, so I tried his name with the term "Cherry Valley" included in the search. I fully expected to come up blank, especially since he was living under a new name there. Imagine my surprise when I actually got a hit.

The site was for a motorcycle restoration business called Penelope's Restorations. Apparently, they had a blog—doesn't everyone these days—and they listed Caleb Jenkins as a new hire a little less than a year ago. There was nothing else mentioned about him, but I wrote down the name of the place and the address on a slip of paper. If nothing else, it was something to go on.

I closed down the laptop and carried the note to my purse, where I put it with the wallet Justin had given me. I was pretty sure I was the only person involved in the investigation who knew David's other name, which meant I would be the only one looking into his place of employment under said name. I wasn't sure whether it would help me understand what happened to him, but at least I'd be out of Paul's hair, and Buchannan would be out of mine.

"Idaho is a long way from England," I told Misfit as I headed for a box of puzzles. I was feeling surprisingly energized after my discovery. I'd have to send a gift to Justin for coming to me with the wallet instead of taking it to the police. If they'd gotten hold of it, I never would have learned anything about it until after the case was solved.

"If it ever will be," I said, setting the crossword book onto the counter while I went to make a coffee. I removed a pair of Jules's cookies from the box that was still sitting on the counter—one to eat, one to soak in the coffee. Yum.

I busied myself for the next hour, actually forgetting

about the murder and any other troubles I might have as I worked on the puzzles. I didn't know whether Paul was going to get back with me tonight, and right then I was okay with either. If he showed again, I'd give him the wallet and tell him someone had dropped it off mysteriously on my doorstep.

I absorbed myself into the words—working in pen, of course—and sipped the coffee until all that was left was the gooey mess at the bottom. That, I ate with a spoon.

I finished the first puzzle, contemplated going to bed— it was already well past ten and I needed some sleep since I had to work in the morning—and then turned to the next, anyway. I felt too good to waste the energy on sleep.

A loud bang seemed to shake the entire house, sending Misfit, who'd been dozing next to me on the counter, off like a rocket. I instantly hit the floor, puzzle and pen flying. Lucky for me I'd finished my coffee and hadn't been holding the mug, or else I might have broken it.

I lay on the linoleum, knees and hands throbbing from where I'd smacked into the floor, listening. Had the loud sound been a gunshot? *Was someone shooting at me?* I suddenly wished I'd taken Paul's advice long ago and kept out of the murder business.

My breaths came in shallow gasps as I waited for something else to happen. Time ticked by. There were no other sounds but the barking of a dog down the street. I chanced a look up over the counter but saw nothing. I looked for a hole in the wall, or a busted window, telling me someone had indeed taken a potshot at me, yet if there was one I wasn't seeing it. I knew for a fact the sound had come from somewhere nearby, not down the street, not down the hall or in my bedroom, even. It had been *right here*.

I waited another five minutes before rising on unsteady legs. My heart rate had slowed to about the pulse of a racing horse, so I figured I wasn't going to die of a heart attack right then and there. I crept slowly around the counter, eyes wide and alert, as I scanned the windows, watching for a shadow or telltale flicker of light.

There was nothing. "You're okay, Krissy," I whispered to myself, needing the reassurance. I tiptoed across the room to the front door, hesitated, and then backtracked to the hall closet where I kept my broom. I carried it with me back to the door, fingers clutching so hard that they were starting to hurt. I knew what I was doing was dangerous. If someone was really out there shooting at me, I should have immediately called the police and waited safely behind the counter for them.

But the thought of Paul Dalton rushing in to save the day again was almost too much to bear. I wasn't going to be one of those women who needed saving all the time.

I flipped on the outside light, opened the door, and took a quick peek outside, darting my head out and then back in so fast that if anyone was actually out there waiting for me, they wouldn't have time to shoot before I was gone. No loud bangs followed my peek, so I got braver and opened the door wider. I scanned the yard, the driveway, but no one was there.

And then my eyes fell on the large rock sitting at the edge of my front stoop. It was about the size of a fist, gray like most rocks, and had a folded piece of paper taped to it. I scanned the yard once more to be sure I was truly alone and then opened the screen wide enough that I could scuttle out onto the stoop for the rock, broom clutched in one hand and held at the ready.

No gunshots were immediately evident, so I eased my grip on the broom as I looked down at what I held. The tape was coming off the rock, presumably from the impact of being thrown up against the house. I turned to find a large dent in my screen door.

"Really?" I said loudly. If whoever threw the rock was still out there, I wanted them to hear me. It wasn't the smartest of moves, but I was angry. "You couldn't have aimed for the stoop?" Then again, I guess a dented metal door was better than a busted window. And if they were looking to scare me, they'd succeeded.

I pried off the tape and removed the note from the rock. I leaned toward the outside light where bugs were buzzing about, minding their own business. The note was hand-written. The writing itself was sloppy, slanted in a way that looked cursive but was actually printed. It simply stated, "Leave it alone." Unfortunately, there was no signature to give the culprit away.

It wasn't too hard for me to figure out what the note was referring to. Chances were good I was getting close to the killer somehow and he or she was getting nervous. I was just glad they decided to leave me a message rather than leave me *as* a message. Small victories, right?

I stood on my stoop and scanned the yard closer this time, hoping to spot a footprint or lost item. Of all the nights not to have Buchannan sitting outside my property in his cruiser, this had to be the one. Or perhaps that was why the rock thrower attacked tonight instead of earlier. They'd have to be pretty dim-witted to make such a move with someone watching.

My eyes immediately darted toward Eleanor Winthrow's house. Buchannan might not have been there to see who-ever threw the rock, but I knew someone who might have. An inside light was on in her house, and I could see Eleanor silhouetted at the window. She was watching me, and for once I was glad.

I set my broom aside and marched across the yard. The

light snapped off even before I was halfway over, but I was determined. There was no Buchannan here to save her this time. She was going to talk to me.

The house was silent as I stepped up to the front door. I knocked on it for a good minute to no result.

"Eleanor!" I called, knowing she could hear me. I wouldn't be surprised if she was pressed to the door, listening. "I know you saw something. Let me in so we can talk."

There was a moment of silence before a faint "Go away!"

I knocked on the door some more. "Eleanor . . ." It came out sounding a lot like how my mom would say my name when I was in trouble as a kid. "Open this door right now so we can talk. I need to know what you saw."

Another long stretch of silence.

And then the answer I dreaded.

"I've called the cops."

My forehead hit the house with a solid thump. Of course she would call the police. Why couldn't anyone actually just talk to me like a normal person?

I turned with a sigh. With the rock still in my hand, I sat down and calmly waited for the police to arrive.

23

A cruiser coasted slowly down the road and parked just inside Eleanor Winthrow's driveway, almost as if the driver was afraid to get too close to where I was sitting. The overhead lights and siren were still and silent. Only the headlights illuminated me where I sat on the front stoop of Eleanor's house.

A long stretch of silence followed. The cop didn't get out of his car, nor did I make a move toward it. I didn't have to see him to know who was in the car. This was my life we were talking about. Who else would it be?

Finally, the cruiser door opened with a faint clunk and Officer John Buchannan stepped out. He hooked his thumbs into his belt and gave me a knowing smile as he sauntered over to where I sat.

"Well, well, well. Krissy Hancock," he said. "Looks like you can't stay out of trouble."

I rose, leaving the rock with the note trapped under it on the stoop. I was pretty sure if I had picked it up, Buchannan would have taken it as an aggressive sign and tackled me. I'd end up sitting at the police station, taken in for premeditated assault with a deadly weapon or some other trumped-up charge. I was quickly beginning to realize this was just the way Buchannan worked. Did that make him a bad person? I wasn't so sure. It just didn't make him likeable.

"I only wanted to ask her a question," I said. "She's overreacting." I held my hands up before me. I felt stupid standing like that, but there was little he could do to me as long as I didn't make any sudden moves or antagonize him by calling him foul names.

"Miss Winthrow claims you tried to break in."

"I simply knocked," I said, keeping my voice steady despite my irritation. "Someone threw something at my house and I wanted to know if she happened to see who it was."

Buchannan was standing about three feet away, so despite the shadows cast by his hat, I could still see his left eyebrow raise. "Threw what?" he asked, sounding like a real cop for once, thank the Lord.

I gestured toward the rock on the stoop. "That," I said. "The note beneath it was taped to it."

Buchannan regarded me for a long moment before walking past me to the stoop. He picked up the rock, hefted it in his hand, and then snatched up the folded slip of paper before it could blow away. He eyed me speculatively before opening it.

I already knew what the page said, yet I had to fight the urge to walk over and read it over his shoulder. I satisfied myself with watching his face as he read. Nothing registered as his eyes scanned over the scrawl. I swear he looked at it for a good minute. Buchannan was either a really, really, *really* slow reader, or he couldn't quite make out the words in the gloom.

Finally he looked up, choosing to study me instead. "Any idea who would do something like this?" he asked.

"No." I had a few ideas, and most of them weren't

good. I didn't want to go pointing fingers at any would-be murderers, considering they seemed to know where I lived. If I made a wrong move now, I doubted my next warning would be a simple rock against a screen door. The next one might find my head.

Buchannan glanced back down at the page and frowned. "Why would someone send something like this to you?"

"Send?" The word slipped out before I could stop it.

Buchannan sighed, clearly annoyed. "Okay, who would *throw* something like this at you?" He looked like he wouldn't mind doing it himself.

I almost told him that it wasn't actually thrown at me but rather at my door, but it felt a bit nitpicky. "I really can't tell you," I said with a shrug.

"You haven't been doing anything you shouldn't, have you?" he asked, knowing I'd been doing just that.

"Um . . . no?"

He heaved a sigh. "I have half a mind to bring you in."

"For what?"

"What do you think?" He scowled. "You are the prime suspect in a murder. You sneak around at night causing mischief and mayhem. You antagonize your neighbors and people involved in the murder case itself. And now, this." He tossed the rock into the air a few times, as if weighing it.

"I had nothing to do with this." And half of what he said wasn't quite true. I mean, most of it was, I guess, but not to the extent he was thinking.

"Someone wouldn't go to the trouble of leaving you a message like this unless you were doing something you shouldn't."

I lowered my eyes. He was right, of course. Hadn't Paul said nearly the same thing to me just a little while ago? Could I really be doing more harm than good?

Nah. I was helping. Right now it might seem like I was

getting in the way, but once I solved this thing, they'd see how valuable I was. They were simply struggling to appreciate my version of helping.

"Could you at least ask Eleanor if she saw anything?" It came out pleading, but I was past caring. If I could figure out who threw the rock, I was positive I'd have the killer in hand within a day.

Buchannan heaved another clearly put-out sigh before nodding. "I guess I should."

Thank you, Jesus. It was probably the best news I'd heard all day.

"But you're staying out here."

"But . . ."

He didn't have to say anything to get me to back off. One hard look and I was simpering like a puppy. Still, he said it anyway, like he didn't trust me to do the right thing.

"Stay. Here."

I nodded as Officer Buchannan walked past me, rock and note still in hand. He knocked on the door and glanced around, as if taking in the scene. It was only a few seconds before the door opened and Eleanor poked her head out.

"I'm so glad you're here, Officer," she said in her best "the crazy woman is going to kill me" voice.

"Let's go inside and talk, ma'am." He glanced meaningfully at me as he spoke.

Eleanor stepped aside, letting Buchannan in. She gave me a good, hard glare before closing the door forcibly behind her, leaving me standing alone by her front stoop.

Even though I'd been sitting outside, alone before Buchannan arrived, I suddenly felt exposed. What if the killer was still lurking out there somewhere? Now that I was spotlighted by the cruiser's headlights, I'd make an easy target.

I eased sideways, into the shadows, but it didn't make me feel any better. Now I was standing where no one could see me if the murderer were to sneak up on me. At least with the headlights illuminating me, someone might see something. I glanced toward my house and considered running for it. But what if the killer was inside, waiting for me? I hadn't locked the door when I'd left.

"Stop it, Krissy," I reprimanded myself. Whoever threw the rock was long gone, and it wasn't even a sure thing they'd killed David Smith. If our rock thrower hadn't run off before Buchannan arrived, they surely would be gone by now.

Unless John Buchannan is the murderer.

I had to admit, a part of me hoped it was true. If I could point the finger at him, everything he'd ever done to me would come to light and I would be deemed a hero. Again.

But Buchannan was an officer of the law who had done nothing but do his job, albeit a bit forcibly and perhaps with a little too much zeal. It was only wishful thinking that he could have anything to do with the murder, yet I couldn't help daydream about it.

I considered walking home to grab the wallet. I could give it to Buchannan, which would get it out of my hands.

But I knew Buchannan well enough to know he would probably accuse me of killing David and stealing the wallet. It would be yet another piece of evidence he could use against me, and while I could tell him about Justin, I wasn't quite ready to break my promise to him yet. No, it would be far better if I waited until I talked to Paul again.

I turned my focus to who might have killed David. Buchannan was unlikely, as much as it pained me to admit it. And while Justin knew where I was, it didn't quite track that he would bring me the wallet and then warn me off the case.

That left the members of the book clubs. I was positive Rita knew where I lived, but there was no way she could have killed David, no matter how angry she had gotten. The same went for Georgina and Andi. Those two women were as harmless as they come. I couldn't imagine a pair of old ladies taking down a bigger man like David Smith.

That left Jimmy and Cindy as the only Pine Hills members who could have done it. Cindy was too taken with David to have killed him, though if she'd discovered his secret, then perhaps she could have grown angry enough to kill. No one likes to be deceived. And if not, Jimmy might have grown jealous enough to attack David, blaming him for what went on in his own bed.

Still, I just didn't see it. That meant I was looking at someone from Cherry Valley. Albert was the obvious answer, though why he would kill one of his own, I had no idea. Orville and Vivian were as unlikely as Georgina and Andi. If Sara learned about David's real name and past, she very well might have gotten angry enough with him to kill him. And Dan had the obvious motive of getting his book club spot back, as well as remove someone he clearly detested.

But how would any of them get inside Death by Coffee to kill him? I kept coming back to that and had no answer.

Could it really be someone from Death by Coffee?

I didn't want to believe it, but I did have to start to consider it. Aside from me, Vicki, Mike, and Lena were the only other people with keys. None of them had a reason to kill David as far as I was aware.

The only thing I could think of was that one of them had let David and the killer back into the store sometime that night. Whether it was because they claimed they'd forgotten something inside, or it was by complete accident, I don't know. Perhaps the killer placed something in or on the door that prevented it from locking properly. That made more sense than anything else I'd come up with so far.

And what if one of them had indeed lost a key? Would they have told me? Could they have lost it but found it again almost immediately? The killer could have taken it, copied it, and then returned it before anyone was the wiser.

It seemed unlikely, though. How would the killer get hold of the key without anyone noticing? It just didn't make sense.

I heaved a sigh and looked for something to kick. I was frustrated by the case, frustrated with Buchannan, and frustrated with myself because I couldn't come up with a solution that would end this entire mess.

The door to Eleanor's house opened before I found anything that wouldn't break my foot if I were to kick it. Buchannan stepped outside, still chuckling from something Eleanor had said.

"Thank you," he told her. "I'll have to take you up on that sometime."

The door closed and Buchannan turned to me. His smile faded and he actually looked somewhat chagrined as he spoke. "It appears as though your story pans out."

"Why wouldn't it have?" I asked, annoyed. Why couldn't he ever believe me?

Buchannan ignored the question. "Miss Winthrow says she happened to look out her window just as the car pulled up at the end of your drive. A man, dressed in black, got out, ran forward, and heaved the rock at the door. He fled before it ever hit."

My ears perked up. "Is she positive it was a man?" If she could confirm the gender, it would eliminate Sara, as well as Lena, Vicki, and the older women of the book clubs. That would significantly reduce the list of suspects.

Buchannan shrugged. "That's what she tells me. She was pretty sure the culprit was one of your scorned lovers, so she didn't pay much attention. There is a distinct possibility we are dealing with a woman here, dressed so as not to give herself away." He paused. "Do you know of any women who might be upset with you because you slept with their boyfriend or husband?"

"What?" I stared at him, dumbfounded. He didn't just ask me that, did he?

"Any old lovers seeking revenge, perhaps?"

"I . . . No . . . There's no one." My face reddened. I didn't want Buchannan to know about my sex life—or lack thereof.

Buchannan nodded as if that was exactly what he'd expected. Ass. "Then there is someone very unhappy with whatever it is you are doing here in Pine Hills. I suggest you stop before you get hurt."

"What about the car?" I asked. He could suggest whatever he wanted. As long as he wasn't arresting me, I was going to keep looking into this thing until the murderer was caught. To do that, I needed more information.

"What about it?"

"Did she give you a make or model? A color maybe?" Even that bit of information could go a long way in solving the case.

"She didn't say."

"Is she even sure it was a car?" I asked, starting to grow frustrated.

"She wasn't certain."

I threw my hands up in the air, giving in to the frustration. "How is that even possible?"

"It was dark," he said with a shrug.

Great. So we had a witness who saw what could have been a man, but might have been a woman, who threw a rock at my house and got into a car, or possibly a truck, shrouded in shadows. That was a *huge* help, thank you, Miss Winthrow. The only thing I learned was that it wasn't a motorcycle or a scooter and that the rock thrower was human. It was something, I guess. No biker alien attacks for me.

"I want you to stay inside tonight," Buchannan said. "Lock your windows and doors." He turned toward his cruiser. "And whatever you do, stay out of trouble."

"What about the note and the rock?" I asked. I really wanted them back so I could study them further. Maybe the rock was from a quarry somewhere, or distinctive in some way that would help. I should have considered the fact that there could be fingerprints all over the rock and note, and my handling of it could have contaminated the evidence. Then again, Buchannan should have thought of it as well.

He paused at his car door and shrugged. "Evidence," he said before tossing the rock into the backseat as if it was nothing more than a souvenir.

Without another word, he got into his cruiser, started the engine, and backed out.

And then he was gone.

I felt oddly empty as I went back home. This should have been a defining moment in the case, one where something extraordinary was discovered, yet I was left with nothing. I just wanted to crawl into bed with a bag of popcorn and my fluffy orange bed warmer. Nothing else was going to get accomplished tonight. I still had to go to work tomorrow, but afterward . . . that's when I was finally going to make some serious progress.

Either that or take a rock to the head.

With the way my life was going, both were just as likely.

24

The bell above the door jangled. I looked up, worried we had yet another customer. Death by Coffee started out the morning busy, and it hadn't slowed down for the two hours since. Lena was at my side, filling orders as fast as I could take them, when she wasn't up in the bookstore. Vicki wouldn't come in until later, which meant it was just the two of us for the time being.

I breathed a sigh of relief as Mike Green waltzed in, looking as if he didn't care about the line that was still almost to the door. Every table was occupied and dirty. It was as if the entire town had up and decided to pay me a visit just to run me into the ground.

"What's happening?" Mike said, coming around the counter for his apron.

Before I could answer, the man at the counter did it for me. "J&E's is closed today. They're redoing the floors."

Ah, well, that explained why everyone was coming to Death by Coffee. I just hoped after sampling my coffee, many of the customers would decide to keep coming back.

Just not all at once. I don't think I could take another morning like this.

Mike tied on his apron and slouched his way over to the coffee machine to pour himself a cup. He leaned against the wall and took a casual sip.

"How about you clock in?" I asked, flustered. I couldn't remember if the man at the counter had ordered a mocha cappuccino or a French vanilla. I turned and asked him as Mike answered.

"Nah, man. I got another three minutes 'til I'm due."

"French vanilla," the customer said.

"Just do it already!" I shouted, spinning for the cappuccino machine.

"Man . . ." Mike grumbled as he made his way over to the register to clock in.

With him there, things ran just a little smoother. I handed the register over to him and went about filling the orders, leaving Lena to handle the customers upstairs. It felt like all of Pine Hills was there, buying coffee and books as if they were going out of style. I wasn't complaining about the money we were earning. In fact, I was thrilled by it. But the work that it was taking to earn said money had my feet barking and my back aching.

It didn't slow down for another hour. By then, it felt like I'd been beaten on the back with a crowbar after walking barefoot over hot coals. I was quickly beginning to wonder if I'd be mobile enough later that day to go all the way to Cherry Valley to snoop around like I'd planned. Chances were good that if lunch was as insane as breakfast, I'd be in a coma.

"Take over for me for a minute," I told Mike. He gave me a nod as he turned to a new customer. I headed back into the kitchen to whip up some cookies. The case was barren, and I'd had to disappoint a few kids who'd come in specifically for the cookies. This seemed like it might be the only time I'd get to take care of the baking before the dreaded lunch rush.

I'm not too proud to admit it—I took longer in the kitchen than I normally would have. I mixed up the batter, placed it on the sheets in round balls, and then shoved the sheets into the oven. Then I sat on the counter to give my feet a break while I waited for the cookies to be done. It didn't appear as if I was going to get a real break anytime soon, especially since I'd have to give one to each of my employees. By the time they had their breaks and Vicki came in, it would be time for me to go. And when I left, I wasn't going home to my warm bath. This was the only moment of relaxation I was likely to get.

I was anxious to get off work, but I wouldn't leave Lena and Mike hanging just so I could run off to Cherry Valley. I didn't know where David lived, but I hoped that after investigating his workplace, I'd find out. If there was any evidence of who David Smith really was, I was positive I'd find it there.

The timer on the oven dinged. I leapt off the counter, wiped my butt down as best as I could—it was covered in flour—and removed the cookies. My stomach grumbled at the smell, so without waiting for them to cool down, I snatched one off the cookie sheet. I sucked in a breath in a vain attempt to cool the lavalike chocolate with every bite; swallowed the steaming goo, which scorched my throat all the way down; and then, satisfied I wasn't going to starve to death, carried the cookie sheet out to the front, calling "Hot cookies!" as I went.

"Oh, there you are!"

My first instinct was to vanish back into the kitchen as if I'd suddenly forgotten something, but it was already too late. I plastered on a fake smile and carried the cookies to the front display case, where I began to shovel them into place. Rita scooted down the counter so she could talk to me face-to-face.

"I've heard the most horrible of rumors," she said, peering in at the cookies as if she didn't quite trust them.

"Really?" I asked, knowing that whether I said anything or not, she'd tell me all about it.

"I heard you were brutally attacked by one of your boyfriends out in the open where the world could see! Are you okay? He didn't cut you too deeply, did he?" She darted her head back and forth, apparently looking for a gaping wound in my scalp.

"I'm fine," I said. "It was just a rock, and it was thrown at my front door." I paused. "And I don't have a boyfriend."

She waved a hand at me. "Well, I *know* that. I could tell that just by looking at you."

It took me a moment to realize what the comment implied. "What do you mean by that?"

Another hand wave. "Never mind. I came here to let you know that we will be resuming our writers' group meetings next week. There was some talk of taking a week off after the exertions of the book club, but I said, 'No! We have to have the meetings for those unfortunate not to be a part of the club.' Meaning you, of course."

"Of course."

"I hope to see you there." She sighed dramatically. "Well, I best get going." Rita glanced toward the menu as if she might order, but she shook her head instead. "No time for coffee today. I'll see you soon." She waved and scurried out the front door.

Mike snorted a laugh from over by the register.

"It's not funny," I grumbled. I carried the cooling sheet

to the back, deposited it by the sink for Mike to wash, and then went out to join him.

"That was pretty crazy," he said, leaning on the counter. His hair stuck out in every direction from beneath his hat, obscuring his eyes. It was a wonder he could see.

"She can be, yeah."

"No, man, I mean the rush. Never seen the place so busy." There was a gleam in what I could see of his eye, like the endless stream of customers had made his day.

"I like seeing so many people here, but I sure hope it doesn't get that busy again today." I rubbed at the back of my neck. It was sweaty and sore and in severe need of strong hands to rub the pain away.

Mike nodded as if it was the wisest thing he'd ever heard. "True dat."

I eyed him a moment and then shrugged. It was like he was talking in a foreign language sometimes. I at least got the gist of that one.

Lena came down the stairs with a groan. "My feet are killing me." She rubbed at the side of her face where a fresh scrape ran across her cheekbone. It was ironic, because she never once complained about her skateboarding wounds, despite the fact that they looked far worse than a couple of sore muscles and blistered feet.

"I think we're all suffering," I told her with a weary smile.

She came to stand on my other side. "Hey, Mike, how about you clean the tables? Some of the customers are leaving."

"Aw, man." Mike grabbed a rag from beneath the counter. "Whatever." He strode out to where there were now two empty tables.

I turned toward Lena. There had been something to her

tone that set alarm bells ringing in my head. I wasn't sure whether it had something to do with David Smith or something else entirely. Either way, I was anxious to hear what she had to say.

"I'd keep an eye on him," she said at a near whisper. She nodded toward where Mike had gone.

"Who? Mike?" I asked to be sure.

"Yeah."

My heart did a little hiccup. "Do you think he could have killed Mr. Smith?"

Lena gave me a sideways glance. "What? No." She shook her head. "Or at least I don't think so. But I do think he's up to something. He acts weird when he thinks no one is looking. And do you notice how he likes to run the register more than anything else?"

I nodded, a frown creeping over my face. I hadn't noticed it before, but she was right; Mike was almost always working the register, even when someone else wanted to do it.

"You don't think . . ." I trailed off, not sure I wanted to voice my suspicions.

"Don't know," Lena said. "But I thought it might be a good idea to let you know."

I thought back to when I first started noticing the lack of funds coming into Death by Coffee, despite the uptick in business. As far as I was aware, Vicki saw nothing out of the ordinary in the books, but what if Mike was skimming from the top? Could he be cancelling orders after taking the money, shoving it in his pocket instead of the register?

My heart plummeted to my feet at the thought. If he was stealing, then not only would I have to let him go, I'd have to tell the police so it wouldn't happen again. But he did have to pay child support, which meant he was probably barely making ends meet. Could I really do that to him?

But if he *was* stealing, I couldn't let it continue, no matter how bad I felt for him.

"Thanks," I told Lena.

"Any time."

I started to turn away when I thought of something else. "Hey, has your key come up missing lately?"

"My key? No. Why?"

"Just wondering." My gaze traveled to Mike. "Go ahead and head upstairs. I'll handle things down here."

Lena hesitated only a moment before she turned and went back up into the bookstore, where a few kids were playing around in the stacks. I could hear her yell at them, though she tried to keep her voice down. From the way the kids acted toward her, I was pretty sure she knew them.

I tried to get back to work, but my eyes kept going to Mike. He lingered out among the customers, wiping down tables and chairs, as if afraid to come back to where I stood. I didn't know whether he knew that I knew what he'd been doing or if it was something else. Even when a new customer came in, his head didn't rise. He looked so forlorn, lost in his own miserable thoughts, it just about broke my heart.

Finally, I couldn't take it anymore. The next time he looked up, I motioned for him to join me behind the counter.

"What's up?" he asked, not meeting my eye.

"I was curious about something," I said. "Has your key come up missing lately? Or did you let someone borrow it, perhaps?"

"What? No." He looked genuinely upset I'd even think it. "I'm more careful than that."

I gave him a reassuring smile. "I was just checking," I said. "Can't be too safe."

He made a noncommittal sound and eyed me skeptically. "That all? I have a few more tables I can scrub down."

I almost let him go then, but I decided I couldn't do that. I had to know if what Lena said was true. "Yeah, uh, Mike." I swallowed. This was going to be tough.

A worried expression passed over his face. "Did I do something wrong?" he asked, sounding as if he was afraid I was going to fire him on the spot.

"Well . . ." I glanced toward where Lena was replacing some books that had been taken from the shelves before turning back to Mike. "I've noticed a decided lack of income lately." My mouth went dry, and I felt myself start to blush. God, I hated this. "And you tend to work the registers, so I was wondering . . ."

Mike's jaw tensed. "Wondering what? If I took it?"

I shrugged before nodding.

"No, man, I would never." He looked away as he said it. "That's stupid."

"I had to ask," I said. "You have to understand." I could tell he wasn't happy with me, but I wasn't quite sure if his unhappiness was because of my accusation or because he'd been caught. "I want us to trust each other, but in order for that to happen, I need you to be honest with me. We can work something out if you are in need."

"No, I'm cool." He looked toward the ceiling. "I just want to get back to work, if that is okay with you?"

"Sure."

He strode out to wipe down more tables. He looked miserable and I felt bad, yet it had to be done. Maybe if he had been stealing, he'd stop now that I was onto him. If he didn't, well then, I might just have to fire him. It was something I really hoped I could avoid.

The lunch rush came and went. Mike avoided me during that time, though he was forced to help at the register while I filled orders. I tried to keep an eye on him, but it wasn't easy, since I kept having to run to the back. Eventually, Vicki came in, as chipper as I'd ever seen her. I don't think there was anything on God's green earth that could have wiped the smile from her face as she joined me behind the counter.

"It's a great day," she said, practically swooning.

I gave her a noncommittal shrug.

She hardly noticed. She swept past me and headed for the back. I followed her, feeling like a royal jerk for what I was about to do, but she deserved to know.

"Vicki?" I said, closing the door quietly behind us. The office felt cramped, which caused me to break out into a sweat. It was either that or my nerves that I was about to get what could very well be an innocent man into trouble. "Can I talk to you a sec?"

"Sure." She pulled her hair up into a ponytail.

"It has come to my attention that Mike might, um . . ." This was almost as hard as confronting the man himself. "He might be stealing."

Vicki frowned. "Stealing?"

"The register has seemed light lately, hasn't it? I think he's been skimming a little. I'm sure it has to do with his other troubles and he doesn't mean anything by it. And I don't think you should say anything to him; I already did. But you should keep an eye on him just in case he's doing it." I looked down at my feet. "I thought you should know."

Vicki was silent for a long moment before saying, "Okay, thanks."

I didn't know how to interpret that, and didn't care to think too hard about it. I so wasn't the confrontational type.

Every time I tried, I ended up getting myself into trouble, or making a fool out of myself. Actually, I usually end up doing both.

Vicki went back out into the store, a troubled look on her face. I wanted to stick around and make sure everything ran smoothly, especially with Mike, but I really wanted to get to Cherry Valley before Penelope's Restorations closed for the day. I should have asked Vicki about her key, and still could, but I decided I'd put enough on her for the day. I could always ask her tomorrow.

Mike watched me, almost sulkily, as I headed for the door. Lena gave me a reassuring nod, as if telling me I'd done the right thing. Vicki was standing beside her, staring out at nothing. I guess I could indeed ruin her good mood.

"See you all tomorrow!" I called, putting as much cheer into my voice as I could. All it earned me was three half-hearted waves. Knowing it was likely all I'd get, I turned and headed out the door.

25

Cherry Valley wasn't much different than Pine Hills. They were about the same size, though Cherry Valley felt larger due to the fast-food restaurants and the large shopping mall downtown. Many of the houses I passed coming into town were cozy and white, with well-tended lawns. It was the kind of place you'd imagine retiring to, where everyone knew everyone else, where shopping was close by but didn't overrun the area. It felt as if it came straight out of one of those old television shows like *Leave It to Beaver*.

A pair of women walked dogs with curly fur that matched the women's own permed white hair. They waved as I drove past, smiling as if nothing in the world could bother them.

I'm not sure what I'd expected to find in Cherry Valley. A part of me thought it would be full of old houses with paint peeling from the siding, windows broken and boarded over, a road with potholes large enough to swallow an entire car. Maybe it was the fact that David was living under a presumed name, so I automatically thought of an inner city where something like that might be more common. Instead, I found myself in a place I might actually like to visit every now and again—just as long as it wasn't full of murderers.

I continued on through the town, taking in the scenery. I passed by more tidy little houses and bumped over a set of old railroad tracks that no longer appeared to be in use. The houses here were a little older, a little more run-down, but it wasn't as drastic as it could have been. This wasn't the stereotypical "wrong side of the tracks." In fact, despite the older homes and businesses, I didn't feel threatened here at all.

Penelope's Restorations was on the far end of town. It sat between a pair of empty-looking warehouses that didn't appear derelict as they could have. The small bike repair shop was squashed between them. A half-dozen motorcycles sat outside, none with riders evident. The building itself could have used a fresh coat of paint. The old red, white, and blue had faded and chipped away long ago, though it still didn't look as derelict as you might expect. The garage door that led into the area where the restorations took place was up, and I could see someone crouched next to a bike that looked as if it had seen better days.

I pulled into the parking lot and came to a stop next to the motorcycles. I felt out of place here, knowing nothing about motorcycles or the type of people that rode them. And if the people who worked here were anything like the bikers on TV, I was pretty sure they wouldn't appreciate my showing up and asking questions.

I gathered my purse, not trusting to leave it unattended in the car, locked or not, and got out. As soon as I closed the door, the figure in the shop rose and turned my way. As it happens, it was a woman.

"Can I help you?" she asked. Her voice was surprisingly sweet, something I wouldn't have expected out of someone who worked on motorcycles. She stepped out of the shadows cast by the garage, and I saw that she was pretty. Her face was smeared with grease, as was her brownish blond hair, yet I could see through it to the delicate features that would normally put her on a runway rather than under tons of machinery. She even had the figure for it, the curves that spoke of someone who could easily have become a seductress. She wore dark blue coveralls with the arms torn off, exposing biceps that would make quite a few men feel inadequate.

"Um, yeah. I'm looking for Penelope, I think?" It came out as a question.

She chuckled. "You think?" Before I could answer, she went on. "I'm Penelope. And you are?"

"Kristina Hancock, but everyone calls me Krissy."

Penelope wiped her hands on a rag she pulled from her back pocket. The thing looked as if she had dunked it in oil before using it, so it did little to remove the grime on her hands. She looked at the dirt and grease under her fingernails, shrugged, and then held out a hand. I took it and shook.

"What can I do for you, Krissy?" she asked. As she pulled her hand back, she wiped her arm across her brow, smearing what appeared to be motor oil across her forehead. I tried hard not to stare.

"I have a few questions about a man named Caleb Jenkins."

"Yeah?" she said. "And why would I know him?"

That took me a little aback. "Your website says he worked here at one point. I figured you could tell me something about him."

"Does it, now?" She bit her lower lip and looked over my head as if she could see the website somewhere in the clouds. "I don't really recall the name."

My heart sank. If Caleb hadn't worked here long, it would be easy to forget him.

"What about David Smith? Does that ring a bell?"

Penelope shook her head slowly. "No, but now that I'm thinking about it, I think there was a Caleb who worked here for about a week before he up and quit on me."

"Do you remember why he quit?"

She laughed. "Honey, if I could remember that far back, I wouldn't keep misplacing my wrench every damn time I set it down." She grinned. "I hire enough people here that I can hardly recall who still works here and who doesn't on most days. There's a lot of people looking for work, what with the economy and all. I tend to get people who breeze into town and work for a month or so before moving on down the road. The only reason I remember Caleb now was because he actually seemed to know a little something about bikes."

I thought back to the photos on Facebook. I supposed a scooter was close enough to a motorcycle, though I imagine there were also major differences. Maybe he knew something about both. I didn't know what he did for a living in Idaho, so I supposed it was possible he could have worked at a repair shop there as well.

"What more can you tell me about him?" I asked, hoping she could remember something else.

Penelope gave me a long look as she shoved the rag into her back pocket. "What's this about, anyway?"

I hated being the one to break the bad news but saw no way around it, not if I wanted to get anything out of her. Penelope seemed like one of those people who would talk only if they felt they could trust you. Lying was no way to earn trust.

"Caleb was murdered a few nights ago."

Penelope winced but didn't say anything.

"I was hoping you could tell me a little about him. When he came to Pine Hills, he was going under a different name, making it harder to pinpoint who he was, where he lived, and so on."

Penelope eyed me, a frown creeping over her pretty features. There was a hint of distrust there, for which I didn't blame her. I was a stranger here, asking about someone she'd barely known. She had no reason to trust me, and I hadn't given her any reason to.

She ran her fingers through her hair, darkening it with the grease and oil still on her hands. "You a cop?" She asked it in a way that made me think she might turn around and walk away if I was.

"Nope," I told her with what I hoped was a reassuring smile.

"A dick?"

"Uh, a what?"

"A PI? You know, investigator or something."

"Not exactly," I said. "I've helped on a murder case before, but this time I'm doing it on my own time. He died in my shop, and well . . . I'd really like to know why."

"Ah, that's cool, then." Penelope rubbed at her chin as if considering what to tell me before turning away. "Wait here a sec."

I did as she requested. I was anxious to hear what she had to say, hoping she would know something about the man I didn't already know. Even if she just had a different perspective, it might help me understand who he really was.

A dog barked in the distance, sounding angry. The shadows began to lengthen as the sun neared setting. I had maybe an hour of daylight left, which was fine by me. Once I was done here, I was going to head back to a McDonald's I'd seen on my way in. I was craving a Big Mac something fierce, having gone without for so long. It would go to my hips, I was sure, but I could deal with that. I still couldn't get past the fact there were no fast-food places in Pine Hills. It was a tragedy, to be sure.

Penelope returned ten minutes later, a dirty manila folder in hand. She opened it as she neared. "Not much I can tell ya," she said.

"Anything you have could help."

"Caleb came in from out of state, asked for a job, and I gave it to him. About two days in, some chick rolled in, asking for him. He saw her coming and begged me to tell her he wasn't around, so that's what I did. Completely forgot about the little incident until now."

"Who was she?" I asked, interested. Had David, as Caleb, been running from someone? It would be a good reason to change your name and try to move on. It's harder to find someone if you didn't know what to look for.

"Just some girl who was upset about her man running out on her, I figure. I didn't much care for her type, I can tell you that. She was all dolled up, acting like she farted rainbows, demanding I tell her where Caleb had gone. Called him Cal, I think."

"Do you have a name?"

"Nah. I told her to beat it and threatened to wipe my hands down her pretty pink dress. She glared at me from the safety of her little convertible before wheeling it on out of town. Think she's long gone by now."

I racked my brain but couldn't remember seeing a convertible or a girl who matched the vague description Penelope had given me. If she'd come to Pine Hills to kill Caleb, she did so without my noticing, which really wasn't all that hard to do, to be honest. I didn't keep tabs on everyone who popped in and out.

"Was that the only incident involving Caleb, then?" I asked, hoping for a tale about some rough character showing up, looking for him sometime in the last week.

"Pretty much," Penelope said, dashing that hope. "A few days after she left, Caleb didn't show up again. I figured he'd simply moved on. Happens all the time."

Well, crap. While the story was interesting and all, it didn't help me much. I was starting to feel like I'd made a mistake coming here, when Penelope spoke.

"I do have one thing that you might be interested in." She stepped up next to me and turned the folder my way so I could see it better. There was a scanned picture of Caleb's driver's license, the same one I had in my possession. Beneath that, written in a decidedly girly scrawl, was a local address.

It looked like my trip wasn't wasted after all.

Penelope let me have the entire folder, which contained very little else. Since Caleb was dead and not coming back, she didn't need it any longer. I carried it to my car like a trophy from a hard-fought match. It was the best lead I'd had in a long time. I'd been worried I'd have to question half of the town to find out where Caleb had lived.

I got back into my car and waved once to Penelope, who was watching me as I backed out. The address she'd given me didn't mean much at the moment, since I had no idea where anything was in Cherry Valley. Good thing I was hungry. It would give me some time to look up a few things on my phone.

I headed for the McD's and pulled into the parking lot. I snatched the page with the address out of the folder and headed inside. A sign on the door proclaimed free Wi-Fi, which was another good reason to do my research here. I ordered my Big Mac with large fries. Grudgingly, I ordered a Diet Coke to offset the calorie and fat intake, knowing it was a futile exercise. Water would have been better for me but far less tasty.

I carried my food to a corner table, pulled out my phone, and brought up Google Maps. From there, it was a few simple clicks, a little typing with grease-stained fingers, and ta-da! I checked the route, memorized it as best I could so I wouldn't have to keep looking at my phone as I drove, and then put it away, satisfied I knew where I was going.

And then I dug in, relishing every last bite.

26

Night had fallen by the time I found Caleb's house in the maze of unfamiliar roads. Streetlights lit up much of the road, including where I sat in my car. Small, leafy trees lined the sidewalk, casting periodic shadows across it. Houses, spaced evenly apart, ran down either side of the street. They were all pretty well maintained, and that included the cute little cottage I was looking at.

I don't know why, but I fully expected to find the house in shambles, a wreck of a place that had been taken over by the homeless, or at least nature. I thought I'd find knee-high grass, shingles drooping on a roof ready to collapse.

Instead, the house was a near pristine white with a small front porch, a painted white swing hanging from the ceiling. A mailbox sat near the sidewalk, standing straight up and seemingly empty, telling me either he received no mail or someone was getting it for him. There were no lights on inside, but that meant little if he was living with someone who went to bed early.

I glanced at the clock on the dash. It was a little past nine, so I guess it wasn't really *that* early. I'd seen a pair of teenagers walking down the street the other way just before I parked, but I had seen no one else since arriving.

No cars had drifted by, and no curious faces appeared at a window. It was eerily quiet in this suburban bliss.

I shut off the engine and listened. I was parked across the street, between a silver Cadillac and a blue Chevy. Both looked well tended. No sounds were immediately evident, which was unnerving in itself. I expected a dog to be barking or the sound of someone's television blaring too loud.

I checked my rearview mirror for about the twentieth time since I'd arrived ten minutes prior. I hadn't seen anyone, but my brain kept warning me that Buchannan could be lurking out there somewhere, waiting for me to make my move. If he were to catch me snooping around Caleb's house in the middle of the night, there was no way he would let me off easily. I might as well book the downstairs cell for the next few months.

But I hadn't seen or heard any indication that Buchannan had followed me. Trust me, I'd checked.

"It's now or never, Krissy," I said, focusing on the house again. I could sit here forever, but where would that get me? If I wanted to find out something about Caleb before he'd become David, this was my best chance.

I sat there a few minutes more to calm my nerves. I was hoping David had lived with someone and they'd be willing to tell me something about the man, something that would help me understand why he'd been killed. After a few deep breaths, I shoved my purse under the seat as far as I could, just in case.

I opened the car door, quickly stepped out, and closed it as quietly as I could, hoping the sound of the dinging and the clunk of the door closing hadn't drawn anyone's attention. I might only be there to talk, but that didn't mean I wanted everyone in the neighborhood to know I was there, especially if the killer happened to be around. The street was quiet, but that meant little if there was someone silently watching me from behind a tree.

The thought didn't help. I glanced wildly around, almost positive I'd catch sight of Buchannan's grinning face or, worse, a gun aimed at my head. If anyone was out there, however, they were doing a good job of keeping out of sight.

"Stop being so paranoid," I whispered, hoping the sound of my voice would calm me down. It didn't.

I crossed the street and headed straight for David's front door—I decided I was going to call him that from now on. This whole David or Caleb thing would drive me batty. Four steps led to the covered porch, which helped shield me from easy view, thanks to the lack of light. I moved to the outer screen door and knocked.

As I waited, I looked behind me, just in case someone was creeping up on me. No one was. I turned back to the door and knocked again.

Still no answer.

"Well, darn," I muttered. Either David lived alone, or whoever lived here with him wasn't home or was dead to the world. *If not flat-out dead.*

I shuddered at the thought. Maybe what I was dealing with here went beyond a book club or relationship gone bad. Could he have been involved in something that got more than one person killed?

I looked at the door and willed it to open. I'd come all this way, and I didn't want to turn around and head back home empty-handed. I knew that there had to be something inside the house that would help me. I needed a way inside.

I glanced around the front porch. There were no flowerpots sitting around in which a spare key might be hidden, so I headed back down the stairs and checked the mailbox instead. A neighbor I once knew kept her spare key taped to the inside, on the top, at the far back. I hoped David would have done the same, but the mailbox was empty.

And as I'd assumed earlier, there was no mail inside, either.

A nagging voice in the back of my head warned me that David might not even own this place anymore. I hadn't done any real research to check, not that I would know how to. For all I knew, he'd sold the place almost as soon as he'd bought it. I could be poking around some old man's property.

But I had to find out. I couldn't just walk away now, not when I was so close.

The front of the house was a bust, but that didn't mean I couldn't find another way in. Not everyone was careful about locking up, especially if they had someone else coming to take care of their mail for them, which I hoped was the case here.

I headed for the side of the house, shoulders hunched. I wasn't quite sure when I'd decided I was going to break in and have a look around, but that's exactly what I planned to do. It might be the only way I'd learn anything. I just hoped I wouldn't end up sitting in another jail cell, this time where I didn't know anyone.

It was practically pitch black between David's house and his neighbor's, which worked just fine for me. The ground sloped slightly downward here, away from David's property, causing the footing to be suspect. I stood on my tiptoes but couldn't quite see into the two windows that were there.

But I could still reach them. I tried the first, pushing up on it gently. It didn't budge, though dirt and debris rained down into my face just as I breathed in. I very nearly started sneezing as I sucked the dirt up my nose. I pranced around, eyes squeezed shut, as I tried not to give myself away in a sneezing fit. The urge passed, though tears filled my eyes, making them sting.

I was more careful with the next window. I stood on my tiptoes and pushed upward on the frame. It actually moved an inch before getting stuck. Determined, I shoved harder, knowing that if I wasn't careful, I could break the glass. With a grind, the window broke free of its paint trap and started to rise.

Allowing myself a silent whoop of joy, I grabbed the windowsill and tried to hoist myself up. I lifted off the ground all of six inches, feet scrabbling at the side of the house, before letting go. There was no way I was going to be able to drag myself up there without help. I looked around and found a metal trash can near the back porch. Bugs ran up and down the sides of it, and a horrible rotten smell was coming from inside. Proof that David had lived here alone? Or simply that whoever lived here now wasn't too careful about cleaning out his trash can?

I didn't know, and right then I didn't care. I grabbed the trash can and carefully carried it back to the window, holding it out in front of me as far as I could. I set it down with a slight squeal as a bug ran up my hand and onto my bare wrist. I shook it free with a shudder.

I was making far too much noise. Someone had to have heard me by now, though I prayed they wouldn't investigate. I knew if I wanted to do this, I needed to get inside, and I needed to do it fast. Ignoring the bugs, I put my weight onto the lid of the trash can. It seemed as if it might hold, so I grabbed the windowsill and pulled myself upright. Once standing, I pushed the window open the rest of the way, leaned inward, and pulled myself inside, somehow not kicking over the trash can in the process.

Instead, I fell into a sink.

All of the air gushed out of me as my stomach met the faucet. I rolled away, bucked my hip off the counter, and then tumbled to the kitchen floor with a heavy thump.

I lay there, stunned, for a long minute. I didn't think anything was broken, but my hip felt as if it were residing somewhere in my kneecap. I sucked in deep breaths until it felt as if I could move without pain. Once I felt steady, I pushed myself up off the floor, feeling good about myself.

It might not have been the most graceful of entrances, but I was inside. And no one had come running to investigate all the noise I'd made. I'd call that a win.

The kitchen was one of those eat-in jobs, cute and tidy. The sink was thankfully empty, or else I would have made a much louder racket, and probably impaled myself on a knife in the process. A table sat against the far wall, two chairs pushed in beneath it. A stack of mail sat on the table, unopened, further assurance that David had someone bringing in his mail for him and that no one else lived here.

The house wasn't as dark as I thought it might be, thanks to light trickling in through the windows. All of the curtains were parted, which was fortunate. I hadn't thought to bring a flashlight, so this was going to be tricky. It would be hard to make out much of anything with the limited moonlight sifting in.

I checked the mail first, not touching anything. My eyebrows rose in surprise when I noted the letters were addressed to David Smith, not Caleb Jenkins.

"Interesting," I whispered as I moved from the kitchen into the living room. He must have changed his name but didn't change his address. I was also thankful that I had confirmation that he still owned the place and I wasn't about to walk in on a couple of strangers.

A couch and chair faced a large television hanging from the wall. A coffee table rested in front of the couch. Nothing sat atop it but dust. The end table by the chair was likewise empty. There were no pictures on the walls, no paintings. I got a vague impression that David hadn't spent a lot of time here. The house didn't feel lived in, almost as if I were looking at a mock-up of a house rather than the real thing. I wasn't sure what that told me. As far as I knew, David had spent all his time at Sara's place.

A set of stairs led up to the second level. I took them carefully, running my hand over the banister, just in case a step was loose or an unseen cat lay sprawled across one of them. I'd had my share of tumbles thanks to Misfit, and I didn't want to repeat the process here, even if it meant I might leave a print or two. It wasn't like I planned on stealing anything, so as long as I was careful, no one would know I was even there.

I reached the top of the stairs without trouble and paused to listen. I was pretty sure I was in the house alone but couldn't be positive. It was dark up here, though I could make out three doors, all of them open. No snoring came from any of the rooms. There were no sounds at all, in fact. There was nothing to do but move forward.

The first room was a bathroom. There were no windows, making it as dark as a tomb. I decided to risk it, knowing that if I was going to find anything, I'd need the light. I flipped the switch. Soft white light illuminated a sink that held only the most basic of supplies, and a tub and toilet that looked practically unused.

I turned and headed to the room across the hall. It was

set up to be an office, I think. There was a desk with one of those short-backed office chairs pushed beneath it. A banker's lamp sat on the edge of the desk. It was currently off and I had no intention of turning it on.

I crossed the room and opened the desk drawer, but all I found were a couple of pencils that rolled around loosely inside. There wasn't even a pad of paper to write on as far as I could tell. When I checked the closet, some old rolls of wallpaper fell out, startling me, but that was all.

I was beginning to feel as if the trip was a waste of time. I went into the final room, David's bedroom, with little hope of finding anything useful. The bedroom held a dresser and a bed, but nothing else. The bed was made and looked as if it had never been slept in. I went to the dresser first and opened the drawers. I wasn't in the least bit surprised to find only a couple pairs of socks, a pair of jeans, and two pairs of tighty-whities. Moving to the closet, I found only four or five shirts sagging on hangers.

I turned, frustrated. There was nothing here, not one scrap of evidence that would help me learn who David Smith really was, or who might have reason to kill him. It looked like it might have something to do with the book club after all, something I didn't relish one bit.

I was about to leave when I thought of one more place I hadn't checked. I turned, got down onto my hands and knees, and peered under the bed.

And there it was, sitting pressed up against the wall beneath the bed: a shoebox. As far as I knew, it contained nothing but a pair of dirty old sneakers, but my pulse ratcheted up a level and my head started swimming. Could this be my big break? Something about how the box sat there, seemingly innocent, convinced me that this was exactly what I'd come all of this way for.

I reached across and dragged over the box. I scrambled to my feet, anxious to see what was inside, and hurried to the bathroom where I had some more light. I set the box onto the counter and then opened the lid.

Jackpot.

First I found at least a dozen different IDs. All of them had David's face smiling at me. Or perhaps it was Caleb's. Or perhaps it was Jerry, or Calvin, or Stegman. Each ID had a different name, a different home address. There was one from Maryland, one from Indiana, another from South Carolina. I sorted through them quickly, my interest growing.

Who was this man, really? Some sort of criminal mastermind who changed his personality every week? A secret agent who needed all of the IDs to keep his cover? Or was he just some guy with a troubled past who was determined never to be found?

It took me a moment to realize the fake IDs weren't the only thing in the box. I set them aside and looked down at the square book that remained. It looked like one of those small scrapbooks you'd find at any hobby store. I picked it up, not sure what I'd find inside. More fake IDs? Some sort of collection of newspaper clippings, the kind you'd find in a serial killer's house?

A shudder ran through me as I flipped open the book. I was confronted with pictures of naked women.

A lot of naked women.

The first dozen pages held one photograph each, taken by a Polaroid camera. Beneath each photograph was a name, followed by a state.

My mind raced. This was exactly the same sort of photo as I'd found in David's room back at the bed-and-breakfast. I had a feeling that if I pulled one of these photographs free,

I'd find a name and number listed on the back. I flipped through the first twelve and stopped on the empty page thirteen. Was Sara's picture going to end up here?

These women, all twelve of them, were David's conquests. I couldn't think of any other answer that made sense. I didn't know the women, and since they were naked I couldn't pick up clues from their clothing, but I had a feeling all of them had money, money David had more than likely taken from them. Was he a con man, then? A drifter who went from state to state, collecting pictures of naked women and then taking their money? Was he blackmailing them?

If so, I'd wager that it was a pretty good motive for murder. The only question was, who took that fatal step?

Paul would want to know about this.

I considered calling him right then and there, but my phone was in my purse, which was in my car. I supposed I could go out and call him, but then what? How was I going to explain how I'd gotten in, or even why I was there in the first place? I could leave the shoebox under the bed, go home, and then call the police. They could find it on their own.

But how would I explain how I knew where to find it? An anonymous call might work, but I didn't believe for an instant Officer Dalton or Buchannan wouldn't know who'd placed the call.

No, best take it with me. I could go home, do a little research, and then call the police to hand it all over. If I could give them more than just the box, like a motive for murder, then maybe they wouldn't look too hard at how I'd come by the information.

I shoved the photograph album back into the box, followed by the IDs. Once that was done, I checked to make sure I'd forgotten nothing, and then flipped off the bathroom light. I hurried down the stairs, too overjoyed by what I'd found to think about being quiet. I mean, it was like I'd hit the lottery of investigation. Everything I needed to solve the case was right here, waiting for me, all this time.

I'd just reached the living room when there was a loud knock at the door.

"David?" A male shape appeared at the window by the door. "Is that you?"

I didn't move, afraid that if I did it would give me away. There was faint light coming in, but I was clear across the room, hidden by the shadows. I didn't breathe, didn't so much as twitch. Whoever was out there knew David, and probably was keeping an eye on his house for him.

Which meant he might have a key.

The shape vanished from the window. There was a creak as he moved back in front of the door.

"Please, no. Please, no." I repeated it like a mantra, just under my breath. If he were to open the door and find me standing there, my goose was cooked.

A dozen seconds ticked by. Two dozen.

And then the heavy thump of boots as the man walked down the stairs.

I waited there, unmoving, for what felt like an hour. I fully expected him to come back, this time with the key, but after a few minutes my muscles started aching and my head was pounding so that I had no choice but to move. I walked slowly, quietly, into the kitchen and considered the open window, and then deciding there was no way in the world I was going to climb up onto the counter to get back out that way, I turned toward the back door. I unlocked it, and then stepped outside.

A rustle from a nearby tree caused me to yelp, but apparently it was just the leaves on the breeze. I closed the door behind me, sweat pouring down my face, and hurried between the two houses. I checked to make sure no one was out on the street and then ran for my car, like a criminal who was about to be caught in the act. I got inside, tossed the box on the passenger seat, and then started the car.

And then I just about had a heart attack as I looked up to find a cop car bearing down on me.

27

The cruiser rolled by. The officer's eyes were cast down to the glowing phone he held in one hand, fingers typing away. He barely glanced up as he passed.

I breathed a sigh of relief and pulled out onto the road. I made sure to drive a few miles per hour below the speed limit, just in case. I didn't think a cop would care what I had sitting in the seat beside me, though they might give me a funny look if they were to check. Still, I didn't want to take a chance. I'd taken too many of them already.

It was past midnight by the time I got home. I parked, got out of the car, and carried the shoebox into my house. Eleanor's windows were dark, telling me that for once, I'd managed to do something without her watching me. It was enough to bring a near smile to my face.

What I should have done was crawl into bed and get some sleep, or perhaps call Paul Dalton and tell him what I'd found. I was exhausted from my trip, but wired all the same. If I had a good excuse, I very well might have called him, but as it was, I could hardly think straight, let alone come up with an elaborate story that would convince the cops that I hadn't broken any laws.

Instead of risking jail with a call, I went to my computer, booted it up, and browsed the web for information on the women whose pictures I'd found in David's conquest book. All I had were first names and the images I could only bring myself to glance at, so it was next to impossible to come up with anything. I was sure the police would have programs that could match the features with someone online, but I was hoping to find something on my own.

After only an hour of browsing, I clicked off the web and carried the box to a closet, where I shoved it behind a stack of dishtowels, just in case someone came snooping around in the middle of the night. That done, I decided to head for bed and sleep on what I'd found. Maybe I'd come up with a solution overnight.

Sleep didn't come easily, which meant morning was not a welcome sight. I could have slept in since I wasn't due for work until midday, but I decided to get up since I was already awake. I dragged myself out of bed, showered, got dressed, and had a quick breakfast of toast and coffee before heading out, conquest book in hand. I wanted to talk to Sara one last time before calling the police about what I'd found.

Tonight was the big book club talk or competition or whatever they called it. I wanted to get Sara alone before that happened, so I headed for Ted and Bettfast. I hoped everyone would be tucked away in their rooms, reading *Murder in Lovetown*, or practicing their speeches, giving me the opportunity to go about my business without everyone watching me. Besides, it would be much easier to tell

Sara what I knew about David without the others lurking about.

My mind flashed to the photographs. I'd been forced to look at them enough in my search. I had all of the women's faces memorized. I was positive none of them was in Pine Hills, or at least hadn't come into Death by Coffee while I'd been there. If one of them *had* killed David, chances were good they were long gone, which meant nothing I did now would matter.

Which, in a way, was why I was bringing the photos to Sara. If she recognized one of the women, had been accosted by one of them, then maybe I'd have something to go on, some bit of information I could pass on to the authorities. I wasn't about to go chasing after some vengeful ex-girlfriend from another state, not when I had trouble enough at home.

I pulled into the bed-and-breakfast lot, found a place to park, and then headed for the front door. I was nervous— as anyone who was carrying naked pictures of pretty girls around would be. If I were to drop the book and some well-meaning soul were to pick it up and see what it held, I would just die.

Neither Ted nor Bett were outside today, which was something of a relief. The fewer people I had to talk to, the better. I might lose my nerve otherwise.

I walked right in, past a startled Jo, and peeked out toward the pool. Sure enough, Sara was lounging in one of the chairs, my dad's book in hand. Orville looked to be asleep on the other side of the still water, face tinged red from the early morning sun. It was going to be a hot one, that was for sure.

I opened the door and went straight for Sara. Albert and Dan weren't around, but I didn't know how long that would last. I didn't want either man snooping while I was talking to her, especially since I didn't fully trust either one, Dan especially.

Sara's eyes lifted from the page as my shadow fell across her. She squinted up at me, and a frown creased her features.

"Yes?" she asked, clearly annoyed, as anyone would be. I'd hounded the poor woman enough. It was a wonder she didn't throw the book at me and storm off at first sight.

"Sorry to bother you again, but there's something I think you should know."

"Can it wait? I have to finish reviewing the book before tonight."

"No, it can't." Without asking, I took the seat next to her, propping myself on the edge just in case she decided to attack me when I told her the news. It wouldn't be the first time the messenger got smacked around for delivering news someone didn't want to hear.

Sara heaved a sigh and scooted up in her chair so she was more or less upright. She closed her book without using a bookmark and turned her annoyed gaze on me. "Okay, fine. Have it your way. Tell me what you have to say so I can get back to work."

My eyes flickered toward the back door. Jo was standing there, watching us. As soon as she saw me looking, she turned on her heel and walked away. I hoped she wasn't going in search of one of the men. I'm not sure why she would, especially since she knew why I was there, but with the way my luck was going, I wouldn't put it past her to call Buchannan on me. I had to be quick.

"I know you and David were an item," I said, speaking slowly, uncertainly. This wasn't going to be easy for her to hear, nor was it easy for me to say. "You might even have loved him."

Sara's jaw firmed. "I did." She took a deep breath and it

came out with a shudder that told me she was on the verge of tears. "But that's no reason to give up living, if that is what you are about to say. He would have wanted me to move on with my life, and that is what I intend to do."

"It's not that." Though I did wonder how she could sit here, mere days after David's death, and plan for a book club event. If it had been me, I would have been locked in my room, bawling my eyes out into my pillow for days, if not weeks. She was still upset by his death—that was obvious—but not nearly as much as I thought she should be, especially if she truly did love him.

Could it be because she found out about his past and killed him for it? I wasn't sure, but I planned on finding out.

"Well?" Sara asked, clearly impatient for me to be gone. She crossed her arms and gave me an expectant look.

"Did you know that David Smith wasn't his real name?"

Sara went still. "What are you talking about?"

"I've found . . . information that says he has gone by other names. Calvin. Jerry. But I think, without knowing for sure, that his real name was Caleb Jenkins, a man from Idaho, not Britain."

Sara blinked slowly at me, as if what I'd said had come out in Swahili.

I didn't blame her. If someone would have come to me and told me the man I'd loved, a man recently taken from me in the worst way imaginable, was living under an assumed name, lying to me, I would have thought them crazy. You get close to people and can't imagine them as anything but how you know them. This sort of thing happened only in movies and books, never in real life.

Or at least, I'd always thought they did, until moving to Pine Hills.

"I have no idea what you are talking about, Ms. Hancock,"

she said after a long moment, voice hard. "Do you have any proof of this claim?"

I cursed myself for not bringing the other IDs with me. They were sitting back at home, including his wallet with his Idaho license. "Not on me," I said. I looked down at the book in my hand. I so didn't want to do this but felt I had no choice if I wanted to get to the bottom of his murder. "But I have proof that he might have been using women for their money for a long time now."

Sara's eyes went even harder than they had been before. "I would appreciate it if you wouldn't speak ill of the dead, especially with such lies."

"I wish I were lying." Oh, how I did. I turned the book over in my hand a few times before holding it out to Sara.

She stared at it as if it might be a snake for a good thirty seconds before finally reaching out and taking it. I could see the curiosity in her eyes, the fear that what I was saying was true. There was pain there, a pain that just about broke my heart.

"I have to warn you," I said. "You aren't going to like what you find inside."

Sara gave me a quick nod, almost as if she hadn't really been listening to what I was saying, as she opened to the first page. Her hand flew to her mouth and her eyes just about popped from her head as she stared down at the nude woman on the page. She eyed it, transfixed, as if she couldn't bring herself to turn the page, let alone look away.

"I found this at a house in Cherry Valley registered to Caleb Jenkins, who we both knew as David Smith. This book is his." I considered whether to say more but decided I had to if I wanted her to believe me. "I found a similar photograph in David's room here."

Sara looked up at me, dread in her eyes. She knew what

I was going to say but seemed she wouldn't believe it until I actually said it out loud.

"Of you."

She broke down then, slamming the book closed without looking at any of the other photos. I didn't blame her; if I were her, I wouldn't have wanted to see them, either. She squeezed her eyes shut and gasped, "I won't believe it," between sobs.

I was torn between patting her on the shoulder to comfort her and grabbing the book and running. I felt like a royal jerk for making her cry, for telling her the truth about David when she could have lived her life perfectly fine without knowing that the man she once loved had been using her. I would have wanted to know, which was why I'd had to tell her. It wasn't my best moment, but I think she would be grateful in the end . . . If she wasn't the murderer, of course.

So, I just sat there, waiting for Sara to cry herself out. I kept expecting Dan or Albert to come rushing out at any moment, yelling at me for upsetting her, or for Orville to rise and wander over, yet no one appeared. It was as if I was being given a chance to make things right, to either learn from Sara who might have killed David or at least make her feel better about herself.

Sara's sobs turned to sniffles. She wiped her eyes dry, smearing mascara across her face. She gave me a defiant look when she was done, as if challenging me to say something about her breakdown.

"How did you get these things?" she asked. "Are you one of his . . . one of his women?"

I shook my head. "No. I . . ." I didn't want to tell her I broke into his place and poked around without permission. I floundered for a long moment before settling on a lame, "Someone let me into his house."

Sara sniffed disdainfully before looking at the book in her hand. "I guess I'd always known I wasn't the first. But when you get to be my age, you never are. People don't understand how hard it is when you have money and looks. They think everything simply falls into your lap, that men come begging at your feet like dogs."

I didn't say anything. Sara was looking at David's conquest book, talking as if she didn't even remember I was there. I was afraid that if I made a move, she would clam up and I would never hear where this was going. If this was a confession of some sort, I needed to hear it.

"Well, it's not easy." She looked up, giving me another defiant glare before returning her gaze to the book. "Most men take one look at me and assume I'm already taken. I practically had to wear a sign that said I was available just to get anyone to ask me out. And with my money, the men who might be interested are often intimidated. They're afraid of women who can do as they please, who don't need men to buy them nice things because they already have everything they could ever want."

Sara sniffed and clenched her fist. "And when one finally does take a chance, more often than not, he's after only two things: sex and money." She smiled grimly. "I'm sure David was after both. And I was happy to give it to him. I don't want to die an old, lonely maid."

There was a long stretch of silence before she looked up at me again. "Did I know David was living under an assumed name? No, I did not. Did I know he was after my money? A part of me did." She picked up the book and held it out to me. "Do I care?" She shook her head. "No, I do not."

I took the book of women and held it lamely in my hand. This was *so* not how I expected this to go. The crying? Sure, I'd expected that. The anger? Yeah. But I figured it would be targeted at David, not me. But the resignation to her fate? I didn't see that one coming at all.

It was sad in a way. This woman, with her money and looks, was probably the saddest person I knew. She wasn't really all that old, yet she talked as if she were on the verge of elderly. David might have been using her, but at least he'd made her happy.

"I'm so sorry about all of this," I said, pulling the book close to my chest, almost as a shield. "I didn't mean to upset you."

Sara snorted. Somehow, she made it seem ladylike. "Yes, you did." She grunted a bitter laugh. "You thought that perhaps I'd found out about David's other life and killed him for it." She smirked. "You didn't even have to say it; it's written all over your face." She picked up her novel. "I would never have hurt David, even if I'd known. I would have held on to him for as long as I could, hoping all the while that I'd be his last. If not . . ." She gave a helpless shrug.

I just sat there, unsure what to say. I'd been hoping Sara might have recognized one of the women in the book, if she hadn't killed David, but I wasn't about to show it to her again, let alone ask. I was beginning to wonder if any of this had anything to do with David's love life at all, or even his secret life. Could something else have been the cause of his death, something that was sitting right in front of me this entire time that I was too blind to see?

"Now," Sara said, drawing me out of my ruminations. "I do believe you should go. I have things to do." She opened her book and pointedly looked away.

I rose. "Thank you for your time." It came out flat, but I couldn't manage much more. I felt as if everything I'd known about the case was wrong, that I'd been following the wrong carrot this entire time. If that was the case, I had to reevaluate everything I knew, or at least what I'd thought I'd known.

And if it wasn't one of David's scorned lovers who had killed him, then it had to be someone here, someone I'd met. Whether it was one of the Cherry Valley people, one of the Pine Hills book club members, or someone else entirely, it wouldn't matter. I had to solve this thing soon, because if I didn't, Officer John Buchannan would make sure I was the one who would take the fall.

28

All of the chairs in Death by Coffee were taken. People stood along the walls, talking amongst themselves. Paul Dalton was sitting at a table with his mom, Chief Dalton, and surprisingly Officer John Buchannan. Every now and again, I'd catch one of them looking my way. I pointedly ignored them.

The box with the photographs and David's fake IDs was sitting under the seat in my car. I didn't want to bring it inside, not with all of these people here, but I did want to give it to the chief before the day was out. I didn't have an excuse lined up, but I was tired of holding on to it. The stress was wearing on me and I'd only had the box for half a day.

Besides, the store was busier than it had ever been. Everyone was ordering coffee and cookies. Lena was working as fast as she could behind the counter while I carried the coffees out to the customers, taking their orders and money so they wouldn't have to stand in line, which would have only gotten in the way of the doors. Doors, I might add, that were even now opening to let in a flood of new customers.

"Have you seen Mike?" Vicki asked on her way past with a pair of coffees in hand.

"Not yet." I glanced at the clock. He was already fifteen minutes late. I was worried I'd scared him off by my questions. As much as I didn't like the idea of his stealing from me, I didn't like the idea of working through the insanity without him.

The bookstore part of the store was closed to the general public, meaning it was much calmer and quieter. Only the book club members were up there, each in their own little group on either side of the stairs. A podium had been set up at the top of the steps, and currently no one was standing there.

Everyone had been talking about the book club competition, telling me how excited they were about it, and yet I never quite grasped how big the thing was. I mean, how could you ever take something like this seriously?

And yet it appeared as if half the town was trying to pack into Death by Coffee. On my way past the stairs, I'd heard Jimmy mention that he thought changing venues was a bad idea and had proof that it was now. I had to agree. The library was a lot bigger than my little coffee shop, and people wouldn't be running me ragged gathering orders. Next time, they weren't having it here.

I turned and just about ran into Will's chest. I gasped and stepped back, not sure whether I was happy to see him. Paul was sitting nearby, and I was afraid of what he'd think if he saw us together.

Get it together, Krissy. You aren't dating!

"Will!" I said, deciding I was happy he was there. "I didn't know you were here."

"I almost didn't come." He looked away. There was something in his eye that made me instantly nervous.

"Why? Is something wrong?"

He looked at me and a sad smile crossed his lips. It was the kind of smile that was usually followed up with bad news. "I didn't realize you were seeing other men when we talked before."

My eyes widened. "Other men?" Did he know about Paul? It was only one date! "What other men?"

"I saw you with someone at the Banyon Tree. The way he looked at you . . ." He shrugged. "I didn't mean to encroach."

"You aren't encroaching!"

"Krissy!" I turned to look at the counter where Vicki was pointing at a pair of waiting coffee cups.

"One sec!" I turned to explain that there was nothing between Dan and me, but somehow Will had vanished back into the crowd without my noticing.

"Great," I grumbled, turning to the counter. It would figure that I'd blow my chance with yet another man, and this time I hadn't done anything to deserve it.

As I was heading back to grab the pair of cappuccinos that Vicki left waiting, the doors opened and Mike Green walked in. He wasn't dressed for work, but rather looked as if he were going on a camping trip. He had a backpack thrown over one shoulder and a ball cap turned backward on his head. He scanned the crowd, seemingly surprised by how many people were crammed into such a small space, before his gaze landed on me. He hurried over and held out a folded piece of paper.

"What's this?" I asked, taking it from him.

"My resignation."

"What?" I flipped open the page. The note was handwritten and signed by Mike in his slanted, nearly indecipherable scrawl. I didn't bother reading it. I folded the page and then quickly shoved it into my pocket. "You can't do this to me."

"Sorry, man." He shrugged and handed me his key. "I can't take the insanity."

Great. The busiest day in the history of Death by Coffee and one of my employees was up and quitting on me. That was just my luck.

"Is there anything I can do to convince you to stay for at least today?"

Mike glanced toward where Lena was watching from behind the counter. His eyes narrowed just a tiny bit, and it hit me. It had nothing to do with the work or the crazy stuff that seemed to happen around me. This whole thing had to do with what Lena had said about him, her accusation that he was stealing. Whether he was doing it or not, I desperately needed him to stay.

"I can pay you double."

Mike seemed to consider it before shaking his head. "Sorry." He turned and walked out.

"Well, that's just lovely." I stared after him a moment before a polite clearing of the throat reminded me of the cappuccinos on the counter. I snatched them up and hurried across the packed room to deliver them.

It had been busy like this since the time I'd shown up. Between setting up for the event and serving customers, I'd barely had two seconds of my own to string thoughts together. I was afraid that after tonight, my brain would be too fried to even consider who might have killed David. And once the event was done, the Cherry Valley people would be gone, back home to their own lives. My list of people I could interrogate would instantly drop, leaving me with nothing to go on. Once that happened, nothing would stop Buchannan from taking me in, this time on murder charges. I'm sure he could find some sort of evidence that he could get to stick. I could almost see the anticipation dripping from him from clear across the room.

Well, it was either that or sweat. With so many people packed inside the small space, the temperature was indeed rising.

Another twenty minutes passed. I was running back and forth, barely cognizant of what I was doing anymore. I was about to throw in the towel and go find someplace to die in peace when Rita stepped up to the podium. All orders ceased as everyone's eyes turned toward the stairs. I handed off the last of the coffees and then collapsed against the counter. It was the only thing keeping me from passing out onto the floor.

"Welcome to the tenth annual Cherry and Pine Book Club Book Talk!" There was a polite round of applause, despite the awkward name. Rita's chin rose as she basked in it as if she'd just won Wimbledon. "I'm glad you all could make it," she said once the applause died down. "This year is special. Not only are we reading *Murder in Lovetown,* but we are also holding the book talk in the author's very own store!" More applause.

I rolled my eyes. My dad might have helped get us started, but this wasn't his place. Of course, trying to tell that to Rita would be just about as effective as trying to tell a cat not to shed on your best cashmere sweater.

Rita continued talking, but I tuned her out. Instead, I allowed my gaze to rove over the book club members, wondering if one of them could be sitting there, thinking they'd gotten away with murder.

Georgina and Andi were sitting next to each other, hands politely folded in their laps as they listened to Rita's speech. Beside them, Jimmy and Cindy sat with clasped hands, seemingly over their earlier spat. None of them seemed like a likely culprit. Jealousy? Sure. What man wouldn't be jealous if his wife were taken with another man? But nothing had happened between Cindy and

David, and I was pretty sure it never would have. I think Jimmy always knew that, so why bother killing the man?

No, it didn't make sense. I couldn't see a single Pine Hills group member as the killer, and that included Rita.

I turned my gaze to the Cherry Valley team.

Albert was sitting closest to the podium, glowering. His hair was plastered to his head, further revealing that receding hairline he so desperately tried to hide. He glared at Rita as if she was the bane of his existence. His fists were clenched, as was his jaw. Now, that was a man I could see killing someone, despite his smallish frame. But to kill someone in his own group? If he'd found out about David's past, then perhaps he might have gotten angry. But to kill him for it when it didn't affect the group? I just didn't see it. As long as David was doing what Albert wanted him to do, I was sure he would have let it slide.

Beside Albert were Orville and Vivian. They sat close together, like they wanted to hold hands but were afraid the other wouldn't approve. It was almost cute. There was no way either of them could be involved. It would be like accusing someone's grandparents of murder.

And then my eyes fell onto the last two members of the Cherry Valley book club. Sara sat with her head slightly bent, as if overcome with tears. One hand was pressed to her mouth. The other was being clasped by Dan Jacobson. He was leaning in close to her, whispering into her ear. His right arm was draped across her shoulder, and as I watched, he would squeeze every few seconds, as if in reassurance.

And that's when it clicked.

Dan had once been a part of the book club. He'd spent a lot of time with Sara, discussing books and probably other interests they had in common. Over time, he grew to care about her, to maybe even love her.

And then David happened.

The man who pretended to be British, just so he could impress rich women, bed them, and then steal their money. Dan gets pushed out of not just Sara's life but the book club itself. He has to be jealous, has to be angry. But would that be enough to kill?

Probably not. But what if he were to learn about David's other life? He might have found out where David lived, followed him one night, and then snuck into his house, just like I did. He could have found the book with the other women pictured inside. He could have realized that David was doing the exact same thing to Sara, could have hated the idea of seeing her placed beside those other women.

That, I believed, might be enough to make a man angry enough to commit murder.

I still wasn't sure how he managed to get inside Death by Coffee that night, but it hardly mattered. Looking at them up there, cuddling close, like two lovers finally meeting again after years apart, I knew.

Dan Jacobson had killed David Smith.

I hardly realized I was moving until Rita paused in the middle of her speech to look at me. My foot hit the first step, causing her to frown and cock her head to the side.

"Is there something you needed, dear?"

I ignored her. I walked up the stairs, excitement growing. The entire room had grown silent as I interrupted the proceedings. Dan shifted uncomfortably in his seat, saw me staring, and moved away from Sara as if being close to her was an admission of guilt.

In a way, it was.

I stepped up to the podium, forcing Rita aside, and turned to the room.

Everyone's eyes were on me, including the three police

officers sitting at one of the tables. Buchannan looked amused, whereas Chief Dalton and Officer Dalton looked concerned. I gave Paul the slightest of nods, telling him silently that I had this. I was going to shock them all and once more prove my worth *and* my innocence. I checked for Will's face among the crowd, but I didn't see him. If I wanted anyone to see this, it was him. Maybe then he'd realize I'd been talking to Dan not because I was interested in him but because I was trying to solve a murder.

"I'm sorry to interrupt," I said. My voice rang out over the crowd so loudly, I winced. Lena and Vicki were standing by the counter, looking at me as if I'd lost my mind. I nodded toward the door, eyebrows raised. Lena seemed to understand. She walked over to it and took up position there. No one was going to get in or out unless they ran over her. She might be small, but she was scrappy. I didn't pity anyone who dismissed her out of hand.

"This is most irregular," Rita complained. Once again, I ignored her.

"I have something to say." I cleared my throat, which was thumping in time with my heart, making my words vibrate. With everyone staring at me, I felt as if I were standing under a spotlight on a stage somewhere.

"Well, get on with it," Albert barked from his seat. He was clearly impatient to get this whole thing over with. I didn't blame him. From the start, the odds were stacked against him.

"As you all know, a man died here recently. Murdered." I let the word hang in the air a moment, worried that reminding the public of what happened here might have adverse effects on business, before going on. "We knew him as David Smith. Other people knew him as Caleb Jenkins, among many other names."

Paul stood, eyes going wide. I'd clearly shocked him. Good. The man needed a jolt.

I turned slightly so I could see Sara and Dan. "I imagine some of you already knew this. And because of it, you learned about his past, which was . . . unsavory." I grimaced, thinking of all of those women he'd taken advantage of. "And when you realized he was moving in on a woman you cared about, you snapped."

Dan looked around as if thinking I was directing my comments to someone else. After a moment, realization dawned and he rose angrily from his seat. "You have no idea what you are talking about."

"Don't I?" I asked, savoring the moment. This was when I would tell the entire room what I'd deduced. Dan would crack, would admit to everything. Paul would arrest him, and once Dan was safely behind bars, he would come to me, begging for my forgiveness. I'd give it, of course.

Dan crossed his arms and glared at me. "No, you don't."

"I find it funny that you came here after being kicked out of the book club. David took your spot and you resented it. He was moving in on the woman you very well might love, and you resented that, too. So, once learning what you could about the man, you did the only thing you thought you could do to get rid of him." I paused dramatically. "You lured him here and killed him."

There was a collective gasp from the crowd. More people rose to their feet but kept mostly silent. Both book clubs were standing now, glaring at each other as if it were their fault.

"And when was I supposed to have done that?" Dan demanded. "Before coming here, I was laid up in the hospital. I have a heart condition that needs regular care." To prove his point, he raised his shirt to expose a bandage, just near his heart.

"But I . . ." I trailed off. I'd seen him wearing nothing but a Speedo suit and hadn't seen a bandage. This couldn't be right.

But had I actually seen his chest? He'd had a towel draped over his shoulder, covering that exact spot. It would have been easy to miss the bandage, even if he'd moved in a way to expose it, considering how hard I'd been trying to not look at him at the time.

A murmur went through the crowd. Paul began working his way to me.

"I'm sorry you felt the need to embarrass yourself," Dan said. "I apologize if you feel my rejection of your earlier advances made you feel as if you had to do this to get back at me."

"Rejection?" My mind whirled. *I'd* rejected *him*, not the other way around.

But I couldn't make my mouth work on any other words. I'd been so sure of myself, so positive that this was going to be my moment of glory, I couldn't comprehend that I'd actually been wrong. This was supposed to be *my* moment of vindication.

Instead, I'd made a total ass of myself.

Paul ascended the stairs and took me by the arm. "Come on," he said at a whisper.

"But . . ." I wasn't quite sure what I was butting about.

"He has an alibi," Paul said gently. "If you would have come to me first, I could have told you that."

"But . . ." I dropped my head.

"Come on, Krissy, let's go."

I let Paul lead me off the stage, too embarrassed to look at anybody. I felt their eyes on me. Each one felt like a little pinprick to the back of my neck.

We paused by the door. Lena was still blocking it off, arms crossed. She glared angrily at Paul, and a flood of affection washed over me. Even after I made a fool of myself, she was still willing to defend me. This young girl was quickly becoming one of my best friends.

"It's okay," I told her.

"I'm just taking her home," Paul said. "She's overworked and could use a little time to rest."

Yeah, as if that was the reason I was acting like an idiot.

Lena glared a moment longer before finally stepping aside.

"Thank you," Paul said, before leading me out of Death by Coffee and away from the mocking stares of my peers.

29

Even though I had my own car, Paul drove me home, promising he'd have my car delivered when he got back to Death by Coffee. I handed him the keys wordlessly as he walked me to the front door of my house. I felt awful. More than awful. I felt as if I'd gone and accused an innocent man of murder in front of the entire town.

Oh, wait. That's exactly what I did.

"Krissy . . ."

I looked up at Paul. Tears were in my eyes but had yet to fall. I was so frustrated, I could scream. Was this where all of my hard work got me? I wanted to solve the case so badly, I'd ignored important evidence, refused to talk to the police when in doing so I could have been saved the absolute embarrassment of what had happened back at the shop. It wouldn't surprise me if my meddling got me run out of town at first light tomorrow morning.

Paul lifted a hand, hesitated like he wasn't sure what to do with it, and then rested it on my shoulder. He wasn't smiling. There were no dazzling dimples or any hint of sympathy in his gaze that would make me feel better.

Instead, all I saw was a profound sadness in his eyes. And pity. A whole lot of pity.

"You can't keep doing this," he said. "If you go around accusing innocent people of murder, it will eventually come back on you."

"I know."

"Let us do our job." He squeezed my shoulder. "Please. You might think we can't handle ourselves, but I promise you, the force isn't as bad as it seems."

That brought a ghost of a smile to my lips. Paul echoed it, though the worry was still in his eyes. The man thought I'd lost it, I was sure. He was probably standing there, wondering what he'd gotten himself into by interacting with me, even on the most basic level. If I kept going, I was going to end up proving his doubts about me right. Five years from now, I could easily become that lonely woman who wears a nightgown and slippers all day, feeding an army of felines and staring out my window with a pair of binoculars.

I shuddered at the thought. I would *not* become Eleanor Winthrow.

Paul must have taken my shudder as a hint that I was cold, despite the heat. He pulled me in close for a hug, rubbing his hands up and down my back briskly. I pressed my face against his chest, basking in his closeness. It had been far too long since I'd been that close to anyone.

I thought of Will and wondered if he hated me now. And if he was upset about me being near Dan, what would he think seeing me standing here in Paul's arms? Why did I always have to make a mess of everything?

You need to tell him everything—about the shoebox, the IDs, everything.

"Paul . . ."

He released me and stepped back. "I have to get back to the competition." He glanced toward his cruiser, as if reluctant to get inside. "I'll let the others know I got you here safely." He leveled a finger at me. "Get some rest, okay?"

I nodded. I felt chilled now that he wasn't holding me. Look at me, all sappy and needy. I guess that's what happens to a person when she makes a total fool out of herself—she ends up needing someone there to tell her that she isn't as big of a moron as she thinks.

Paul turned away and slipped into his cruiser. I almost called out to him to tell him to check under the seat of my car, but I didn't. I felt stupid, and I didn't want to add to it. I promised myself I'd call him later, once most of my shame had faded.

Paul sat there for a long moment, staring at where I stood huddled outside my front door. He looked torn, as if he wanted to get back out and hold me some more. I'll admit, I wouldn't have minded one bit. In fact, I longed for it.

Instead, he started the car, gave me a brief flick of the hand that was supposed to be a wave, and then, with the rumble of the engine, he was gone.

I turned and unlocked my front door, lonelier than I cared to admit. I stepped inside and closed the door behind me before Misfit could escape. He turned and strutted off, walking away just like Paul had.

My shoulder felt naked without my purse hanging from it. It was sitting in the back room of Death by Coffee where I'd left it. It was a wonder I'd shoved my keys into my pocket instead of depositing them into my purse before work. I should have grabbed the stupid thing on the way out, but I'd been a little too preoccupied with all of the eyes on me to think of something as simple as the one item that held my belongings.

I heaved a sigh and looked down at myself. I was still wearing my apron. I pulled it off and balled it up, thinking that maybe throwing it against the wall would make me feel better, when I heard something crinkle inside it. It took me a moment to realize what I was hearing.

Mike's resignation letter. Just when everything was going insane in my life *and* Death by Coffee, he up and quits on me.

I pulled the letter out of the apron pocket and unfolded it before tossing the apron aside. I never did read the letter fully. I was curious to see if he gave a better reason than what he'd told me when he'd handed me the darn thing. I had half a mind to call Paul up and tell him about Lena's theory about Mike. If he'd been stealing, then he deserved to be punished, especially after leaving me hanging like that. Of course, I doubted there was much Paul could do about it now. And since I didn't have any actual proof, it would be pointless to tell him.

My eyes scanned the page. There wasn't much to the letter itself. He got straight to the point, saying he was quitting, and then he signed it. No excuses, no warning. I mean, what ever happened to the two-week notice? Quitting suddenly like that was awfully suspicious. It was looking more and more like Lena was right about him.

"Just my luck," I grumbled, carrying the letter farther into the house. Standing by the door all day wasn't going to get me anywhere. There was still a murderer out there, and if I wanted to restore my dignity, I needed to figure out who it was.

I was halfway to the island counter when a niggling started in the back of my head. I stopped and stared down at Mike's scrawl, at how the letters flowed together, making it hard to read. The note was written sloppily but legibly.

Misfit sauntered into the room, head cocked, as if catching the vibes coming off of me. He plopped down on the floor and stared up at me, tail swishing back and forth.

"Why is this writing so familiar?" I asked him. I reread the letter, but nothing in it was pinging the persistent thought that was attempting to break through. I tried to remember if Mike had written something down for me at some point, other than his signature back when I'd hired him. He'd filled in the application, but he'd printed that.

But looking at this writing here now, I *knew* I'd seen it somewhere else.

And then it clicked.

"No way." I looked wildly around, but what I was looking for was gone. John Buchannan had taken it the night the rock was thrown against my front door.

That was where I'd seen the near indecipherable scrawl before—on the warning note that had been strapped to the rock. It had to be.

Mike Green was the killer!

He had access to Death by Coffee. In fact, he closed the store that very night. He'd also been acting strangely lately, eyes darting around as if he was paranoid that people were watching him. I'd thought it had to do with the missing money and Lena's theory, but perhaps he was nervous because he'd killed David Smith only a few nights before and was afraid someone would figure it out.

Like me.

What I didn't know was *why* he murdered a man who was a stranger to him. It wasn't like David would be able to tell me who killed him. And as far as I could tell, there was no evidence pointing Mike's way. What could have happened that night after Vicki left? Was there something I was missing?

The sound of an engine shutting off outside had me running for the door, thinking Paul had come back with my car. If I would have stopped to think about it, I would have realized that it was impossible for him to be back already. He had been gone for only a few minutes at most.

I threw open the door, letter in hand, ready to proclaim Mike the killer, restoring both my dignity and reputation, when I saw what awaited me.

It wasn't my car sitting in the driveway.

And that sure wasn't Paul Dalton walking toward me with a tire iron in hand.

I backpedaled and tried to get the door closed before Mike could reach me, but he was too fast. He thrust the tire iron through the door opening just before it closed. He used his scrawny frame to slide sideways, through the door, despite my best efforts to keep him out. I was too exhausted from work to put up much of a fight, and he was determined. He thrust me away by shoving the door before stepping inside and closing it quietly behind him.

"I knew I made a mistake," he said. "Man, I totally blew it, didn't I?"

"Uh, hi, Mike!" I put as much cheer into my voice as I could manage, which to tell you the truth wasn't much. "What are you doing here? Change your mind about quitting?"

"Don't play stupid," he said. His eyes flickered to the letter in my hand. "So, you figured it out, huh?"

"That you quit? Sure, you told me yourself."

Mike sighed and ran his free hand through his stringy hair. "I'm serious. I like you and all, but I'll hit you with this if I have to." He hoisted the tire iron.

"Okay, okay," I said, backing slowly away, hands held

out before me. Of all the times not to have my purse, this was the worst. I thought I'd be able to make a run for it and lock myself in the bathroom before he caught me. Then I could call Paul on my cell and he'd come and save me.

But I needed my cell phone for that, which was in my purse, which was back at Death by Coffee, where it would do me no good.

"I should have told you my key had come up missing and then just come in and told you I was quitting, rather than leaving you the stupid letter," Mike said, smacking himself in the temple a few times with the palm of his hand. "I wasn't thinking, you know? I don't have a computer or anything, so I wrote the thing out, hoping I wouldn't have to speak to you, but that was the wrong thing to do. I realized my mistake almost immediately, but when I returned to take back the note, you were already gone."

"We all make mistakes," I said. "I forgive you."

He snorted. "I'm not sure your forgiveness helps me much."

Okay, so talking my way out of this wasn't going to work. I needed to buy time until Paul, or at least somebody he trusted, came back with my car. I didn't know if they'd be arriving in ten minutes or two hours. I wasn't sure I had enough time either way.

"Why'd you do it?" I asked, figuring that as long as I kept him talking, he wouldn't have time to kill me.

Mike chewed on his lower lip a moment before answering. "He caught me," he said with a shrug, as if it explained everything.

I should have been thrilled. He'd just confessed to David's murder in a roundabout way. But if he'd killed a man he'd hardly known, what was stopping him from doing the same to me, especially since I posed a greater threat to him?

"Caught you doing what?" I asked, taking another step back.

"Stop," he said, hand tightening on the tire iron. "No farther."

I did as he said. "I just want to know why you did it."

With a sigh, he answered, "I was skimming from the register, man. I'm surprised you didn't know."

"I was working it out." There was no way I was going to tell him Lena had pointed it out to me. If he finished me off here, I didn't want him to go after her once he was done disposing of my body.

"Well, I'd ring stuff up, delete it, and then pocket the money. It wasn't hard, since no one really paid much attention to what I was doing. And the money really wasn't all that good. But it was enough to get by. Living is expensive."

Living was something I wanted to keep doing, but I kept that to myself. "And David caught you?"

"Yeah." He shook his head, almost as if the thought of anyone catching on to him surprised him. "He watched me, I guess. The dude seemed like it was the sort of thing he'd done before. After I closed that night, he came up to me and confronted me. I thought for sure he was going to turn me in. Everyone was right there, getting into their cars."

"But he didn't?"

"Nope. He wanted a cut."

I raised my eyebrows at him. A cut of what he was skimming wouldn't have amounted to much.

"Told the dude to meet me at the store later that night, once everyone was good and gone. I was totally going to pay him and hope he'd simply go away. I was done after that, for sure."

"Didn't work out that way, did it?"

Mike's eyes narrowed. "Nah. The dude came in, took

his cut, and then demanded more when he saw how little it was. I was like, 'Whoa, dude, chill,' but he was insistent. Put his hands on me and shook me a few times like he thought I was hiding the extra bills in my hair or something."

I cringed at the bad lingo but refrained from commenting on it. I glanced from side to side, looking for a weapon within easy reach. He had me out in the open, out where if I made a move one way or another, he could get to me before I could grab anything. Misfit was sitting nearby, watching the proceedings with mild interest. I doubted he would be much help.

"He wanted everything, man." Mike shook his head, almost sadly. "He was going to wipe the place out, steal every last thing he could reasonably sell, including that stupid teapot, and wanted me to help him. When he turned his back, I don't know, I just sort of snapped. I clunked him on the head, hard enough to knock him out. I was going to leave him there for the cops, but I realized he'd just turn me in when he came to. So I hit him again. And again." He moved the tire iron into a two-handed grip.

Something had come into Mike's eyes as he spoke. It was as if remembering David's death was enough to send him into a murderous frenzy. I knew then that no matter what happened, what I did or said, he was going to come at me.

I wasn't going to stand around and let him do it.

Mike took a step forward. I feinted toward the kitchen, which seemed to be the best place to go. I figured Mike would think the same. He moved to cut me off, and I immediately changed direction and darted toward the living room. I snatched up one of those solid candle holders that are about the size of a small cup. I turned and threw it as hard as I could, aiming for Mike's head.

It smashed into the wall about three feet to his left. He snarled at me and charged. I started for the hall, realizing there was nothing I could use against him in the living room, unless I wanted to try to beat him over the head with my TV.

Mike spun around a chair and swung his tire iron. I jerked back, avoiding the blow, but my lamp wasn't so lucky. It shattered on impact, spraying glass and ceramic pieces all over my freshly cleaned floor.

I screamed and scuttled backward, right into the TV I'd considered using as a weapon. It was one of those HD flat screens that should normally be bolted to the wall or a stand of some sort. Unfortunately, I'd done neither. I hit it hard enough for it to crack back against the wall and then heave forward. I made a mad grab for it and realized that in doing so, I'd be giving Mike a chance to clock me a good one, so I shoved on it instead. Mike managed to leap back before it came crashing down at his feet.

"Break all you want," he said. "It won't help you." He wasn't even breathing hard, while I was panting.

I looked for a way out of my predicament. Misfit, who should have been hiding somewhere due to all the noise, was sitting in the dining room, watching us with his ears pinned back. It appeared he was my final hope.

"Attack!" I yelled at him, startling Mike. He jerked back, clearly expecting a massive dog of some sort to come flying at him. All he found was an orange cat giving him a curious look.

"Traitor," I grumbled as Mike chuckled. The cat was going to be of no help.

Mike came at me then, tire iron held above his head, poised to strike. I shoved on the coffee table as he neared. It didn't move much, but Mike's leg clipped the edge of it, anyway. He tripped and fell into the stand that used to hold my TV. He went down hard.

I bolted between the coffee table and couch, thinking I'd caught my break and could get out the front door before Mike could right himself. Too bad I was watching Mike struggle to his feet instead of watching where I was going.

When I'd moved the coffee table, it had not only turned to get in his way but also cut off the clear path to the door between the table and the couch. My knees hit the corner of the table at a full run, and I went tumbling over it. I hit the floor hard and skidded across, giving myself some serious rug burn in the process. I came to rest near where Misfit had been sitting a moment before. At some point, he'd taken off and left me to fend for myself.

I tried to scramble to my feet, but before I could so much as get to my hands and knees, Mike was atop me. I spun and kicked out, hoping to hit him where it counted, but instead I ended up kicking the wall. My leg went instantly numb, and pain shot through my foot as one of my toes snapped. I was on my back, Mike atop me, his hands on my throat.

He'd lost the tire iron in his fall, apparently, which would have been great if he didn't have all of the leverage and was choking the life out of me instead. I beat at him with my hands, but it was to no avail. If he'd been any stronger, he could have crushed my windpipe and been done with it. As it was, he was cutting off my air, which might be slower but would make me dead just the same.

And then, thankfully, that was when the blessed sound of sirens filled the air.

Mike's grip lessened on my throat as his head jerked up. I sucked in a gulp of air, which burned going in but felt good. It might be my only moment of reprieve, and I needed to take advantage of it.

"Oh, man." Mike jumped to his feet and started to run for the door.

There was no way I was going to let him escape. Despite the pain in my foot, despite how every breath felt as if I were swallowing fire, I rolled over onto my side and grabbed for his leg. The grab was wild, but I caught him. Mike went down hard, nose cracking the floor. I held tight to his foot, even as he began kicking at me.

"Let me go!" he shouted as the siren reached a crescendo outside.

"Never!"

There was the clunk of a door slamming closed, and a moment later my angel stepped through the door. Paul scanned the scene, gun in hand, looking as if he wasn't quite sure what he was looking at.

"He killed David Smith!" I shouted. "And he tried to kill me!" I hoped he would do something before Mike's foot finally found my face. He was bucking wildly even now.

It all seemed to click at once. Paul's face went hard, and since Mike was ignoring the gun in his hand, he did the next best thing: he tackled the already prone man, and zip-stripped him up faster than I could blink. I let go of Mike's foot and rolled over onto my back, panting and in pain but alive.

And at least this time, I didn't pass out.

30

The parking lot to the theatre was so full, I had to park down the street and walk. I got out of the car, limping, as I made my way back toward the large brick building. I was dressed as if on a date—a cute, light blue skirt and white blouse—but unfortunately no man was going to meet me, much to my disappointment.

My toe had indeed been broken in my fight with Mike, but it was worth it considering David Smith's murderer had been caught. I'd turned over all of the information I had on David, including the conquest book. It didn't really help the police in their case against Mike, but hey, whatever. I didn't want it.

Of course, Paul wasn't happy I'd been holding back on him. I couldn't blame him, really. I did let him know that the only reason I hadn't told him about what I'd found was because of how he'd been treating me. He looked rightfully abashed, but I do believe it was also the reason I was going to this thing alone.

I reached the front doors to the small brick theatre at the same time as Chief Patricia Dalton. She was wearing her uniform, though the top two buttons were undone and the stiff hat she always wore was missing. She looked as if she'd just come off duty.

"Hi, Chief," I said, leaning against the side of the building to catch my breath. In the week after Mike's arrest, I'd pretty much sat on my butt, thanks to my toe. I was quickly assuming the shape of my recliner.

"Well, hello there, Miss Detective." She said it with a teasing grin. "How's the foot?"

"Better." I wiggled it in my loose-fitting sandals. I couldn't get it into anything else.

"Good, good." She paused. "Talk to Paul?"

"Not really." Other than when I'd given him the information I'd found, he hadn't spoken to me at all.

"He tell you why he came back that day?" She was grinning as if she'd been dying to tell me since the moment it happened.

I shook my head. He hadn't brought my car back, either. I'd had to convince Vicki to pick me up and take me back for it. Let me tell you, a freshly broken toe and the gas and brake pedals aren't compatible. It took me five times as long to get home, but darn it, I was determined not to ask for any more help.

"Your neighbor called us. Dispatch forwarded the call to me, not quite sure what to make of it. Miss Winthrow was ranting about you having rough sex with a minor. She claimed it was disturbing the entire neighborhood and someone needed to come in and break it up."

"What?" I practically shouted it, drawing the eyes of a few stragglers who had yet to enter the theatre. "He's over twenty. And we weren't having sex!" The eyes of the gawkers widened as they hurried inside.

"I know." Chief Dalton chuckled. "Good luck convincing

everyone else of that. Between Eleanor and her friends, it is all over town now." She turned and walked into the theatre, still chuckling.

Great, just my luck. I solve yet another murder and instead of being a hero, people were going to look at me as if I was some sort of child molester. Buchannan was probably already having a field day with that one.

With a grumble, I entered the theatre. The old building sagged from seemingly everywhere but looked sturdy enough. A woman in a little booth just inside the door took my five dollars and handed me a little piece of paper that would serve as my ticket into the play. I thanked her and headed inside to a nearly packed room. I caught a glimpse of Jules Phan and Lance, sitting down near the front, but there were no empty seats around them.

I scanned the crowd with a frown. There were people standing at the back, apparently unable to find seats themselves. There was no way on God's green earth that I was going to stand through this thing. My foot would probably fall off first. But I wasn't going to miss it, either.

I found Will sitting with his bowling buddies, Darrin and Carl. I considered going down to talk to him but decided I wasn't quite ready for *that* conversation, especially with the rumors flying around. Maybe once they died down, I could look him up and explain.

I was about to give up on finding a seat when I finally found an empty pair. One was an aisle seat, and the other was two seats down the row.

And between them sat Rita Jablonski.

I groaned. Of course those would be the only spots available.

I limped my way to the aisle seat and sat down, hoping she would somehow overlook me.

"Oh, Lordy Lou!" Rita exclaimed as I took my seat. "You look a pitiful sight."

"Thanks." I stretched my leg out as far as I could, which wasn't much. The rows were too close together, and there was enough traffic up and down the aisle, I couldn't use it for space. Still, it was better than standing.

"I'm sorry I haven't been in lately," Rita said, talking a mile a minute. "Not that you've worked much, I'm sure. I've been so busy as of late, and what with the teapot going to Cherry Valley, I haven't felt all that great, either."

"They won?" I asked, mildly surprised. With losing one of their own and my later accusations, I would have thought they would have been too distracted to discuss the book properly.

"Oh, Lordy, no." Rita flapped a hand inches from my face. "They took the silver teapot home due to the murder clause within our rules."

I stared at her blankly. "A murder clause?"

"Of course, dear. We've never invoked it before, so no one thought about it. In the event of a sudden death, due to unnatural means, the team who suffered the loss wins by default."

"You didn't think of this before having the big talk?" Boy, it would have saved me a whole lot of stress if they would have figured this out before now. I could have focused more on what was going on around me and might have caught Mike sooner.

Rita snorted. "*I* did, of course. I just didn't see it as a big-enough reason to give the teapot to a team that was clearly going to lose, so I kept my mouth shut. That Albert . . ." She made one of those "Ooooo" sounds, like she was going to smack him upside the head with a news-paper the next time she saw him.

"At least you got the teapot back from the police," I said. It was the best I could do to console her.

"Dented, of course." Rita huffed. "Well, I'll never understand why the police didn't replace the thing for us. It's their fault it is ruined, so they should be liable."

Mike was really the one to blame, but I wasn't about to tell her that. There was no reason to egg her on. She'd probably go to a lawyer to see if there was some way he could be forced to pay for it.

"We'll win next year," Rita went on. "And you'll help."

"I will?"

"Sure you will! You're part of the reason we lost this year in the first place. It's the least you can do."

I wasn't so sure about that, but I nodded anyway. I'd just have to make sure to come down with a bad case of the flu this time next year.

"Oh, did I tell you that James is back in my bedroom? I missed having him there so much." She sighed dreamily. "I dressed up in my best lingerie to celebrate, despite what the police did to him while he was in their custody."

Right about then, I tuned her out. Part of it was because of what she was talking about, because, ew. And the other part was because my roving eyes had landed on the back of a sandy brown head of hair I instantly recognized as Paul's. As I watched, he lifted his arm and placed it on the backrest of another seat, which was currently occupied by Shannon, the waitress from J&E's Banyon Tree who had always teased him about never bringing a date.

The entire world went away for a few brief moments as I watched them. Paul leaned over and whispered something into her ear. I could hear her laugh from where I sat, despite the noise of the room.

Blessedly, the lights dimmed then and the actors—including Vicki in all of her glory—stepped out onto the stage. The play began, and for the first time I thought to look at my ticket to see what exactly I was about to watch.

And Then There Were None.

Agatha Christie.

I should have known.

With a shrug, I shoved the ticket into my pocket and then leaned back to enjoy the show.

Please turn the page for an exciting sneak peek of
Alex Erickson's
next Bookstore Café Mystery

DEATH BY PUMPKIN SPICE

coming in October 2016!

1

The pleasing aroma of fresh baked pumpkin cookies filled the room as I removed the pan from the oven. Halloween was one of my favorite times of the year because that was when the world turned into a pumpkin lover's bliss. I leaned in over the pan and breathed in deeply. It was a challenge not to give in to temptation and sample the cookies as I carried them to the front to place within the empty display case.

"Some have just come up!" Lena Allison said from her place at the register. She held up two fingers and gave me a relieved smile as I slid two cookies into a bag.

Death by Coffee had been buzzing since we'd started selling pumpkin items. The cookies were gone almost as fast as I could bake them and the various coffees were constantly in need of refills. It was running me ragged, but it was worth it.

As Lena rang up another order, I finished filling the display case and carried the cooling cookie sheet to the back. I deposited it in the sink where it would need to be washed before I could use it again, and then headed back out front to make a coffee of my own. I filled the cup three quarters of the way full, added some pumpkin spice flavoring, and then plopped in one of the recently baked cookies.

"Ugh." Lena turned up her nose as she leaned against the counter. The line was gone for the moment, giving her a few seconds to breathe. "I still don't see how you could drink that. I hate pumpkin."

I took a sip and grinned at her over the rim of my cup. "Yum."

She laughed and shook her head, causing her purple hair to bounce around her ears. Her chin was clear of scrapes, though her elbow had a pretty nasty scab that she'd covered with a pair of Band-Aids. Her skateboard was parked in the back room, and it looked just as beat up as she often did.

Still, I wouldn't trade her in for anyone else. Since Lena had started working at Death by Coffee, she's made my life a whole lot easier. She's a smart girl, and friendly to boot. She was saving up to go to college and I privately hoped she stuck close to home when she did leave. I'd hate to lose her.

The bell above the door jangled and in came Rita Jablonski, bundled in a coat lined with fur I hoped was fake. She was a short woman, on the plump side, and was the biggest gossip in all of Pine Hills.

"It's getting windy out there!" she said, coming straight to where I stood. "They're saying we could see some pretty serious storms over the next few days."

I glanced out the window, and indeed, the leaves were blowing around as if a tornado was itching to come roaring down out of the cloudy sky. The reds and yellows were beautiful, but I'll admit, I did miss the warm sun and full green of mid-summer, though I wasn't a fan of the sometimes oppressive heat.

"I hope it won't be too bad," I said. If the power went

out, there'd be no more cookies or coffee. And that meant no more business.

"Well, as long as it spends itself before this weekend, I'll be happy." Rita glared out the window as if the rain could hear her and comply. "The church is having our annual Trunk or Treat and I for one plan on being there, rain or shine. We are participating this year, just like last, and I won't let a little wet weather ruin it."

I narrowed my eyes. "We?"

She looked surprised for a moment before smiling. "The book club, of course! We talked about it during our last meeting." She paused and a look of understanding passed over her face. "That's right, you weren't there." She leaned forward, pressing against the counter as she spoke. "We're holding it at the church on Sunday evening. Cars will be parked in the lot, trunks filled with candy. The kids walk around and trick or treat like they normally would. It's safer than going from house to house and the costumes are a little less . . ." She grimaced.

"Scary?"

"Disgusting, more like. You don't want to imagine what some of the teenagers dress up as when left to their own devices."

Oh, I could imagine all right. I'd lived near a college campus for a few years. Halloween was always a lesson in the perverse, especially since most college kids took any opportunity they could to drink and party. Add in costumes dreamed up over a drunken weekend, and let me tell you, it didn't take long before I made sure not to be anywhere near the campus on Halloween.

"I do hope you get the night off," Rita said. "We start at six."

"I'll check with Vicki," I said. "But it should be okay. We aren't open much later than six anyway."

"You do that."

I was surprised to realize I was actually excited about the event. It sounded fun, and Vicki was always pressuring me to get out more. It might give me a chance to meet more people in town, and maybe advertise just a little.

The door opened and I glanced up just as Will Foster walked in. He paused just inside the door, looking as uncomfortable as any man could, before his eyes landed on me. He strode across the room, right past Rita, and came to a stop in front of me.

"Krissy." He coughed to clear his throat. "Could we talk for a moment?"

I was so flustered, I almost didn't answer. Will was a dream to look at normally, yet today he seemed to positively glow. His dark brown eyes, his near-black hair, and skin the color of a creamer-rich coffee was enough to cause me to break out into an instant nervous sweat. His coat was one of those long black button up jobbies that all the stylish men seemed to wear on magazine covers. I couldn't see his shoes from where I stood, but I was pretty sure they'd be polished to a shine.

"Krissy?" he asked. "You okay?"

"Huh? Oh! Yeah." I hurriedly set my coffee down before I spilled it. "I'm just surprised to see you." The last time I'd seen Will, he'd left thinking I was seeing another man, not knowing the man he'd seen me with had been a suspect in a murder investigation. The guy had hit on me and made a scene, but I'd never even considered going out with him. I hadn't had time to explain what really happened before Will was gone.

He flushed a little and looked down at his hands. They looked strong and manicured. "Well, I . . ." He cleared his throat and looked around me like he was afraid looking me in the eye would cause me to start yelling at him.

As hurt as I was about him vanishing like he had, I let him off the hook. "Let's go upstairs so we can talk privately." I glanced at Lena. "You'll be okay for a few minutes, right?" She nodded with a grin. I turned to Rita. "I'll be back in a minute. Feel free to order and take a seat."

I stayed behind the counter as I headed upstairs to where my best friend and co-owner of Death by Coffee, Vicki Patterson, was showing our newest hire, Jeff Braun, how to ring up a book sale. He was a slow learner, but I had no doubt he'd get it eventually. Vicki glanced toward where Will was walking up the stairs across the room and then raised a delicate eyebrow at me.

I shrugged and tried to hide my grin as I walked past her, around the counter, and went to where Will was waiting between a pair of bookshelves.

"What did you want to talk to me about?" I asked.

"First, let me apologize," he said. "I was stupid. I jumped to conclusions and didn't let you tell me your side of the story. I'm an idiot."

"No you're not," I said. His apology had my insides jumping up and down for joy so much, I felt sick.

"No, I am." He took one of my hands and clutched it in both of his. "I shouldn't have walked away like that. And then with what happened after . . ."

"It's nothing," I said, willing my glands not to overreact. His hands were so warm and strong, and yet soft at the same time. It was all I could do to keep from shaking.

Will sighed and smiled. "I don't know how you can forgive me so easily. I should have come before now, but was afraid that after I'd made such a fool of myself, you wouldn't want to see me."

"That's silly," I said. "Of course I want to see you."

A gleam came into his eye. "I know that now." He laughed. "But you know how things are. I felt stupid, was afraid you'd call me on it the moment you saw me, and with work being so hectic lately, I used it as an excuse not to come see you."

"But you're here now."

"That, I am."

It was as if a hole had opened in the roof and a beam of pure sunlight had washed over me. I felt warm all over, and had an intense desire to squeal in joy.

"You didn't need to apologize," I said, doing my best to contain my excitement. "I should have been more upfront with you about what I was doing."

"You didn't owe me anything," he said. "We'd barely had a chance to speak, which was my fault entirely. If I'd given you more time, then maybe I wouldn't have let my imagination get carried away with me. It's a fault, I know."

He didn't need to tell me about it. My imagination had a tendency to get me into more trouble than I cared to admit. It was a wonder it hadn't gotten me killed yet.

Will let go of my hand and cleared his throat again. "Now that that is out of the way, I have something I'd like to ask you."

My heart started pounding. "Okay." It came out as a little squeak.

"Because I was such a knucklehead, I'll completely understand if you say no."

"I won't." I cringed and forced a nervous smile. "I mean, I won't say no just because of that."

That caused him to laugh. "All right, then." He cleared his throat yet again. He appeared almost as nervous as I felt. "I would like to make up for my ignorant actions by taking you to a party."

"A party?"

"A Halloween costume party, to be exact." A devious

smile crooked the corner of his mouth. "Unless you are frightened."

"I . . ." Fear clenched at my core. I might love Halloween, but I'd never been one to dress up in a costume. Any time I tried, it was always an unmitigated disaster. Pieces would fall off constantly, or I'd end up wearing the same thing as a dozen other people. Then there was the one time when I'd worn a rubber nose and broke out in a horrible rash that spread over half of my face.

A look of worry crossed Will's eyes. "If you aren't interested you don't have to go," he said. "I have an invitation and thought it might be the perfect way to say I'm sorry."

"No!" I said, worried he would take it all back and leave, never to return. "I want to go. I'm just not sure I have anything to wear."

Relief washed over his face. "That's okay. The party isn't until Friday night. You have a couple of days to find something appropriate." He reached into the pocket of his coat and removed a folded piece of stationery. "Here," he said, holding it out to me.

"What's this?" I asked, taking it.

"It's my number. My cell, actually. In case you have any questions."

"I . . ." It was my turn to clear my throat. "Thank you."

He looked amused as he said, "It's no problem at all. And if you wouldn't mind, I have my cell on me and can input your number now in case I need to contact you before the big night."

"Of course!"

Will whipped out his phone and handed it to me. It was one of the really nice ones that cost a fortune. I always opted for the free phones that came with a two-year contract.

My fingers shook as I typed in my number. Once it was

in, I saved the contact and handed him his phone back. He was grinning as he glanced down at his screen, before shoving the phone in his pocket. He then checked his watch and frowned.

"I need to get back to work," he said. "I'll call you tomorrow sometime so we can work out the details."

"Okay." It was about the only thing I could manage.

He turned and started to walk away but stopped. "Is he supposed to be doing that?"

I followed his gaze to the upstairs table where people could sit to read. The black and white store cat, Trouble, was standing on his hind legs, front paw reaching into the eye socket of a jack-o'-lantern, trying to bat at the light inside.

"He'll be fine," I said. "The candle is fake." Though the pumpkin wasn't. If he were to knock it off, I'd end up having to clean it up.

"Ah." Will watched the cat a moment longer before chuckling. "I'll talk to you soon." And then he was gone.

I floated over to Trouble and picked him up. He meowed in surprise as I gave him a quick hug, before he started squirming to be put down. I carried him across the room and deposited him on top of one of the four-foot-tall bookshelves, where he glared at me before lying down to wash. I patted him on the head before going back downstairs to where Rita still stood, eyes focused on the front door Will had just exited. She turned to me with a surprised look on her face.

"Well, well," she said. "William Foster now, is it?"

I couldn't keep the stupid grin off of my face as I answered. "He asked me to a costume party."

Rita's eyebrows tried to leap from her face. "Really? You?"

I was too happy to be miffed. "Yep. Me!"

She made a sound that was part incredulous and part impressed. "There are quite a few women who would kill to go somewhere with him." She paused, eyes widening. "Did he say what party?"

"No," I said, wondering what all the fuss was about. "He said he had an invitation and he wanted to take me."

Rita looked as if she might keel over right then and there. "Oh, Lordy Lou! He's taking you to the Yarborough party! I can't believe you of all people get to go!" She paused. "You did tell him you'd go, now didn't you?"

Annoyance started to seep into my voice as I answered. "I did. And how do you know which party he was talking about?"

She rolled her eyes. "Everyone who is anyone always goes to the Yarborough party. It's by invite only, you see, and I'd wager it is the *only* one someone like William Foster would go to."

"I didn't think it was all that big of a deal."

Rita's eyes widened. "Not a big deal? Where have you been? It's a huge deal!" She leaned onto the counter and lowered her voice. "I'm just surprised they are having it this year after . . . you know."

"No," I said. "I don't."

"The party was always Howard Yarborough's baby," she said, keeping her voice down as if she was sharing some deep, dark secret. "He was an architect, you see. He designed his house for this very occasion. He loved Halloween, did Howard, and he made sure to show it."

I noticed the past tense. "He's passed?"

"Just a few weeks ago, if you can believe it." Rita shook her head sadly. "He was a strange man, believe you me, but he was always kind. His wife, Margaret, never was big into the costume parties, but Howard loved them, so she put up with them. I can't believe she's going to continue on the tradition without him, especially after what happened."

Some of the air went out of me then. What I'd thought of as a chance to get to know Will better, was now starting to sound more and more like it might end up being a somber affair where Howard's wife and friends would lament his passing by holding the party he'd held so dear. I would feel like I was imposing, not having met the man.

Rita leaned forward even more so that she was only a few inches from my face. "And let me tell you something about William Foster . . ."

I held up a hand before she could go on. "No," I said, taking a step back. "Just, no."

"No?" She said it like she'd never heard the word before. "No, what?"

"I don't want to hear it." I picked up my cooling coffee and took a sip, shaking my head all the while.

"I don't know what you could mean?"

"No gossip," I said. "No secrets. I want to discover these things on my own."

Rita stepped back, looking mildly offended. "I don't gossip!" Someone sitting at a nearby table snorted. She glared over her shoulder at him. "Well, I don't."

I knew for a fact that Rita spent most of her life gossiping about the people of Pine Hills, but decided not to press the issue. It would get me nowhere but on her bad side, which in turn would turn me into a major target of her gossipy wrath.

"Well, I should run," Rita said, hand going to her hair. She'd recently curled it, though with the coming rain, it was starting to sag. "You *must* tell me how the party goes."

"I will," I said, knowing I wouldn't have any choice. I'd either tell her everything, or she would find someone who would. At least if I told her, I could make sure everything she heard was true.

She gave me a simpering smile before walking away.

"Party?" Vicki asked, startling me. Apparently, she'd come downstairs at some point during my conversation and was standing behind me. "What party?"

I turned away from Rita, and with a grin that nearly split my face in half, I began to tell Vicki all about it, hoping I was going to finally have my chance to make a good impression on Will.